FAULT
by ~~Lumen Reese~~

Lumen Reese

Congrats on winning the
giveaway,
Shayla!

Author's note:
This book is dedicated to the letter b.
I never knew how important you were until I lost you, 2/3rds of the way through this book, and had to copy and paste you the rest of the way. What a pain in the utt.
And to Elon Musk: Fuck that guy.

Book cover designed by Mihai Costea

ISBN: 978-1-952373-12-1 (Print)
978-1-952373-11-4 (Ebook)

Also by Lumen Reese:
Trial of the Lovebird Butcher
Monarch Falls
Claire Got Herself in Trouble
The Undesirables
Monster Midwife
The Bride Hunt of Elk Mountain
Fire Fields (Monarch Falls Sequel 2023)
To You Shall All Flesh Come (2024)

Follow the author on Twitter @ZoominLumen
Or, opt-in to her mailing list by emailing
lumenreese@gmail.com with 'join' in the subject line.
If you enjoy this book, please review! Reviews matter.

Part One
The Grieving Mother

Chapter One

The Thing swam out of the magma in the Earth's core, and clawed its way up through the San Andreas Fault, on the night that a chunk of the California coast sank into the Pacific. Whether it was woken from an ancient hibernation by the earthquake and driven mad by its hunger, or whether it had been placidly swimming around in an ocean of fire -and subsisting on God knows what else is down there- when it saw its opportunity, or whether it got bored and caused the rift in the first place, no one can know.

I think the last is true. The rift in that fault should not have been possible, not the way that it did happen. That's what scientists have said. That massive divide that formed, the vibrations shaking structures and toppling them, supports snapping like twigs. The lava surging up from between the two plates, and the western one shifting so fast that buildings that did survive became watery graves for so many. All because that Thing decided to come up. That's what I think, although at the end of the day it doesn't matter how and why it happened. All that matters is that millions died, including my children. Two little girls, Astrid and Josie, too little to look after themselves in the panic, left with a nanny who was qualified and highly recommended but who ultimately was not their mother, and who broke for the surface the second that the water came crashing in, driven by instinct. She probably thought only of getting back to her own child, as I would have.

It was chaos those first few days. I was in Helena, Montana on business; I couldn't get a seat on a flight that would bring me anywhere close. The government had the coast on lockdown, enacted a no-fly zone and sent in the National Guard and the Navy. They weren't sure what else might come out of the rift, which was still spewing orange lava rolling into the sea and cooling, turning black, dyeing the coast. There was even speculation of them planning to nuke the area, in the beginning.

So I had to hire an amateur pilot with his own bush plane. We were stopped for fuel somewhere in the desert when I got the call from Regina the nanny. She was sobbing as she told me that the children were in bed, of course, when the rumbling started, the earth shifted in huge slabs and the waves came shattering through the windows. My own body went cold. My voice came out level as I asked, "Are my children dead?"

Of course I had been running through the possibilities. Would it be better if they had been crushed, or drowned? People like to say that drowning is peaceful, but I almost drowned once, as a child, and I remember the fear and the pressure I felt before my mother scooped me off of the bottom of the swimming pool. Of course I had needed to believe that there was a chance. And Regina's call, her inability to say the words, her apology so strained and simpering had made everything come crashing in, just like that Thing had dropped a building on me, or flung me into the ocean. I wished that it had. Or that my mother had not noticed me at the bottom of the pool until it was too late.

It became clear to me that my children were not among those who made it to the surface, were rounded up at the shore, waiting in tent cities or on Navy vessels. They were dead.

I acted harshly. I screamed at Regina that she was supposed to be watching them. She was responsible for their deaths. I think I even said the words, 'You killed my children', to a woman clearly falling apart with guilt. I collapsed in the dirt alongside the air strip and sobbed for a long time. I don't even know how long.

Losing a child is like losing a limb. Worse. It's the kind of pain that makes a whole life seem like a cruel joke.

The pilot approached me after some time. He was a northwestern farmer in his fifties with a large gut, red in the face and kneading his CAT baseball cap in his meaty hands as he crouched beside me. His name was Tommy. "The plane's refueled, Ma'am, if you'd like to go ahead..."

That poor man, he gave me a tissue to wipe the snot and tears from my face, and helped pull me to my feet. I was in dress pants and kitten heels, a sleeveless blouse. I was supposed to be meeting with the board of directors of the company for which I was the chief mechanical engineer. I had my favorite navy suit jacket in my hands when the phone call came in, and I was content to leave it in the dirt, knowing my time in boardrooms was done, but the pilot scooped it up and carried it back to the plane for me. He set it on my lap and reached across my unmoving body me to strap me in.

"Pardon my reach, Ma'am... Safety first."

"Take me back to Montana," I heard myself say, before I had even pieced together what I was going to do next.

"Are you sure?"

"There's nothing left for me in California."

"Is there someone you could reach out to? Family?"

A mother with dementia back in Reading. A brother I hadn't spoken to in years. He never even met Astrid and Josie. Then, there was James... "There's no one."

We took to the air, a bumpy flight on that little puddle jumper, heading back north. I found myself staring at the ground miles below and hoping that the engine would fail. But the engine did not fail, and

Tommy and I landed at his large farm outside Helena. The propellor still whirring out in front of us, the little plane rolled along the bumpy ground and into the open mouth of the enormous barn peeling with red paint.

Once the racket from the engine cut out, everything was too quiet. I was used to city life. Sirens all hours, low riders with subwoofers rolling past. The last few turns of the propellor whipped up dust and hay, then it all started to drift back down, silently. It was all too quaint. It didn't feel like real life.

Tommy helped me climb out of the plane, and I stood in the square of afternoon light streaming in the open barn doors. I looked out at the bright day, the rolling land, fields of immature corn, and I did not want to go out there. I looked back at Tommy standing further inside the dark barn. There was plenty of ceiling height, a loft on each side, a large green tractor in one corner and still so much empty space.

I stood in the open doorway for a few minutes. Tommy eventually joined me. I could see my rental car parked in the distance, on the dirt driveway connecting the two-story, white farmhouse.

Tommy touched my shoulder. "Can I make you something to eat, Ma'am?"

"Ceely," I said. "Short for Lucille."

"Ceely. Will you come up to the house?"

"Alright."

We walked up the path and then I found myself on hardwood floors, in a little foyer. Tommy pointed out the first-floor bathroom at the end of the hall, then slipped into a kitchen straight out of the 1950's, where he washed his hands in a deep sink basin before cracking open the fridge. Across the foyer was a traditional dining room.

It took being in the powder room, seeing the toilet to realize that my bladder was full. Washing my hands in the sink put me in a kind of trance state. I soaped and rubbed and rubbed and rubbed, mind drifting to my girls and hardly noticing as the water heated up, then suddenly my hands were red and stinging. I hissed; it hurt enough to bring the tears back up.

My girls were still in our home. In their bedroom. Not hurting anymore. It was some comfort, but I knew that before long they would become fish food, they would be decaying and bloating by the hour in the warm water. Just like that, I knew what to do. It helped me find my way out of the powder room, into the kitchen where Tommy was slicing two ham sandwiches diagonally.

"Not fussy, are you? I gave it the works." He offered me the plate, complete with a handful of potato chips.

"No. Not fussy. Thank you."

Tommy was clearly not used to having guests. "Want to sit in the dining room? I usually eat in front of the tv…"

"I'd like to see what's happening."

"Are you sure?"

I nodded. Through the dining room to the living room, we sat on the couch and Tommy produced tv trays from the seventies. The event was on every news channel. Drone footage played and replayed of the creature's two-clawed mantis-like forelimbs bursting out of the fault, hauling its massive body out, molten, shaking lava off and revealing its white skin. It didn't seem to have eyes in its oblong, prehistoric skull. Experts agreed that it would have no use for them in the earth's core. As it dragged itself further and further out, they estimated it as being almost a mile long. It had no hind legs, finally ending in a massive two-fluked fan of a tail, not unlike a whale's but much larger.

The president held a press conference in the rose garden. "This is a tragic day for the United States, a day filled with grief and fear for many Americans. My administration is making all efforts to move the refugees of this massive earthquake, to reconnect them with their loved ones, and to recover the bodies of those who lost their lives. We have phone lines set up to contact families of survivors. We ask that you give us time to facilitate safe reunions.

"At this time we cannot allow any civilians to enter the containment zone. We have our country's best scientific minds determining the physiology of the creature which emerged from the San Andreas Fault, and working on how to track it, subdue it, and potentially kill it. We have troops amassed alongside the boundaries of the containment zone and aircraft monitoring the rift at all times. In the event that another creature should appear, we need to be ready and willing to defend our population by whatever means are deemed necessary. Do not attempt to enter the containment zone. I'll now take a few questions. Go ahead."

Tommy changed the channel to another news station. They had a woman on the street holding her phone up, and on its screen was a map of what had once been the California coast, not yet updated to show Los Angeles and other cities underwater. She was midsentence.

"-I saw it moving, and I thought, 'Thank God, he's okay!' He must be on his way home, you know?" Her face fractured, her lips pinched, and she sunk her teeth into them, they were already bleeding. Her big eyes shined with unshed tears which came through in her strained voice. "But over the next few hours, it drifted out and came back in again. It was too fast for someone swimming, and the boats wouldn't be taking people back out. I think it's inside the creature."

She was talking about her boyfriend's or husband's phone, I realized. And of course, those are never far away from us. It was swallowed by the creature when her partner was swallowed by the creature.

"It's eating the bodies," I declared. My voice sounded like it belonged to somebody else.

In his green armchair, Tommy's mouth dropped open. He covered it with his hand, tossing half his sandwich down. He was clearly appalled. I, however, lifted my own sandwich and took another bite, continuing to munch methodically through it. My mind was turning again, forming plans, I knew what I had to do. And once I knew what I had to do, nothing would stop me.

"Do you have any beer?" I asked. "Or whiskey?"

"I have beer, sure." He grunted as he leveraged himself out of the chair, then lumbered into the kitchen and brought back two bottles. He must have been thirsty, he downed half of his right away.

"Thanks…" I sipped. Waited for it to hit Tommy's bloodstream. Commercials rolled. I started in gently. "Do you live here all alone?"

"Yes. It's my family home, I grew up here. Lived here all my life. There's… there's plenty of spare rooms, if you'd like to stay for a little while, figure out what to do next."

I hid a tiny, bitter smile in the glass bottle. He was too eager to not be alone in the big house, for once. I didn't even need to get him drunk. Pressing the cool and damp bottle to my warm face, I nodded. "I would like to stay, and I have a proposition for you. I'll pay you five thousand dollars, I'll be gone in a week, or maybe ten days. Definitely not more than two weeks. I need to build something. I need space in your barn. I'll have to buy all sorts of material and tools and have them delivered here, and when I'm done, you can keep the tools, you can have whatever is left. How does that sound?"

His brow furrowed, his mouth became a tight, worried line. "What is it that you want to build?"

"A submarine. I need to go down and get my children's bodies." *And if I kill that thing while I'm down there*, I thought, *All the better.*

"I don't know… it sounds dangerous."

"I'm going to do it with or without you. One of your neighbors will take me up on my offer, if you don't. Five thousand dollars. At least a few thousand dollars' worth of equipment. What do you say?"

Still, he hesitated. "I wish you wouldn't."

"Do you have any children, Tommy?"

"No… never blessed. Would've liked some, but it wasn't in the cards. Jessica couldn't have them. And she died a few years ago…"

"Where is Jessica buried?"

"Out by the pond, under our favorite tree." His voice sounded far away, his mind wandered out that way, too.

"My girls are Astrid and Josie. I need to go and get them before that thing eats them. I need to know where they're buried. It's the only thing that will help me, now. Do you understand?"

Looking at me for a long moment, he slowly nods. "Alright. You can use my barn. You can stay as long as you need. But I won't take your money. I don't need it. I do just fine."

11

I would find a way to leave him some money. I suspected that I wouldn't need it, either. It was impossible to plan for a life after losing my girls, but if there was one, it was different than my busy, glamorous, sun-drenched California life had been. I took Tommy's hand, wrapped it in both of mine. "Thank you."

Color rising to his face, he nodded, and looked away embarrassed. "Of course."

Chapter Two

I started making calls, I knew sleep would not come. I got the heavier duty equipment ordered, paying any price to get it to rural Montana in two days' time. Metal, welding equipment, an engine I could alter and a hoist for it, pullies and winches. I was not concerned with comfort, or visuals, no temperature control and no life support. The sub would not need to be lived in for extended periods of time, nor survive high pressure. It just needed to be airtight, it needed to have arms and grip controlled from inside, and it would need to have a deep freezer chest, to keep the girls' bodies from further decay. I was already on a tight schedule. The girls would be unrecognizable by the time I found them, but they might still be whole.

The first night, my body and mind were exhausted as I laid out on the lovely queen bed in Tommy's guest room. There were flowers on the quilt, flowers on the wallpaper, doilies on the nightstands. The bed was an

13

old iron frame and reminded me of the one in my first house in Reading. I closed my eyes and tried to shut my brain off. I reached out and touched the cold metal. The pole in my hand rotated freely in place, squeaking.

James Bender and I put that bed together the first night we lived in the house on Bailey Street, falling into it as soon as it was done. We didn't get anything else assembled or unpacked that night. It felt like the bed was all we needed. Was it fifteen years ago? Was that possible?

James was passionate, intelligent, honorable. He was strapping and bearded and his head was covered in thick, dark waves of hair that I loved to stroke, pull, run my fingers through. I loved finding his hair on my pillows. I didn't even mind cleaning it from my shower drain, it was so beautiful. We met in college and stuck together like glue. I was going to be an engineer, and he was going to be an architect, and maybe teach someday. He came from money and was always planning trips for us over breaks, to Portugal, to Thailand, to New Zealand to see the locations from the *Lord of the Rings* movies.

He doted on me; he treasured me. It was the storybook love I never knew that I wanted. Planning for a future with someone else instead of only having to look after myself was an adjustment, but I thrived in the challenge of shifting my lifestyle. Then the pregnancy scare happened, and everything changed. In no uncertain terms, James did not want children. It had been a maybe, but suddenly it was a no. And when the test came back negative, my maybe became a screaming, careening, life's-trajectory-altering 'yes'.

I went after a better job, I moved to California, I had my two babies on my own with the same anonymous donor's material. I never regretted it for a second. I missed James every day, in some quiet moment or another, in the early morning before I went to wake Astrid and Josie up, or after they were in bed as I sat alone with a glass of wine.

My cellphone was turned off. I wasn't ready to field dozens of inquiries about my health, explain the deaths of my children and, therefore, my failure as their mother. I found it and turned it on, and its light blinded me for a second in the dark room. My fingers were typing his number before I had even thought of what I would say, or what I wanted to get from the conversation.

James answered on the second ring. Of course he was awake. He had always been a night owl. "Ceely? Oh my God, I've called you ten times."

His voice sent a pang through me. He was going to pry more tears out of me without even trying. "My phone was off," I managed, and my voice was already breaking.

"But you're okay. Thank God."

"I'm-." I tried to say that I was not okay, but I had already dissolved into tears.

Listening to me sob, James was attentive and patient. "Oh no. Ceely, I'm so sorry." It seemed he knew without me having to say. He knew I had two daughters, he knew their names, how happy they made me. We kept in touch on holidays. He knew me; he knew that I would not have broken down over just my house sliding into the ocean.

I tried to talk before I was quite finished crying, sputtering and gulping down breaths. "I- I was in Helena... I was working. They- they were home with a- with a nanny. I shouldn't have-. I should've-."

Over my next cascade of sobs, James tried to reassure me. His own voice was tight with emotion. "It's not your fault, Ceely, you can't blame yourself. It's a terrible tragedy. Nobody could have seen this coming... I'm so sorry. Let it out. It's okay. I'm right there, with you."

His familiar voice, his reassurances eventually helped smooth me over. Even when he was not speaking, just hearing him breathe and knowing he was waiting on the other end of the call soothed my spikes of pain into manageable little barbs. I blew my nose with no modesty, mopped up the mess I had made, and rolled to the other side of the bed.

"I don't know what I'm doing," I sighed. My voice was raw and husky. If I told him about my idea to build a submarine, he would be frightened for me. Maybe even concerned enough to interfere. Maybe I wanted him to.

16

"Where are you?"

There it was. I had known it was coming but it still made my heart start to pound, the idea of seeing him. I could fall back into our life together too easily. The Ceely of the past led a life that was less full, but it was familiar. "I'm in Montana. On a little farm with a pilot I met this morning, when I was still trying to get home. Tommy."

"Are you safe?"

"Yes."

"If you need someplace to stay, to figure things out, to heal, you should come to Reading. Get the first flight out that you can, I'll come get you. Just come home, Ceely."

I pressed my eyes shut. Every cell in my body hummed at the idea of James, home, even mom. Familiar streets, familiar buildings, landlocked, mundane, Reading. He still lived in our old house, as far as I knew.

"Aren't you seeing someone?"

"I am..." I could hear the indecision. "But I think you need me. I'll do whatever I need to do to help you get through this, just come. Please. I want you to come."

It would be too easy to say yes. But my equipment was on the way. My girls were still under the water. If I left them there, they would waste away or end up in the creature's stomach, dissolving, eventually be shit out and become ocean sediment. Or maybe their tiny

17

particles would mingle with the water and be evaporated, enter the water system, and I would feel guilty every time it rained for the rest of my years.

"I can't."

"Okay… Why don't I come to Montana, just to be with you for a little while?"

"I don't think we should. I'm throwing myself into a new project, I don't think I can find the time." It would hurt him, but it was the only way. He would understand my need to work on something, and in the end, it would only hurt more if he came out and I had to send him away.

We stayed on the phone a few hours, late into the night. Neither of us wanted to say goodbye. Eventually I must have drifted off with him still on the line. I woke up to the sun shining in the window, and the phone still in my hand, and a text from James wishing me deep sleep and peaceful dreams.

I turned the phone back off, after that, and left it off.

I worked like a woman possessed. Sleep would not come, not for more than a couple of hours and only when I physically collapsed. Tommy brought me coffee and meals a few times a day, I stopped to eat with him and joined him inside for dinners at his request. We didn't talk much, but I felt his concern and tried to assuage his fears. Soon I looked forward to his visits to the barn. When he asked about my progress, and I repeated out loud to him everything that I had accomplished, it helped to fight back the nagging fear

18

that I was moving too slowly, that I would never finish in time.

I did not call James again. I did not bother answering messages from friends. If I came out on the other side, I would deal with it all then.

A week passed and I had mostly assembled the crude, metal body of a tiny submarine. The engine and propeller were in place and functional. The ice chest and single overhead light were wired to the battery. The arms with contractable prongs to grab with were giving me the most trouble. Their composition was significantly more complex than anything else on the vessel.

In a normal assignment, I would be of more than high enough caliber as an engineer to create such a machine. But the sluggishness of my brain and the desperation were both weighing on me. I don't know how long I had been leaning on my work station, staring into the wiring of their slender arms when I shifted my weight to my other side, and just that small movement managed to knock over my empty coffee mug and send a box of screws toppling to the ground. It exploded on impact, black screws danced across the wooden floor, seemingly to every far corner of the room.

I felt a surge of disappointment, puffed out a big breath, then my hand shot up to my chest. Those hints of anger and sadness were only the tip of a long, cold blade of rage and grief and guilt that worked its way deeper as tears welled in my eyes. I sank to my knees once again and a sob tore its way out of me. Just a spilled box of screws, but I was weeping again, unable to rise, unable to drag myself out of swirling, crashing despair until minutes had passed, my tears had run dry, and my pain had faded to a numbness once again. Then I thought that I was ridiculous, sitting on the floor, crying over screws. I started scooping up the runaway screws, swore to myself that I would not break down like that again. But I knew -deep down- I had no idea who I was and what I was capable of anymore.

Tommy stepped into the barn. Looking past him, I realized it had gotten dark outside.

"You didn't come in for dinner. It's Taco Tuesday."

He set a plate of three hard-shell tacos and a beer down on my workbench beside me. Reached down and took hold of my arms, pulling me up.

"Thank you..." I steadied myself, my knees were shaking. I stuck my hands back into the guts of the mechanical arms. Its wires, like arteries, would leave me dead on the table if I left them for even a minute; I couldn't do it, I had found the metaphorical bleeder and needed to seal it off before it darted away like a fish in a river. "I have to finish this, I'm sorry."

"I understand." He went on standing there with his hands in his overall pockets, watching as I soldered the loose wire. Then he spoke his mind when I finally took a bite of taco. "You don't look well, Ceely. You should come inside and get a full night's rest."

"I can't."

"I know it seems like you need to keep working, but your brain is no good when it's exhausted. It only thinks it is."

My shoulders slumped under a weight I wasn't even previously aware of. "You're right. I'm too tired. That's why I'm not making the progress I should be."

"You'll get some sleep?"

"Yes."

I did try, even if it was in and out, tossing and turning, bad dreams filled with darkness all night. I was out in the barn again before dawn, with a large mug of coffee, and I did feel like I had a clearer head. And by the end of the day, the prongs were closing on my mechanical arms, they were welded in place along with a full circle of spotlights.

The final pieces of my submarine were in town, waiting. Tommy took me in his old Chevy truck. One massive, custom windshield twice as big as any you'd find on a vehicle and more than five times as thick, and two of the largest harpoon guns that money could buy, shipped in a wooden crate.

"I don't think that's a good idea, Ceely."

"I knew you wouldn't approve," I said. "But it's better to have it, and not need it, than to need it, and not have it."

I had no way of knowing, of course, whether the massive spear tips would even puncture the white, calcified-looking skin of the creature. It could withstand heat, that was obvious by the way it shook off the lava as it burst out of the fault. But the way it moved was also perfectly fluid, the skin was not really rock, although it gave that appearance. I supposed it was possible that down there, it had no natural predators, that it would not have evolved to withstand something sharp.

I also asked Tommy to take me to the local branch of my bank. I made a withdrawal of the money I would be leaving with him, sliding it into my purse in an envelope and not mentioning it to him as I climbed back in the passenger's seat. It was late in the afternoon by then.

"Should we grab a cheeseburger?" I asked, putting my sunglasses back on, brushing my brown hair behind my ear. In my boardroom blouse again, I was the most glamorous thing on the streets we rolled through; I knew that it would have made me happy at some point, to attract stares, to think of myself that way. I didn't care about any of it anymore, but Tommy beamed with pride whenever he waved to somebody he knew. I was no A-lister, not model material, but in this place, I would have been a beauty queen.

Cheeseburgers, fries, and strawberry milkshakes, eaten in the cab. As long as I was eating, with my gaze trained out on the grassy hill and trees of the lot next to the parking lot, I managed to keep my mind blessedly empty. The warm breeze blew over my face, carrying scents of cooking food and fresh cut grass, and it felt almost peaceful; I hardly existed. Then a child screamed as its sibling chased it around a picnic table, and my moment of blissful nothingness was shattered. I was a mother without a child, again.

My girls should be here with me now, I thought, *and that is the most unnatural part of all of this.* At least to me. More fundamentally wrong than a creature clawing its way up from the center of the Earth, shifting entire cities into the sea, killing millions, eating their bodies.

Tommy must have noticed my face pinch. He sighed. "I wish you wouldn't do this," he said, for probably the dozenth time. Then, ignoring the judgmental gazes of generations of strong, silent men who had come before him, he dug deep to try and make me understand. "I know you feel like you have to, but burying Jessica didn't make it hurt any less. It didn't make any of it make any sense. It certainly didn't bring her back."

I just cleaned up our wrappers. "We have to get back. I still have to mount the guns and windshield, do some final system checks. -Are you finished?"

He sighed again, started the engine, and drove us back to the farm without another word. I worked through the night. Lit by a single bulb overhead swaying in the cool wind blowing in the open barn door, and the faint glow from my torch. A final touch, I took a can of bright yellow spray paint to the body of the submarine. I drew my girls' names, stared at them for a long moment, and then covered them up like they were never there.

The yellow made the thing look a little bit like a toy. I had sudden fears that it would sink like a stone when lowered into the water. Worse, I would be a mile down among the wreckage of the city and I would spring a leak, or the engine would stall, and I would fall to the bottom, powerless.

I could swim to the top, probably. Abandon ship. There had already been reports of arrests; grave robbers rowing out on little boats, holding onto stones to sink down and find abandoned valuables. Scuba divers, too, popping up and being caught by roaming spotlights of the Naval vessels stationed nearby. But then, they were young. I was almost forty, exhausted, I hadn't gained too much weight with either pregnancy but was certainly not the hard-body I had been in my youth; hadn't been to a gym since Josie was born more than five years ago.

Damn. Astrid's birthday was in less than a month. She would have been eight.

Letting the paint dry and trying to trust in my own skills, I laid my jacket on the hard ground and stretched out. Cradling my head, I tried to sleep for a few hours, and must have drifted off at some point, because beeping of the flatbed backing up woke me before dawn. The sky had begun to lighten to a periwinkle blue. My body felt heavy at first as I dragged myself up, had a brief discussion with the driver that was meant to take me to the coast, and watched as he and two other men set up the straps and winch that would haul my submarine onto the truck. They were young men who all called me Ma'am and seemed delighted by my little vessel; asking to take pictures with it.

Tommy came out with a to-go mug of coffee made for me, and offered it without saying much.

"Thank you... Can I convince you to take the five thousand that I offered you?"

He had a small smile, and shook his head. "No, you cannot."

I had already left it tucked up under the visor in his truck. He would find it eventually. The sun would shine in his eyes one day as he climbed in, he would lower the visor, it would fall into his lap, and he would know. It was a nice thought to take with me, never expecting to see him or his farm ever again. He could sell off the tools I had left him with, too, and scrap materials.

Tommy held out a hand when we had nothing left to say. I pushed it aside and gave him a hug. I felt next to nothing in my waking moments -it had become like walking through a dream- but in my logical mind I knew that I had hardly been shown such kindness at any other point in my life, and certainly never by a complete stranger who wanted nothing from me. And I thought Tommy had found someone to care for when he needed someone, something.

Sometimes, things work out that way. He closed his arms around me and patted me on the back.

"Take care of yourself, Ceely."

"You too."

I rode in the front of the truck's king cab, while one of the movers drove and the other two sat in the back. We crossed Idaho as the sun rose behind us, and I kept stealing glances over my shoulder to make sure that my submarine was still there, that it hadn't fallen off the back of the truck or been a figment of my imagination. Every time I looked, there it was, glinting in the sunlight.

Down the coast of Oregon, to a little town at its southernmost point. With some difficulty we unloaded the sub into the water; it bobbed when it finally slid in, but it stayed afloat. A bit of tension dropped from my shoulders. Still tethered to the flatbed, it couldn't drift away. I shook the hands of the three men in the moving crew, they wished me luck although they had no idea what it was that I was planning.

I got the sense that I would be discussed around the water cooler, maybe a strange story to tell their families: "Once I brought this woman from a farm in rural Montana to the coast in Oregon with what looked like a homemade submarine. She was some big-shot engineer. She was never seen again. Pass the potatoes?"

My boots tapped the wood of the dock. I had brought my purse with me on my voyage, not having a reason to but being a woman it was unnatural to be out in the world without it. I slid its strap high on my shoulder. If it all went wrong, it would be good to have identification near my body. The sun was hanging in the western sky, out in front of me. Sky blue, with sparse, white clouds. The water of the Pacific was a deeper shade, rippling gently. It was fair weather for sailing, or submarining.

With one foot on the dock, I reached out the other, got it on the gently rounded top of the hull. Centering my body, bracing myself, I swung and leveraged my weight to get over. The sub drifted slightly with my momentum; I went down on my hands and knees to keep from toppling over. I undid the last tether, opened the top hatch, and then descended the ladder down into the chamber.

Closing the hatch, sealing myself in, I felt a crushing fear, a prickle of excitement. The ceiling of my metal tube was low, I had to hunch to move forward -past the ice chest, under the single light bulb- to get to the pilot's chair. It was a ripped old leather office chair I had taken from Tommy's barn. I took the wheels off and welded it to the floor at their four points. The control panels were simple, a wheel attached to the rudder, an ignition switch, two joy sticks which correlated to the robotic arms I could see tucked against the body of the submarine in front, through the broad windshield. A harpoon gun mounted to each, controlled by a single switch.

Settling into the utilitarian captain's chair, I pulled my legs up, crossing them, centering myself. My knees weren't what they used to be, but they would afford me a few minutes. I tossed my purse under the console. I shut my eyes and listened to the sound of my heart beating.

I reminded myself that I could climb out, swim to shore, let the submarine drift away. I could start over. Attend group therapy, learn to cope with my grief... I could have more babies, or adopt if that ship had sailed. I could get hired to a team working to kill that thing, be the one who designs the net that ensnares it and rips it from its watery wonderland, hauls it into the sky, dripping, screaming if it can scream.

I could do it all. I could do anything. I could buy a 1964 Aston Martin DB5 and road trip across the country, or down to South America. I could hot air balloon around the world. I could open a burlesque club. I could go home to Reading, marry James Bender and we could flip dilapidated houses, which he liked to do in his spare time. I could start mainlining heroin. But no matter what I chose, my girls would stay down there. Until the thing came and ate them, or a million little fish did it, piece by piece.

I flipped the switch to start the engine, thinking just to test it out. But the thing whirred to life, the submarine started to propel through the water, still at the surface with the gentle waves lapping at the top of the glass, but moving, humming, filling me with frenetic energy. I gripped the controls, opened the ballast tanks to let water into them, and dove.

The sea floor was not far, so close to shore. Greyish sand illuminated white by my ring of outward facing spotlights. Tufts of green seaweed rising a few feet up, washing inward and outward with the tide. Picking up speed, fish becoming aware of me and darting away, I found myself smiling as I dove through the Pacific, a yellow knife slicing through the increasingly dark waters, heading south toward home.

Chapter Three

After a few hours of steering south and charting my estimated position by my speed on an outdated map of the coast, I surfaced for fresh air. Standing with my feet in the rungs of the ladder, I opened the hatch on top of the sub and heaved it open; my arms were sore, from heavy lifting the last few days and from tension as I'd sat at the controls the last few hours. Water sloshed off of the hatch and salty droplets sprayed my face as I emerged, the warm breeze smelled clear and clean and I could see shoreline in the distance, nothing but blue waves and white froth and the gold reflections of the early evening sun on the other side.

I ate a peanut butter and jelly sandwich out of plastic wrap, chugged water and just breathed deep the sea air, let it inflate my lungs, and then exhaled, letting tension go. It might be the last time I saw the sun. The thought made my heart start to rattle, but I kept breathing, cleared my mind. I was scared that I might die, but I took in the sight, the smell, the feeling, absorbed the moment and felt truly right, righteous in what I was doing. There was nothing else to do. I ducked back inside, sealed the hatch, returned to the captain's chair.

A few more hours, a few hundred more miles with the water getting darker and more suffocating around me. My tension grew, the longer I sat behind the wheel, the less I could see into the ocean around me. Soon, my spotlights were only reaching a few feet out in front. I had to slow my pace to keep from colliding headfirst into something, as buildings were beginning to appear; I had come up on the outskirts of Los Angeles, to what was once the coast.

Some squat buildings had survived, little one and two-story shops and restaurants, plenty of others had been crushed by skyscrapers collapsing in the shift, like a prolonged earthquake just shaking them until their supports snapped and cement crumbled, steel bent, jagged pieces sticking out of crooked, gnarled buildings and a thick carpet of glass twinkling under my lights as I drifted over and between it all.

My measurements were only approximate; I had to find some sign to tell me where I was.

It took nearly an hour of aimless drifting before a green sign on a pole reflected white letters back to me. Pulling out my paper map, I found my location. My brain on autopilot, I immediately set to finding the way home via the interstate, before realizing my mistake and huffing angrily. I rested my eyes a moment, I breathed, I reminded myself that I was not in a car, heading home to make dinner, ask the girls about their day, about school, give the girls a bath, tuck the girls in for bed, have a glass of wine and enjoy the quiet hour before I turned into bed, myself. I was in a submarine. I could cut across most of Los Angeles as the bird flies, or as the fish swims, without worrying about evening traffic. I was going home to fetch my daughter's bodies, so they could be buried, so they would not be eaten.

I tilted the sub upward, getting over the tops of the buildings that were left standing. I cruised southeast, picking up speed and keeping my eyes peeled, staring into the black distance until my vision blurred. Some minutes I propelled through the water, thinking that the tiny flecks of white that were reflecting my light and zooming past the windshield were like stars outside of the Millennium Falcon as it jumped to light speed.

My lights fell on a white wall and my arms yanked back on the controls. My foot slammed down on an imaginary brake pedal. Letting off the throttle meant that the submarine slowed very little in the seconds before impact, I pinched my eyes shut and braced myself by grabbing the shelf on which my controls were mounted; still the force flung me forward over it, I cracked my forehead hard on the metal, my ribs jammed the edge of the shelf.

My eyes opened to catch sight of the white wall of rock rushing past my windshield which was miraculously unbroken. It was no wall at all, it was the creature speeding away. Its massive two-fluked tail sliced through the water and the water rippling sent my sub tumbling, I hit a wall, bounced, hit another wall, felt a crack of a rib, turning head over feet. Finally the spinning stopped, the sub stabilized, right-side-up, and I was laid out flat, gasping for breath with swirling pain closing in all around me once the shock lost its hold.

I had enough sense to reach up for the controls, fumbling for the light switch for a moment and finally pushing it. Darkness descended. I found the engine shutoff next, it was chugging along, sounding distressed, and then it was silent except for the gentle swish of water moving past the sub's walls, the crunch as the vehicle settled down onto the gravel and broken glass of the new seafloor.

"Fuck," I muttered to myself. "Fuck me."

That thing had no eyes, I was certain. It hadn't seen me coming, maybe it had some kind of sonar or maybe it detected my movements, the whir of the engine or some other way and came to investigate, or maybe it was just sniffing out bodies nearby and some little bug had bumped into it. A bug I was, to that thing. My little submarine could not have put a dent in that thing's side at full speed, couldn't have really hurt it. Certainly not like it hurt me.

Every breath was painful, even just laying still in the silent darkness for what must have been an hour. I had to give that thing plenty of time to swim away, to

33

go and find a meal or investigate a Navy ship further off the coast. I would stay closer to the bottom, even if it meant that I had to travel slower.

When I rolled over and hauled myself up, a groan tore itself out of me. I bit my lip and silenced myself as I settled into the captain's chair once again. I'd had worse. I had a long way to go, still.

My air was beginning to feel a bit warm, smell stale and sweaty when I came upon familiar streets. I had plenty of time before I would have reason to be concerned, would need to resurface once I had the girls' bodies, anyway, to put them in the chest freezer. In the back of my mind, I had known that would be part of the night, but really considering it made me let up on the throttle. If I hadn't lost my mind already, then cradling my daughters' surely bloated and nibbled on bodies, smelling their rot would do it.

I am going insane tonight, I thought, and repeated it like a mantra as I pushed forward and the sub picked up speed. *I am going insane tonight.* Maybe insanity would be bliss. It would have to be more peaceful than endless grief.

At least an hour to our old neighborhood. The kids always wanted to go into the city. Astrid was old enough to know that we didn't really live in LA, even if we said that we did, and had begun to call our area 'the suburbs'. Josie copied everything her big sister did, I might as well have had twins. They griped -and I had loved my updated apartment in the heart of downtown,

34

when it was just me and Astrid- but I wanted them to have a yard where they could grow and get dirt on their bare feet.

My mind had wandered as my hands steered the chugging submarine toward home, having to rise to clear some buildings and debris and lowering again as soon as I did. I knew that I had to focus, keep my eyes peeled. The ring of spotlights on the top of my craft did not illuminate enough water, the windshield did not provide an unobstructed view; the creature could come from the side, or come up behind me. The sub might not survive another hit.

I stayed low. Before long I was damp with sweat, my arms were shaking as I held the controls out in front of me. Whether it was the night's tension, the approaching horror of handling my children's bodies, or the past week's insomnia, stress, grief finally taking its toll, I couldn't know. My eyes were bleary, too. I reached up to rub them, feeling static behind my lids and demanding their compliance for a few more hours.

I was on our old block. Streets were familiar, soon I was passing houses I recognized, our neighbors. I puttered past cars parked forever on our sunken street. One had a bloated, wilting white face like a melted ice cream cone still in the driver's seat; had he run for the car when the rumbling started? Had he had a heart attack inside, or had his seat belt been stuck, door gotten jammed, and trapped him inside when the water washed over this place?

The house next door to ours had its second level caved in. Ours was a ranch style, orange brick and white stucco. As I finally came face to face with my home, it looked like I could walk in the front door and my girls would come running to greet me. Only a few brown clay shingles had fallen from the roof, the front windows were shattered, and their glass scattered on the turf. I had not considered, in all of my planning, how I would get inside the house. I hoped the sub could fit through the big bay window in the living room. If not, then the integrity of the house had to be compromised, after a week underwater. I could hit it hard from above.

I steered slowly and carefully around the building, taking down the wooden fence between our yard and the neighbor's, uprooting posts and cement from softened ground. Dirt stirred up from the new seafloor and briefly obscured my vision. I held my position as best I could, but the wall of the submarine scraped along the wall of my house, sending rasping echoes around my narrow chamber. The sediment particles cleared from the water around me, and I made it to the picture window, also shattered.

Jagged chunks remained in the frame. The wooden floors of my living room shined under my lights, and my body arrested the sub's movements before I had decided to. I stayed there, struggling with tiny adjustments to the controls to keep the machine level, without hitting the ground or drifting upward. My heart was suddenly in my throat, my eyes were flooding with warmth and my nose was prickling. I could hardly breathe.

I couldn't even shut my eyes to meditate, I just had to grip the controls harder and steer myself in. My gasping breaths hurt my chest and I was crying, trying not to sob, gritting my teeth and seething, feeling saliva flick out onto my chin. I had to go in, or I never would. Waiting would only make it worse. My air was stale, my sweat was warm under my armpits and across the top of my back, dripping down my spine, making me feel even warmer and damper and worse. Of course I knew it wouldn't be a basket of roses, but I hadn't imagined just how bad it all could feel.

Inside my living room. Demolishing the ceiling fan, with the blades drifting down around me. I went high because of the furniture, but when I scraped the ceiling, and white powder clouded my view once again, my hands automatically course corrected downward and I landed on the wooden coffee table, smashing it to bits. The couch got shoved out of the way, surely gouging its legs into my lovely, wooden floors, but that hardly mattered anymore. I was fighting my way through the living room, to the narrow hallway which would prove an even bigger problem.

If I fit at all, there would be impact involved. The plaster of the walls would be crumbling into the water all around, a thick cloud. My view would be impaired, and the doorway to the girls' room would be even narrower, I'd need to break through a few inches of wall. If I didn't have momentum, I could easily become wedged at any of several points. But a big enough knock could dislodge something in the engine, I could be stranded and have to abandon the mission, swim for the surface. If I made it, I would surely be picked up by a Navy ship or caught once I reached the shore, there would be questions, maybe federal charges. If I didn't go to prison, I would certainly be monitored and never have another chance.

Controls forward, the sub surged into the hallway and bounced off each wall in succession, gouging chunks out and filling the water all around with clouds of white. I both hear and feel the impact of crushing my little hall table, the mostly decorative, green, glass cake dish surely shattering and shards drifting in my wake. The engine whirred, struggling, my progress slowed, momentum robbed in each impact, I could see the end of the hallway and the open doorway to the bigger bedroom the girls shared. I jerked the controls and the propellor spun me and gave a new burst of speed that shot me through its archway; one final crunch and I broke free into the room.

My heart still thudding in my chest was the only indication I had that I was still alive. My extremities felt cold, heavy. I didn't want to look inside the room, but my eyes would not shut. Pastel pink walls, white dressers and a white vanity table with the mirror still somehow intact. I locked on it; I don't know if I thought that my children's dead bodies would turn me

38

to stone if I looked at them directly, or if -because it was all reversed- the room inside the mirror looked like it belonged to somebody else.

The girls' bunk beds were empty, their covers tossed to the floor, stirring gently as water was displaced with my intrusion as though they were swaying in a summer breeze. Manipulating the submarine to inch closer to the mirror, the angle changed and more of the ceiling came into view, and there they were, floating. White bodies in white nightgowns, with dark plumes of hair fanning out and waving.

I felt my lip quiver, my eyes pinch shut. Bile surged up my throat, burning its way out and I heaved on the metal floor at my feet. The revulsion spread out from my stomach to my slumping shoulders, my weak arms, my trembling hands holding my hair back. But as my vomit stopped, my shivers dissolved, I sat back and I felt clearer headed than I had in days. I had to do it. I was their mother, and nobody else was going to take care of them, if I didn't. It was almost over.

I spun the sub around. Looking at my girls through my own eyes, angling the sub upward and activating the mechanical arms which were held close to the body to protect them. I had to keep one hand on the steering mechanism at a time, while with the other I maneuvered the arm slowly out, nudging Astrid's body first down off of the ceiling. It bobbed back up before I could get the machine's prongs around it; its putrefaction floating it, gases being released by her decay wanting to bring her up for the birds.

Lake Superior never gives up its dead; but this is the Pacific.

I knocked into the ceiling, brought her down, rotated the two pinching mechanisms skillfully and getting them around her abdomen, then sliding them closed. That was Astrid, my first baby, secured. I could almost feel the squishiness of her flesh, her coldness, through the metal. But I was bringing her home.

Josie was smaller. It took three tries, nudging her down from the ceiling, accidentally scraping it with the mechanical arm's two claws, rotating them and inserting them into the space around her, closing them as gently but firmly as I could on her rounder, more childlike belly. It deflated under my claws. A few bubbles of some trapped gas rushed out of her mouth. I shuddered.

That was both of my girls, secured. I found myself speaking, out loud, as if they could hear me. As if they were the ones who needed comforting, when really, it was me. "It's okay. Mommy's here. Mommy's got you." I caught my breath, pressed a hand on my chest to try to soothe the aching muscles, so tight they felt ready to snap. While I was still inside the sunken house, I felt relatively shielded from what lurked in the sea surrounding Los Angeles. But I still had a long way to go, back to safety.

First, I should break for the surface, pull my girls from the water and load them into the freezer. It would feel disgusting, but they would be safer inside, and the cold would keep them from breaking down any further. It was for them. Actually, first I had to make it back down that narrow hallway without getting stuck. I tucked Astrid and Josie as close to the body of the submarine as I could, praying the mechanical arms would hold, and surged forward.

Chapter Four

Out of the house, back in open water, I angled the sub upward and broke straight for the surface. A school of silver fish that had settled in around my chimney scattered. The engine chugged audibly in the rear of the vessel, sounding more labored than it had at the start of the evening, although maybe I was just paying more attention.

I was near the surface when I noticed the spotlight, its white beam cutting through the darkness and flashing right in my eye for a second before continuing its roaming. My hands automatically eased up on the controls, I leveled my craft and started cruising north. They couldn't have seen me and would not be equipped to come and retrieve me even if they had. At least I hoped so. Why were they even in the area? Had they picked me up on a radar somehow? Or…

With my hackles rising all over my exhausted body, I turned the sub so that my limited view was pointed back the way I had come. I cut the engine so that I wouldn't lose any ground -much like a shark, my submarine could not reverse-and I could feel the slight pull of gravity as the sub started to sink; I had at least a minute before I would be in danger of hitting the bottom or any debris. In my own limited circle of light, for a moment, I saw nothing. Then the spotlight from the presumably Navy vessel shifted again, and its tunneling white light illuminated the broad side of the creature. Its long skull was angling toward me, its massive body with rippling white skin flexed and it propelled forward with a flick of its tail.

Of course, the Navy was tracking the creature, the creature was tracking me. It was either curious of the vibrations I gave off or it was hungry for the snacks I was carrying through the water, with microscopic bits flaking off and leaving a trail in our wake. The pit in my stomach did nothing to help me, I was on my own and had a second to decide what to do. My mind whirred like my struggling engine. Keep the engine off, kill the lights and let myself sink? It worked last time, the creature did not come and find me on the bottom. But another hit as I sank could find me stuck there, abandoning ship and my daughters.

Without really deciding it, I started the engine again, and was immediately propelling through the dark water toward the creature, heading for it as it headed for me. My clammy hands squeezed tighter on the controls, index fingers pried loose from the rest and hooking like claws into the triggers for my harpoon guns. Maybe that thing was coming to investigate the noises, or maybe it smelled rotting flesh and was coming to rip my daughters out of my hands once again, this time eating them in front of my eyes. I would ram it head-on with everything I had, imploding my windshield and wrecking my sub before I let that happen.

The few seconds that it drifted out of the Navy ship's light -meandering in a curve in my direction and becoming almost invisible in the dark- were some of the longest of my life. Then it entered my sphere of light, its prehistoric snout appearing first and its gargantuan jaws spreading open, ready to pluck one of my girls or swallow my sub whole. Its teeth were sharp, tinier than expected but there were two rows of them outside of the blackish purple of its gums and throat muscles.

My harpoons were mounted on the mechanical arms holding the girls. I steered my dominant, right hand out instinctively and there was Josie offered out to it, or leading my charge like the beautiful, gnarled wooden figurehead at the helm of a pirate ship of old, and I squeezed that trigger with a jerk of my entire body, clenching my teeth so tight that they could almost explode like tiny defective lightbulbs and seething out between them, "Fuck you!"

The harpoon fired into the cavernous mouth of the creature and I saw a puff of black blood cloud the water before it whipped its big head away and a keening cry

44

tunneled into my eardrums, a blade as sharp as the spear tip of my harpoon. I recoiled from my controls, cupping my head and gasping in pain, and I didn't see what happened next outside in the ocean, but the creature must have displaced a lot of water darting away to send me spinning the way it did. Something was not right about it; sound should not be able to travel through the water like that. I would not understand it until much later.

I tumbled off the side and top of the submarine once again. Flung from my captain's chair, remembering rolling my mother's Cadillac when I was seventeen and wishing I had installed some kind of harness, I took blow after blow, my entire weight landed on my right shoulder first, then my left thigh connected with the protruding metal seam where the pieces of the submarine were welded together, and then I landed on my side and rolled with the momentum I had built as the sub did manage to right itself and coast.

I did not have time to catalogue the damage, to sit with my pain. I flung myself to my feet, almost toppling over or passing out as I stood and banging my head on the ceiling in my carelessness, I hissed, "Fuck," and tossed myself ass-first into the captain's chair again. My engine had stalled, I was sinking, I could not see the creature in the open water in front of me, I had no idea which direction I was facing but the girls were thankfully still clutched in the mechanical arms out in front, no worse for wear.

I flipped the engine's switch off, prayed to the nameless, faceless controlling force of the universe and flipped it back on. A moment's chug, then another stall. I turned it off again and did not ask, but demanded, "Work, God dammit!" I pushed the switch and it fired to life and I was in control once again. Putting the sub into a tailspin, I found the Navy spotlight and the white flank of the creature in the distance. It was retreating to a safe distance but turning and fleeing did not even enter my mind, I accelerated, pushing the submarine to its limits. The creature wheeled back around, its top half flipping upside-down and then rotating in a wormlike way that made me wonder if it even had a spine. Its eyeless face was coming right at me when I heard the first boom, its volume loud enough that I instinctively shielded my head again. Was the Navy firing? Finally given the okay to send that thing to Hell?

Light flashed over the surface, brightening everything in my line of sight for a split second, showing me how the creature's hideous two-pronged legs were lifted out in front, ready to snag and claw and pierce. It was defensively drawing itself upright in the water, so immensely long that it could not even sit up straight, its tail was still behind it somewhere. Its underside exposed, the place where its stomach should be, I twitched and took aim, ignoring what I was now sure was a storm rolling overhead.

Wind had to be whipping fiercely, howling. I could definitely feel subtle changes to the way that the water was rolling around me, roiling, angry, nudging me more strongly than before, but I stayed my course, heading for the thing's wide-open abdomen. I had to get within range. I had only one, comparatively small harpoon left. It was practically a toothpick to that thing. But I had to hit it again, I was itching to. It would not stop coming for my girls.

Thunder boomed overhead again, louder than I'd ever heard before, but I was ready for it and only flinched for a fraction of a second. Lightning struck. A flash of white as far as I could see, showing that thing still holding itself upright and legs poised, ready. I felt the water sing with electricity, sure I felt the current dispersing through my controls and up into my arms, leaving tingles in its wake as I came within range and blood or sweat -I didn't know which- rolled down the side of my face. I steered the mechanical arm which held Astrid out in front, taking aim.

Let this find its heart, if it has one, I prayed. "Please."

I was not sitting anymore, the frantic energy demanded I be on my feet like a rabid dog about to attack, hunched over the controls. I was ready to be flung away again, wreck the engine, break the windshield, water rushing in; whatever happened, happened. I wrenched the trigger. The harpoon spewed from the gun and after a second of sailing through the open ocean and out of the brightness of my circle of lights, the horrible shrieking of the creature pierced my ears again, a cloud of black blood colored the water as it was still ringing in my head and another crack of thunder deafened me, another flash of white lightning lit everything as the bolt seemed to come down, slicing through the water and straight into the metal arm out in front of me, into Astrid, through her.

My own circle of lights popped, white balloons, including the single bulb over my head which exploded and showered me with little shards of glass. Energy surged out of the controls and into my palms and up my arms, burning the entire way and zinging up into my skull, frying me like an egg, killing everything inside, no thought, no me, just pain. The last thing I was aware of was the empty silence where the whir of my engine, the keening of the creature, and the boom of thunder had all just been. But no longer. I was falling.

*

I landed on my side, having lost my bearings but not consciousness, and the only sound was my blood pounding in my ears. I felt wrong; the pain that had run through every cell in my body was gone, making each breath feel like rapturous pleasure in the way that it felt like nothing special. The rest of my pain was gone, too. Blood had dried on the side of my face, matted my hair to the side of my head, my cracked rib no longer tweaked with pain at every movement, my arms and legs were numb and heavy but did not ache. I wasn't sure if I had exaggerated my injuries to myself earlier, or if the lightning strike had killed my nerves, made it impossible for me to feel pain anymore. Would that be the first stroke of luck I'd had since that creature showed up?

My girls were still in danger, I couldn't rest. Knocking pieces of light bulb out of the way, I pushed myself up onto my hands and knees, but then I stopped. Something was wrong. The water outside of the sub was medium blue, I could see fish darting around the tops of sunken buildings in the distance. The creature was gone, disappeared without a trace. The Navy ship was gone. Astrid was still clutched in the mechanical arm pointed out in front of the windshield, but there was no cloud of dark hair in the water around her. Her head was bald, her face was sunken, her skin no longer looked bloated but instead compressed, almost skeletal. Josie was the same way.

Maybe I had passed out without realizing, my brain was scrambled. Maybe it was the next morning, and the girls' bodies had been affected by the lightning strike, and the creature had fled. But I could feel the slow descent of the submarine. I was sinking, seemingly right where I had been when the lightning flashed and struck us. Realizing it, I climbed into the chair, and, without much hope, I flipped the switch to fire up the engine. Surprisingly it came chugging back to life, and I inclined us toward the daylight at the surface.

In my encroaching confusion, I had noticed that the hair bouncing into my line of vision on the side not caked with blood was grey, and it had hardly registered, but with one hand on the controls, keeping us ascending, I reached up and twisted a lock around my fingers. It was as grey as a barn cat you'd call 'blue'. Grabbing another handful of short strands, looking hard out of the corner of my eye, I found them the same. Not just a streak, but my entire head had gone grey. I had heard of a lightning strike or intense fear causing hair to start growing white, but nothing like what I was seeing, not in an instant.

But had it really been only an instant, or had it been a few hours? Long enough for the sun to rise... Reaching the surface, I purged the water from the ballast tanks and opened the channels for them to fill with air. The sub bobbed, floating. Then, lifting the mechanical arms high, I removed my girls from the ocean. Held aloft like that, I couldn't know if they might attract sea birds in their current state, or, if -as I suspected from their appearance- their flesh had been dried and become sort of mummified, aged like my hair. I had to put them inside in the chest freezer, either way.

I grabbed my compact mirror from the contents of my purse scattered around the floor of the submarine along with the broken glass. A suspicion was creeping up on me that something was very wrong with all of it; everything. I needed light, and I needed air.

Climbing the ladder, I unscrewed the hatch and heaved it open with my weary muscles. Fresh and warm sea air washed over me. I felt overcome with the beauty of it, like seeing the ocean for the first time. For the first time since the creature came out of the fault, I thought that there could still be good things coming my way. Just that breeze was enough to make me glad to still be alive. I kept my eyes trained on the horizon. I was not ready to look at my girls, yet, held aloft, offered up…

Instead I climbed up onto the submarine, which swayed as I centered my weight. I sat astride it like an unruly, yellow horse.

Breathing deep, my rib did not hurt, but my breath seemed shallower, obstructed, almost like I had developed pneumonia. Probing my side under my blouse, I felt the ridges of my ribcage, and I could feel where one's arch wasn't quite right. It didn't hurt. It definitely had been broken; that was not all in my mind. It was fully healed, at a slightly wrong angle.

Out in the bright day, with the compact clasped in my hand, I noticed the liver spots on my skin. It added to my unease. But I told myself: *You're being ridiculous.* I found the courage to open the thing up and lift it. The face looking back at me might as well have been my mother's. Her strong jaw and petite nose, brown eyes blood shot and tunneled into a once handsome face. I was easily going on seventy, not forty. I had wrinkles, and not just the laugh lines around my

51

mouth, tiny crow's feet at the corners of my eyes when I smiled. My skin sagged.

My breasts, too, I realized. I could feel them hanging lower on my abdomen, sticking with sweat under their folds, and it was uncomfortable. Sure, they had dropped some after I stopped breastfeeding, but not like that; not thinner and stretched. I had the tits of a grandmother, not a mother.

I never thought of myself as vain, nor a true beauty, but I had liked the way I looked. I liked to accentuate good features with a little makeup. To feel desirable.

When I had been imagining all of my possible futures, there had been many different avenues. Some were absurd. But the thing they all had in common was that I had time. And I had not seriously imagined having more children. If the thought had popped into my head, I had smushed it down; it would feel like a betrayal; I could never replace my babies. But I had known, in the back of my mind that I could have more, naturally or by acquiring them.

I couldn't even walk into an adoption agency in the most war-torn of third-world countries and expect them to give me a child, anymore. It was all gone, and the endless possibility of the golden light reflected on the gentle water of the wide ocean felt like it mocked me. The breeze and sound of lapping waves could seemingly lend blissful oblivion to anyone but me. I didn't scream, or cry; there was no point. It was all gone. Past, present, and future.

I was gone.

Part Two
The USS 'Last Chance' Baton Rouge

Chapter One

It was the strangest little water craft that I had ever seen. Bright yellow, shining as it bobbed along on the tumultuous waves that were thick and dark in the overcast evening. Roiling grey clouds overhead promised a hell of a storm, and that submarine worked its way closer at the rate of a golden Labrador doggy-paddling after a stick.

The lookout had rung a bell in the crow's nest. The old fashioned alarm system was connected by a system of wires to the captain's quarters, the mess hall, the hall outside of the crew's sleeping chambers and -of course- my office. The sound of the tiny bell on my end of the call starting to tinkle as the wire bounced it up and down startled me at first. I was bent over my desk, with papers scattered, and that bell had not chimed in the two weeks I had been onboard. Neither had the modern, electric sirens which would imply a creature attack. That realization calmed me.

The alarm, though, confused me; sleep was hard to come by, with the constant rocking of the ship. I had no natural affinity for the water, no sea legs to speak of, and although the sickness had abated after the first few days as long as I drank my ginger tea, my mind was sluggish.

Alarm, I came to the slow realization. *A generic alarm.* It meant all hands to our stations, whether that was the engine room or the helm or the gunner's turret. Whether it would be wiser to stay in the relative shelter of my centrally located office, or whether I should head to the deck to be more quickly able to evacuate, I did not know. The Captain would head up, and so I decided that was what I would do, as well.

Not only was it my place, my duty to be by his side to record and report any actions taken, but he was the only one in that place whose presence could make me feel something like safe. I took my leather ledger. I never left it unattended, as was the duty of my station.

The narrow hall, metal painted white, shifted below me and I stumbled into a closed door. "Darn," I exclaimed, and just as I had righted myself, the door swung inward with a creak. Three bodies rushed past me and one barreled straight into my shoulder, spinning me to the ground.

"Out of the way!"

The men went running up the stairs and onto the deck. Only one hung back. It was Roshin, the Arab with the tunnel-eyes, rough stubble, and a rangy build. He offered his hand.

"Are you alright, Jacob?"

My head was still spinning, my pen's clip had come off the cover of my ledger. I scooped it up and stuck it into my mouth so that I could accept his hand. His were large and a deep brown, mine were small and white and soft by comparison. He had worked with his hands before stepping onto this boat and he would work with them again if he lived to step off of it. As he pulled me to my feet and steadied me -there had to be muscle hidden under his modest clothes- I grumbled around my pen, "Mm-hm. Thank you."

"Go on. Let's see what fresh Hell…"

It was the most I had ever heard him speak. He kept his voice hardly above a whisper. He sounded intelligent and I found myself stealing a glance back at him as I climbed the stairs; I was not afraid, exactly, but I was not immune to the intensity of his presence. Plenty of the men on the ship were criminals, plenty liked to throw their weight around, but Roshin, I thought, had to have seen more than all of them, and was capable of more than most because of that.

On the immense deck of the freighter, men gathered at the starboard side. Roshin went to join them, while I looked aft and then stern, and found the captain through the glass of the enclosed control room. His smooth head, his face and neck decorated with tattoos, his short but fit body leaning forward over the comm systems. I ran to join him, and he hardly glanced up as I entered. My insignificance stung me anew.

He went on speaking into a handheld, "This is the Captain of the USS *Baton Rouge*, you are approaching a protected vessel, you do not have clearance to dock. Stop and identify yourself, or you will be blown out of the water." His voice was deep and rough, but as easy and steely as the architecture of the ship, as exalted. If it was a terrorist approaching in that yellow sub - environmental or otherwise- then the Captain would sink it without batting an eye.

My heart had begun to pound in my chest. My palms were sweaty as they gripped my leather ledger. I had not seen the ship's guns used, and the idea of it gave me a thrill which turned sickening a moment later. There had been so many wavers to sign, so much talk in the mess hall of the danger of one of these missions, one in three would die, they said, although the actual sum was one in three-point-two-six, and it applied not to individuals within the same mission but to missions as a whole; about one in three ended in shipwreck and mass death. The other two out of three might have an accident at the drilling site, or a flu outbreak that would result in one casualty or medivac out -lost work incidents- but most of the crew would return mostly intact. More than half of the assigned crew had deserted before we shipped out. Then, once we got onboard, there had been nothing but monotony and open water for fifteen days.

I did not want to be someone who wanted to see someone sunk in the ocean for breeching a protected zone around government property. At the same time, I was a representative of the company Carius Industries. And due to their government contract, any failure to fulfill my duty constituted failing the United States as well. If it had to be done, I had to witness and document.

The Captain listened with a headset pressed to only one ear. Hearing nothing, he switched to a different frequency and repeated himself. Again, he seemed to get no response. He switched to the ship's intercom system and his voice blared out of speakers all around. "This is the Captain of the USS *Baton Rouge*, you are approaching a protected zone around this vessel. You do not have clearance to dock. If you come any closer, I am authorized to fire on you. Stop and identify yourself immediately."

The men gathered at the ship's railing shouted, "Shoot it, Captain!"

"Blow it up!"

Roshin looked back to watch the Captain, but his eyes flicked to me and I had to look away. The Captain's mouth was a firm line. His eyes narrowed, making the teardrop tattoo at the right one's corner lift just a hair higher. He was considering, he looked out of the glass encasing us, to where another man was up on the gun turret, waiting for his signal. I could feel the back of my neck prickling, afraid that he would give the signal and afraid that he would not. If the yellow submarine got much closer, it would be within range to put a hole in our side if it self-destructed, or if it had some kind of torpedo under the water line.

I squinted, lifted my reading glasses up off the bridge of my nose so I could see it better. It certainly did not look like something an enemy nation would have sent; it did not look like it belonged in the Pacific at all; it was more suited for Lake Michigan. At its front, where the dark waves lapped at it, I thought I could see two small tubes mounted on protruding metal, square right-angles unlike the rest of it.

"Captain," I found myself speaking, nervous but excited, "I think there are harpoon guns mounted on the front. This might be a small-time fisherman without a comm's system. It looks homemade…"

He looked at me out of the corner of his dark eye. "A poacher. It might be, or it might be a drone filled with C-4. It has no electronic license, and it shouldn't be in these waters…" He moved to the door and called to the gunner, "One shot, non-explosive. Give him a chance to abandon ship."

The men crowded at the railing groaned in disappointment, although Roshin had his eyes shut, his hand clutching a necklace he kept tucked into his shirts and his mouth was forming whispered words. Another man reached out and gave him a shove.

"Knock off that 'Akbar' shit!"

Roshin's tunnel eyes were dark. He moved away, further down the deck, and continued his prayer, this time with his eyes open.

The gunner was switching from one mounted gun to another, loading the chamber with a massive bullet, and taking aim.

"Wait!" I shouted, seeing a flash of white movement somehow in the submarine through the darkness of its wide window. "He's coming out!"

"Hold fire," the Captain ordered, heeding my warning, and my heart jumped up into my throat.

The yellow submarine's top hatch handle spun, then flipped open. A grey head appeared, and out climbed a figure that was unmistakably an old woman with broad shoulders and wide, maternal hips. Somebody's grandmother, alone in a tiny submarine out on the Pacific Ocean.

The men at the railing cackled at the sight of her, one wolf-whistled and some bent over and went to the ground from laughing so hard. Roshin and I found each other's gazes again, and he gave me the slightest nod of his head. It was instantly gratifying, but it was not enough; I looked to the Captain and found him squinting at the woman, arms crossed. He did not look my way as he headed back into the control room and spoke to her over the intercom.

"Woman in the yellow submarine, remain where my gunner can see you. I'm coming over with my bomb technician to search your vessel before you'll be allowed to dock. Do you understand?"

She unmistakably gave a thumb's up, then climbed all the way out of the manhole and sat on top of her vessel, with her legs hung over one side. Her grey hair was cut short and matronly around her square face, but still caught the breeze. She lifted her face to it, looking content and totally harmless.

A bald man probably in his fifties, tall and fit for his age, broke away from the dozen men gathered at the railing. He had not been cheering with the others, more dignified by far. He was just smiling, amused with the afternoon's turn of events. "By 'bomb technician', I take it that you mean me?"

"You are correct," the Captain said. "Get what you need and meet me at the Zodiac."

The bald man -Perry, his name was- moved briskly for the stairs and took them down, while I followed the Captain to where one of the dozen inflatable Zodiac rafts was stored in a compartment under the ship's deck. I was nervous. "Should you really go over there, Captain? What if something goes wrong? I really think our superiors would prefer it if you sent someone of a lower rank for the initial investigation-."

"-Stop," the Captain ordered, as I had been rambling. "I'm going, and so are you. What kind of captain would I be if I left this to someone else?"

The smart kind, I thought, but didn't dare say it. He cared more about keeping the respect of the crew than following policy. "Me?"

"You're going to have to document my flagrant disregard of policy, aren't you?"

I blinked. I wasn't sure if he was being truly adversarial or if he were just mocking my position as clerk, scribe, reporter, snitch. Honestly, if he asked me nicely not to say anything, I would keep my mouth shut. But it wouldn't happen. "I suppose. What makes that man Perry qualified to be your bomb technician?"

The Captain held the tightly wrapped square of plastic out over the edge of the ship, with a single tether tied and expertly knotted to the railing. He pulled a ripcord and it triggered a chemical reaction inside of the raft, causing it to hiss and inflate in a few seconds as it fell to the choppy surface of the ocean. Just looking at it made me feel dizzy. Paddles were stowed nearby, and a rope ladder to get down.

"What makes him qualified is that he's the closest thing to an expert I've got out here."

"Was he Army? Navy? Marines?" I certainly would think so, even watching him as he comes back up the stairs securing a fanny pack around his waist.

"Army."

"And he worked in the field of disarming explosives?"

"No. He just knows bombs."

It did not make me feel any better, and I realized that if I made it back to the *Baton Rouge*, I would be up all night reading personnel files. I should have done it already, probably -to know what I was dealing with- but apart from the Captain, the crew were the least interesting part of my work. They were hardly people to me, just expenses and liabilities and tools.

"After you." The Captain gestured for me to descend the ladder first. He hated me. Found me irritating, at least. Wanted me to suffer.

"Hold that for you?" Perry offered, hand extended.

He meant my ledger, which I was never to let out of my possession. I shook my head, tucked it up against my neck, holding it between my chest and my chin. Then I gingerly swung one leg out, finding perch on the ropes, and started a slow climb down with arms tense and shaking all the way. I was pummeled by wind that made the entire ladder drift with me on it and made my stomach drop. The ladder ended before it touched the water. I had to reach out with one leg to try to hook the Zodiac with a toe, and drag it in. Even sure that it was under me, my transition was graceless. Somehow, I dunked into the water up to one ankle as I flung myself down into the cradle of the raft.

Perry was right behind me, settling down onto his haunches, smiling a carefree smile, inhaling deep the scent of the sea breeze. The Captain came last, dropping two paddles and standing easily with his legs spread as he produced a knife and sliced the tether. It was a small craft made for at most six people.

"Let's go."

Each of the two men began to paddle, alternating sides, while I sat at the back and watched our slow progress. The woman with the grey hair laid down across the top of her submarine. Even from a distance and even with her age, she gave the impression of a sunbathing beauty; she would not burn, the day was not bright between the coming storm and the usual smog. It seemed that even I could appreciate a woman's figure, her glamorous presence, after a few weeks at sea with no female presence around.

The closer we got to the yellow submarine, the more interesting its makeup became to me. With my glasses lifted once again, I squinted and made out its crude seams, single propellor at the back and quite surely single engine, because there would not be room for two. The metal protruding at the front of the vessel appeared to be two moveable arms folded inward, and those certainly were harpoon guns, unloaded, welded on top of them. So she was maneuvering underwater with the plans to grab things, and possibly to spear fish. For food? Or for defense? Those little guns could do nothing against the creature from the fault, except, maybe, make it angry.

Thinking about it made me instinctually look over the edge of the Zodiac, into the water, clear only for a few feet down and growing darker, so deep a person couldn't really comprehend it. That thing could be down there. Other things, too. Other faults in the ocean floor shifted all the time; something smaller could have come up without anybody noticing. Something even meaner. Something that zapped like an electric eel, or stabbed a poisonous barb that could pop our little raft and drag us down…

The sea air washed over a sheen of sweat that had broken out on my face. I felt even smaller than usual. I looked at the captain and just the sight of him eased me a little.

A few long minutes of the two older men paddling feverishly in front of me. Soon their backs were both damp in the indents of their shoulders, their back muscles, the canals along their spines and the Captain's dimples at the back of his exquisitely narrow hips, where a gun was tucked into the waistband of his pants. I never really noticed the heat except on other people, but took the time to roll my sleeves up, trying to keep the cuffs crisp and straight.

By the time we reached the yellow submarine, its grey-haired driver had sat up and surveyed us with hard eyes. "Hello. Welcome aboard." She extended her hand downward.

Lips pressed into a straight line, the Captain loosed his shirt so that it hung over the gun. He accepted her hand, reached up with his other to get ahold of the lip of the open hatch, got one foot midway up the body of the vessel and pushed off. Up he went, dragging himself but also being helped by the woman. He then turned and offered Perry the same hand. Up the big old man went. Their combined weight sank the sub lower in the water.

"Stay in the raft, Jacob."

I deflated, I had wanted so badly to look inside the submarine. But I was nothing if not a follower of orders, and somebody had to say behind, keep the raft nearby. Hopefully there would be time to inspect the submarine later.

The Captain leaned over the porthole to survey the inner chamber of the vessel from above. "Check it out, Perry." The older man climbed down inside, while the other two stayed on top. The Captain addressed the woman. "I'm Captain Alvarado. Who are you?"

"Captain Bennett," her tone was cool, she looked off into the distance. I scribbled a log of the conversation in shorthand, just to be thorough.

"Your vessel lacks an electronic identification, and comms systems, too? What's its purpose?"

"Its purpose? It doesn't really have one, anymore. It's decommissioned." Her answer was slow. I didn't get the impression that she was searching for a lie, maybe she just didn't feel like answering. Her eyes showed irritation, exhaustion.

"Why are you out here? Why did you approach the *Baton Rouge*?"

She considered. "I was lost. I have no navigation, and a storm swept me out. I haven't seen another ship, or any land. I ran out of food days ago."

A sound of a boot on metal, an unzipping, and then Perry's hand appeared out of the manhole, offering a foil-wrapped protein bar. Captain Bennett accepted it.

"Thank you." She tore it open with her teeth, which were nice for her age, big and white but not so white that they must be fake. She must be at least in her sixties, if not seventy years old.

"He came prepared," I observed, and Captain Bennett turned her eyes on me for a moment, examining my ledger and my shirt. Her eyes lingered on my red hair.

"He did…"

The Captain asked more blunt questions, and got blunt answers. "Were you sent here by a terrorist organization?"

"No."

"Were you sent here by any nation's government?"

"No."

"Do you have anything on this vessel that will harm the *Baton Rouge* or my crew?"

She had taken another bite, and chewed it slowly, swallowing before answering. "No."

"Did you come here with the intent of sabotaging the *Baton Rouge* or its mission?"

"No. I don't know what your mission might be. Is it an oil tanker?"

It was, but the Captain said nothing, just looking at her hard. "How's it coming, Perry?"

From inside the submarine, a sound came like a seal being broken, like a refrigerator being opened. Captain Bennett's lips pursed, her slender, arched eyebrow raised. A sound like the refrigerator door closing. The man climbed back up the ladder, his bald head emerging first into the warm sea air. He had a small, black flashlight in his mouth. He stopped there, with one arm propped up on the roof. Took the flashlight from between his lips. "There's a basic engine, very old make. Basic access panel, not trying to hide anything. No room to hide anything, even if she wanted to. Controls are smart, efficient. No chemical residue detected anywhere. No life support, no water supply or filtration system. No food onboard, like she says. I think she was spelunking, got lost in a storm. There's no bomb onboard."

"Are you sure?"

"I guess -since we're talking hypothetically about a bomb in an oil tanker right under where I lay my head at night- I must be pretty sure."

That answer seemed to satisfy the Captain, and he gestured for Perry to go ahead and climb back into the Zodiac raft. "You're cleared to dock your sub with us, Captain Bennett. We'll resupply you and then you can be on your way. Take the lead, head for the aft of the ship, I'll signal them to let you in."

"Thank you, Captain, for your hospitality."

69

"It's not hospitality," he replied. "It's my legal duty. You won't want to stay long. The men call this ship the *'Last Chance'*. Its destination and its mission make it the most dangerous job in America, or maybe the world. It's a skeleton crew of felons and fuckups with nowhere else left to make an honest living, and the jobs are up for grabs because one in three men who work this beat die doing it."

"One in three-point-two-six," I corrected, and all three sets of eyes turned to me. "That's the official figure, although it doesn't so much apply to the individual, it's more that one in three-point-two-six crews get wiped out when their ship is sunk by terrorism or unnatural disaster. There's a roughly one-third chance that everybody dies, and a roughly two-thirds chance that nobody dies."

"Who are you?" Captain Bennett asked, still looking placid.

"I'm Jacob August Bos, Ma'am. I'm the ship's clerk. It's nice to meet you."

"It's lovely to meet you too, Jacob."

Chapter Two

After a more thorough scan with the equipment at the entry bay of the *Baton Rouge*, Captain Bennett's yellow submarine was steered up into the hold, where the ground lifted her as the water rushed out. She was dry-docked, and climbed out to meet a handful of crew gathered. Roshin was not present, I noticed.

"Hello, Ma'am," Jones offered his hand. "Jason Jones. JJ if you'd like."

"She wouldn't like. Out of the way." There was jostling to get within range of her.

"I haven't smelled a woman in weeks."

She slipped out of their throngs and joined our party again, asking the Captain, "Will my sub be safe?"

"To enter it without permission would be a breach of policy," he replied, although he did not say 'yes'. "Jacob, let's work on a report. Perry, why don't you escort Captain Bennett to the galley, get her something to eat, then make sure she makes it to my office."

"Yes, Sir," I said, quietly delighted.

And Perry affirmed, "Aye-Aye, Captain."

I sat across from the Captain on the other side of his wooden desk. His office was unadorned, cool and organized. A single shelf behind him held atlases, navigational equipment and dictionaries in several languages. Captain Alvarado's file I *had* read. I knew that he spoke Spanish, English and Mandarin fluently, first having worked for our company as a translator. It had thrilled me, as I spoke all three and French, too, having to translate official documents from all over during my time at the main office. He had no college education. He had spent two consecutive years in prison in his early twenties. His emergency contact was his mother, who lived in Reno. It was not in his file, but I had heard members of the crew repeat that he had once been shot, or stabbed, or both.

I took down his statement word for word, accepted his signature, and added my own. With the report folded and ready to be faxed, I stood. "Should I go, and return with Captain Bennett when she's finished in the galley?"

"I'm sure it won't be long."

His gruff and vague reply made me think that I should stay. I noticed a chess set in the corner. "Do you play?"

He followed my eyes. Shook his head. "It's decorative. Came with the office." And the pieces were, indeed, finely carved wood, stained black on one side and red on the other, so I believed him until he stood and crossed to the board, bringing it back with him. "Yes, I can play."

I hurriedly cleared a space for the board. "Should we have a wager?" I was not really a gambler, but I thought that the Captain must be more like the rest of the crew than like me, and all but a few played cards every night. Entire paychecks would be lost by the time we finished our mission, signed over upon receiving.

"I'm not allowed to gamble with subordinates," he said. "You move first."

I pushed a pawn forward. The Captain mirrored me for a few moves, then stronger pieces started to break loose. I created a sort of battering ram with my bishops and queen, while he hopped his knights around haphazardly taking pawns. I claimed one of his knights and one of his bishops, and was surprised how uneven he seemed, how unimaginative. But then, Captains were for relaying orders, and I was the one with the head for figures.

I considered Perry being the one asked to inspect the sub for bombs and asked to escort the woman to the kitchen. "Perry... do you trust him?" It was forward of me to ask such a direct question of my supervisor. Maybe foolishly so.

The Captain raised a brow. "I don't trust any of them. I know their backgrounds, their strengths and weaknesses, and if I have to, I make a decision about which one to use in any given moment to minimize risk. It's always a gamble."

It sounded wise and balanced; unlike the Captain's moves on the chessboard. A truly striking dichotomy. The game had shifted in my favor. I started to wonder if I should back off, make it look like more of a fair match. Maybe I should even throw the game… I didn't know enough about him to guess whether he'd be a sore loser.

And while my head was turning, the Captain slid his queen out from where she had been, straight into a nook I hadn't been minding anymore. "Checkmate."

I opened my mouth, but nothing came out. I scanned the board, sure that it was a mistake, not sure if I'd correct it or just let it go. Then I realized: the knights were a distraction. He wasn't playing the game, he was playing me, and getting me to let my guard down.

"Well done," I said. I tipped my king over, as was customary, a show of concession.

A knock at the door. The Captain told them to come in. He was already putting the pieces back in their places, obscuring that there ever was a game, that he claimed victory. He did not care to show off. I helped and then he carried the board back over to its table in the corner.

"Thank you, Perry." It was a polite dismissal, and the bald man closed the door as he went.

I abandoned my chair to offer it to the lady, she accepted with a nod. I sat in one of the spares along the outer wall, under the window. Sometimes, as a scribe, it's better to be set back from those you are recording. Even with my flaming red hair, they would forget that I was there, if I was quiet enough. And I felt certain that the interaction would be better off without me; most were. The Captain would get the woman's story for his own interest, her statement for the record, and I would put a nice bow on it all before I sent it off with his official account.

The Captain made sure that the lady was seated first, before settling down into his chair. "Was the meal acceptable?"

"…It was passable. I'm grateful. Although… maybe you could use a woman's touch in the kitchen."

"I had a woman on my last crew. Didn't sleep for two months, always making sure she was where she was supposed to be, not wandering off alone. Things could happen, you know, it just takes one second. I prefer it like this, everybody takes a shift in the kitchen."

"Even you?"

"Every Friday night. Nobody complains."

"Is this your second time on this 'beat'?" She used the same term he had used earlier. She was comfortable, leaning back in her chair and draping one leg over the other with a slight wince. Maybe her hip was hurting her.

"Third."

"Pushing your luck."

He was unflappable. "What's your given name, Captain Bennett, and would you like a drink?"

"Sure. Ceely. Short for Lucille."

His lips lifted at the corners just a little. He was pulling a bottle of whiskey from the deepest drawer of his desk, and one glass, which he poured and slid across the desk to her. "Ceely. I like that. One of my mothers' names is Lucille. And I'm Caesar, by the way."

It made me blink. I knew his first name, I had read it in his file, but he never introduced himself as such. Nobody ever addressed him as Caesar.

"You have two mothers?"

"Three. First one couldn't hack it. So Lucy and Vita adopted me."

"No father?"

"I had a few of those, too. Took after them a little too much, when I should've been listening to my moms."

"All's well that ends well. You're not drinking?"

"Not allowed, on the clock. Not until we dock back in Alaska. I like to watch other people drink it, though."

She took a sip, obliging. His eyes followed the alcohol to her mouth, then down her throat as the muscles shifted to swallow. I thought that maybe in that moment there was nothing more he wanted in the world. "I was thinking that you said, earlier, you were Captaining a skeleton crew. Well I find myself in need of work. I'm an engineer, I got my degree from Northwestern. I can fix absolutely anything that breaks. Or I can work in the kitchen if you'd prefer."

The Captain's face shifted, became suspicious. "What really brought you out here, Ceely?"

"I was exploring the sunken cities."

"Looking for valuables?"

"No."

"What, then?"

She took another sip of her whiskey. She considered. "I went to find something. Something personal to me. I used to have a house in the greater Los Angeles area. I went back for something sentimental that I'd rather not discuss."

He seemed to take it as truth, but was still confused. "Why did you wait thirty years?"

She exhaled. Her voice was weaker. "I went as soon as I was able."

I had no idea what to make of her story. I just silently scribbled the key points of the conversation in shorthand, knowing I would fill in the rest by memory, later.

The Captain was perturbed by the idea she had presented, of her working on the ship. "I don't like it."

"Because I'm a woman, or because I'm old?"

"Off the record, Jacob." The Captain's stern voice made me nod and immediately lower my pen. He went on. "I'm not doubting your ability... This job requires a balancing act. The men who sign up for these missions are very hard men, who've done bad things. I have to set all of that aside and treat them like they have clean slates -like they're human beings- because the rest of the world doesn't see them that way anymore. And for good reason. Some of them are animals. If I hire you, you'll be in danger every second. You'll need constant supervision. I'll have to abandon this pretense of respect I've created with the crew; the one that fools them into thinking they have a chance at a normal life again, someday, if they walk the line. As soon as I show them that they can never escape what they've done, that incentive for good behavior evaporates and this whole thing crumbles into lawlessness and savagery and mutiny. I fail my mission, I lose my paycheck, my future, maybe my life."

Ceely was listening intently, but was ready with her response. "I don't like hypotheticals. As a woman, I either lock myself away and live in fear or I get to live my life and accept everything that comes with that. Do I look like someone who hasn't lived?"

"Death and worse are very real possibilities for both of us, if I lose control of this ship. It has happened before."

Seeming to sense that he would not see things her way, she tried a different path. "I'll sign any waiver that you want me to sign. I'll be exactly where I'm supposed to be at all times. If that's the mess hall, maybe you can lock me in between mealtimes, say that there has been theft. I'll only need supervising on my walk to my sub or sleeping quarters at the day's end, where I'll stay until morning."

He was still not moved.

She addressed her next statement to me. "I think that your superiors would agree, your mission would benefit from the addition of someone with my expertise."

The Captain looked at me, too, then, and I had no choice but to nod my assent to what she had said. It felt wrong to do; I didn't want to see her harmed any more than he did. But as the company's representative, I had to look at the bigger picture; if her qualifications were what she said they were, then she was a substantial gain, and if she would really sign any liability forms I asked her to, then she presented little risk. The Captain would have to tighten and loosen the reins on the crew as needed, but I had faith in him, as always. Especially after losing to him at chess, I knew he had the mind to maintain his death-defying highwire balancing act.

"...Okay. Alright. We don't have an engineer onboard. In fact, I think Jacob's the only one with a degree, and his is probably in, what? Accounting?"

I nodded. I could feel color rising to my cheeks and tried to calm myself down. I couldn't believe how weighty my presence in the interaction had become, how he had deferred to me.

"There's plenty of room, so you can stay the night. I'll reach out to my bosses and see about adding you to the roster. They'll run your credentials and a background check and probably agree. If anything were to break at one of the drill sites, they'd have to fly in an expert to assess or fix it, and they'll be eager to avoid that added cost. You can work the kitchen until we reach a drill site, and I want you watching the training videos to catch up in your spare time and studying schematics of the equipment. As far as salary goes, what are you expecting?"

"Pay me what you want, just keep my ship docked in your bay, and hooked up to your grid, restock my supplies, and keep your men out of it."

"You built it yourself, didn't you?"

She looked down as she nodded, and his face changed.

"Look at me."

She did.

"This is not a suicide mission. We're all working to go home. You pull any risky shit, endanger anybody on my crew -including yourself- and I'll have you in the brig so fast your head will spin. We're talking about federal charges. Are we clear?"

"Yes, Sir."

"And you understand the risk that you're assuming."

"One in three-point-two-six. Yes. Terrorism and unnatural disasters."

"The creature from the San Andreas fault, that's what Jacob was referring to. The one that sent your home into the ocean, and my mother's, too. Sent her into a downward spiral... It doesn't care so much about ships, but it's attracted to the vibrations from the drilling rigs. They irritate it, work it into a frenzy so that it'll attack anything nearby. It's not a matter of if it shows up, but when, and there are ways of diverting it, but they don't always work. You might end up face to face with it."

"I assumed. I can handle it," was all she said.

"Alright. I bet you can. I'm looking forward to working with you, Ceely." He stood and offered his hand.

She stood, sighing as she pushed herself to her feet, and shook it. "Thank you, Captain."

She downed the rest of her whiskey before starting to move toward the door.

"Hold on. Jacob, go with her. Show her to a room... as close to the mess hall as she can get. Lock your door."

She huffed a laugh as she slid out, and I snapped my ledger closed, hurrying after. It was strange to think of myself as some kind of bodyguard; any member of the crew could snap me in half like a twig, and clearly she thought it was ludicrous that she should need protection.

The crew cabins were down another level, and we walked the length of the first subfloor to reach the stairs. I pointed out my office as we passed by. "That's me, if you need anything and you think I could be of service, just let me know."

"I appreciate that."

Down we went, and to the end of the hall nearest the galley and kitchen. I knocked on one of two dozen, identical doors. "I think this one is empty." Opening it, I stepped into a utilitarian room with a bunk bed, a set of drawers, and a tiny desk. I opened a drawer just to be sure, it was empty except for a folded sheet and pillowcase. "Yes. Empty. All yours."

"Okay. Thank you." It was early in the afternoon, but with the bags under her eyes and the way she sighed as she sat down on the bed, I could tell she was ready to turn in.

"Have a pleasant evening," I said. "And please lock the door behind me, like the captain said."

Returning to my office, I pulled out Perry's file, and it was hefty. I knew that if I opened it, I would read it cover to cover, late into the night. It could wait for tomorrow. Instead, I took Roshin's file out of my cabinet. It was narrower, only a few papers inside. I stared at the photo of his face. His tunnel eyes that had seen so much. His beard was thicker when the photo was taken, and made his face look wilder. I stared at the picture for a full minute before I realized, it was not the kind of picture in the other files. It was taken in front of a white, brick wall, under track lights. It seemed like a mugshot; certainly some kind of staged identification photo taken against his will.

I started to read. Roshin Oder, thirty-two years old. He was born and raised in Syria. He attended Cairo

University, but did not receive a degree. Good grades; he seemed to have dropped out. That was his documented life up until eight years ago, when he was twenty-four.

I turned the page. Lines and lines of blacked out text. It made a pit sink into my stomach. Was it blacked out on my account? Or was it blacked out even when my superiors received it? Only Roshin's name, age and nationality, the date, and a single sentence at the bottom of the page were left exposed.

Cleared for release.

His next documented moves were to New York, Dallas, Mexico City, never staying long. Then to Alaska, working fishing boats. And then he signed up for this mission. Six years of his life was blacked out on that form. Presumably taken from him. And what could have caused such an action to be taken?

I closed the folder and sat back, perturbed with myself. I had no reason to believe that it had been justified. Hadn't there been so many instances of human rights deprivation, all the way back to Columbus? But I worked for the government. It would be easier to believe that Roshin was dangerous, like the rest of them. It was the 'Last Chance' after all. Most of the crew were at the end of their rope, trying to stay afloat. I was not like them. I was part of a crowded field of clerks and assistants, and I wanted to set myself apart, show my willingness to go anywhere, do anything, be a man of the world.

And now, here I was. One in three-point-two-six. About two-thirds chance of making it back. The numbers were my comfort, usually. But they did nothing to ease the knots that were forming in my mind.

I found myself waking my handheld device without deciding to. Opening the communication portal and sending a message to my direct superior, Stephen Scott, asking him to look into at what level the documents became redacted. Was that just on the digital file? Could he secure the original or maybe inquire for a general idea as to what they once contained, only if it would be on the up and up and not much of an inconvenience, of course…

I put the file away and locked the cabinet. Enough of that. Enough of that.

As I walked to my cabin that night and crawled into bed, Roshin's tunnel eyes were in the back of my mind every time I blinked.

*

In the morning the galley's bell chimed out for breakfast. You could roust yourself and eat breakfast, or you could sleep in another hour before the work day began. I rolled out of bed, changed my clothes, and shaved. In the mess hall, strong coffee was brewed and wafted in the air. I poured myself a mug, left it black, then circled past the few men already eating at tables to the serving bar. A metal tray was stacked high with pancakes, another with sausages, and I filled a plate.

Ceely was sitting on her own, and I went over.

"Can I join you?"

"Go ahead."

She was eating with a blank expression, washing her pancakes down with tan-colored coffee.

"You made all of this?"

"Yes."

"Jumping right in, huh?"

"Nothing else to do, this morning."

I nodded. "Did you sleep well?"

"Oh, yes. I was sleeping on the floor of my submarine. The bed was luxurious by comparison."

"I'm glad. These are good! I can't wait to see what lunch brings."

She smiled, her skin reacted all over her face. Her skin was wrinkled, but still fair. She must have had a rigorous skincare routine in her youth, and stayed out of the sun. "Banana pancakes. My daughters' favorites. Every Sunday morning, when they were little... That reminds me, you're probably the person to ask. Are there any allergies I should know about? I was worried about the banana."

"Banana should be fine... No allergies have been declared, no. Roshin, he can't eat pork... He's probably praying right now..."

When Roshin did come in, he sat at an empty table with coffee and a pancake. I didn't even realize I was staring at him until Ceely spoke again, distracting me.

"Does the Captain eat with the crew?"

"Sometimes dinner. Breakfast and lunch, almost never."

"How long will it be before we reach a drilling site?"

"We're almost there. Two or maybe three days."

She nodded, took another sip of coffee. "Have you been to your office yet, this morning?"

"No... Did you need something?"

"Your higher-ups are checking my credentials. They're going to find a very large gap in my life."

It made my throat constrict around the pancake I was trying to swallow. I washed it down with a gulp of hot coffee. "Oh?"

"I've been off the grid for a long time. Thirty years. They might even think that I'm dead... I haven't paid any taxes."

"Hm... Well... I don't think that will immediately tarnish your prospects. There might be some things to smooth out with the Social Security Offices, the IRS. It actually sounds like an interesting challenge. The bosses won't mind, it's like the Captain said, we don't often get engineers or people with degrees wanting to work on the oil rigs. And I love paperwork."

She had a small smile for that, but it faded quickly. Her stare was a mile deep, just like Roshin's... I glanced over at him again, and he was looking at me, so I looked away.

My mind wandered to all the things that the two of them -and the Captain, too- might have seen, lived through, that I never would and therefore could never understand, and I felt strangely insignificant. I was in the midst of doing the only dangerous thing I ever planned to do; I couldn't wait for it to be over. I wished for the millionth time in my life that I was braver, bolder, truer to myself.

I asked Ceely, "Why do you really want to be here? You were on your own for a long time, got lost in one storm, and now you're ready to reenter society through its… well… its dregs." I almost said, 'through its asshole', and it gave me pause. The way the crewmen spoke was rubbing off on me. I couldn't allow it.

"Well, it was frightening, being in my little sub, in a big storm. And I have no money to settle down anywhere."

"No family?" I couldn't help but to ask it.

"No."

It didn't strike a chord for me, her tale of being frightened. She certainly didn't seem like someone who frightened easily. Maybe there was a hint of truth to it, but more likely she was just lonely. She didn't realize, yet, what a lonely place this big ship could be.

"I'll need the schematics and training videos that the Captain mentioned," she said.

"Of course. I'll go and get them right now."

I was finished with breakfast, and left my dishes in the empty bus tub on the way out the door. I stole a glance back over my shoulder, though, stopping in the hall. She was sitting alone, Roshin was sitting alone, and there were six of the crew sitting at a table together. She wasn't to go anywhere alone, but hadn't she already risen, found the kitchen, made the breakfast? And weren't seven men together less likely to do a woman harm than, say, one man with no witnesses?

Perry was coming my way. He was known to skip breakfast, preferring to eat a piece of fruit at the ship's bow, with waves crashing and wind whipping around him. A sailor's sailor, I knew it was his second deployment with the Captain, but he had been on the water for years. "Is our new friend in there?"

"Yes," I said.

I went. My nerves were twisted, but there was relative safety in the galley. Perry was there, now, much more suited to fighting off would-be attackers than I was. And besides, if the Captain wanted to make Ceely's safety my personal responsibility, well, he hadn't said so, and it would be outside of my purview of course.

I found everything she could need to learn the equipment and the job, and brought it back to the galley. A few stragglers shoveled pancakes into their mouths standing up at the coffee station, the big group had cleared out, off to work early. Equipment checks, cleaning the ship, things like that. None of it was strictly necessary, but the Captain liked for everyone to stay busy.

'Idle hands are the Devil's playthings', he had said, once. I should have been paying more attention, I knew. He was a brilliant man. I should not have let him hustle me at chess, last night.

"Here you are." I presented the paper materials to Ceely. "You can watch the training video files on any handheld device... But you don't have one of those, do you? I've got a few old ones in storage, I'll bring one by at lunch."

"And a pair of the coveralls I see some of the men wearing?"

"Of course."

"I hope I'm worth all this trouble."

"It's no trouble at all."

Chapter Three

Perry's file occupied the rest of my morning. He was somehow sixty-four-years-old. He was born in Idaho, raised mostly in Kansas. He had no college education, had joined the Army right out of high school and served for about ten years, earning no significant rank. His thirties seemed a turbulent decade, containing two DUI's, a divorce, trespassing and vagrancy charges in Washington, a simple assault in Texas, a one-year sentence, reduced to six months served in a county jail.

After that, he seemed to have worked with Habitat for Humanity all over the world, doing odd jobs between his trips on fishing boats and working as a janitor on cruise ships. In his fifties, he came to work for our company, first as a security guard at home base, then a ship's mechanic at the port in Alaska, then on flight crews for the rigs. Each post he had held for a few years, before finally signing up for his latest experiment and setting sail with the Captain on the *Baton Rouge.*

If he planned to work the tankers for a few years, like he had with all his other posts, then, well, he would never make it that long. His crimes in his youth did not surprise me; I assumed the assault had been earned, or was at least regretted. It couldn't have been so bad, if he spent only six months locked up for it.

Not like Roshin, who was disappeared for six years...

Perry, more likely, was a bit of a thrill seeker. The army probably warped his teenage brain. I could see how being sent overseas for the first time in your young life to kill brown people -and slowly coming to realize you had no idea why any of it was really happening- could lead to drinking, turmoil, fighting and other risky behavior. And also to the genial and curious and self-contained man who ate fruit on the ship's bow every morning amidst the sea spray.

I closed Perry's thick file and replaced it in my locking cabinet. In a different drawer on the bottom, I found a tablet and charger for Ceely to use, along with two sets of medium-sized coveralls from the hall closet. I was starting to feel hungry, although it was a bit early to head to lunch, I decided to go. Maybe she could use some help.

Maybe I should try to put together a file on her, for my own comfort and for the company's records... for their protection. Something about knowing I had all of their information tucked in those files, at my disposal - under my lock and key- made the crew feel less frightening to me. And she, she was not frightening in her mystery, but not understanding her still irked the meticulous part of me.

At the galley's door, I knocked. After a minute she appeared in the round window, then let me in. Sliding in with arms full, I let the door swing closed behind me and offered the goods to her.

"Thanks. Lunch will be a few more minutes, but I made a pot of coffee…"

"That would be lovely. I stay away from most substances, and usually only indulge in one cup a day, but… I didn't sleep too well, last night."

We settled into seats at one of the pale blue tabletops with our mugs. Ceely said, "I slept better than I have in weeks. It didn't really matter, though. I don't have the energy that I used to."

"I can't imagine sleeping in that little sub of yours, out on the ocean, all alone…" Just saying it made me shudder.

"It was eerie at first. After a few days and nights, I hardly remembered the way that it was before. But then meeting your crew, and having a bunk again, I realized how unnatural and how hard it had been."

"You've got a unique story under your belt, now. It's what I'm doing here, on this mission. Life experience is a good thing to have, when applying for a job or promotion."

"Mm." She murmured her agreement as she sipped. Then, with her eyes seeming to stare at something miles away, she said, "I'm not sure how many jobs there are in my future."

I scoffed as I stumbled on my words. "Well, you can't be sure, especially not when you've been out here for so long... but if you're only here because you're not sure what other choice you have, I think you should really consider catching a ride back to headquarters with the flight crew. Or even returning to the mainland in your sub. It would be safer for you than staying here. I could put in a word for you with my superiors and almost guarantee they'll find you an entry-level assistant or filing job."

She smiled and shook her head, reaching up to tuck messy cropped gray hair behind her ear. "You haven't known me long. I'm better suited to-."

The door swung inward, cutting her off, and into the galley stepped Jason Jones and his friend named Colson. The sight made a prickle of discomfort skitter from the back of my neck all the way down my spine. I hadn't relocked the door behind me, that much was clear, but with it being almost lunch time, I supposed it did not matter.

Both men looked between me and Ceely.

JJ reached back and twisted the lock, closed, open, closed, fiddling with it. Something heavy settled in my guts, static rushed to my legs and I found myself on my feet. Ceely, too, stood beside me.

"There's coffee, gentlemen," I said, pointing to the coffee station on the side wall, decently far from the two of us. I hoped my fears were misplaced but I had a growing certainty that we were in trouble. The men looked at the coffee station and back at us; they looked long at Ceely, then one after the other turned their gazes on me. I was about to have a choice to make. Let them go around me or let them go through me, buy Ceely a second or two with which she could run back into the kitchen. The swinging doors had no latch, let alone a lock. There were knives back there, but ultimately it would make little difference, I decided. And was it really worth sacrificing my body to buy her those few seconds? Was the principle of the thing worth being mangled over? They primarily were interested in her, but men wishing to exert violence on someone of a sexual nature cared more about the act itself than the target. That had to be true, if the glamorous but matronly old woman next to me would do. They just wanted someone to hurt, to scratch some festering itch. If I didn't move aside, I could easily become brutalized as well.

I had nothing within reach but my mug of coffee, so I grabbed it. It was decently hot, it would scald the face enough to stun someone, if not to actually incapacitate. I still didn't know if I was going to make that move or just put my hands up and shuffle to the corner. Indecision and fear had paralyzed me for too long; the men shuffled a few feet closer, keeping their movements slow -JJ in the lead had his hands in his pockets- they came forward like mountain lions hoping not to scare a deer. As it was, neither Ceely nor I bolted. My feet acted on their own, sliding me back a few inches as my heart hammered and I realized I had forgotten to breathe for a torturously long while. I was out of time to figure out who I was; I hadn't moved and I wasn't going to. Not bravery but indecision decided my fate.

Sucking in a breath, it then tumbled back out of me in a quiet, "Fuck."

The door handle jiggled and everybody froze. The advancing men glanced at each other again, while I finally shook myself out of my stupor with urgent thoughts of: *There. People. Help.*

"Coming!" I found my voice as I took two big steps, then Colson who was the nearer of the two men took a step and reached for me. I tried to step faster out of reach of his hands but I was yanked off of my feet with an arm encircling around my throat, cutting off my shout of, "No!"

I was aware of JJ stomping across the room, running toward Ceely who had bolted for the kitchen as I expected. I grappled at the thick arm constricting tighter around my windpipe, feeling blood pounding in my temples and my vision blurring and going black. I had dropped my cup of coffee the moment he'd grabbed me.

A crash from the kitchen. Another. My legs were giving out and I was swimming upward through staticky pain toward the blissful surface of unconsciousness. A few more seconds, I was sure, then it would be over. But the seconds ticked by and I was still suffering, trying to let go but unable.

The next thing I comprehended was the thud of a body dropping to the floor; it was not mine, as I thought at first. It was Roshin landing in a crouch. A vent clattered on the floor, having fallen from the ceiling. Roshin brushed himself off.

"Hello," he declared, and I was dragged back a step by the startled man holding me. The arm around my neck loosened just a little, still holding me in place but allowing me to suck in a gulp of air.

Roshin looked at me; I could see him through the black dots swarming and my vision returning. He looked at Colson. Colson let me go and I collapsed flat on the cold tile. Roshin was only two steps from the door and his eyes lingered on me wheezing on the floor as he crossed to it, slamming a hand down on the handle and popping it open.

Perry stood on the other side, muscular old arms folded. He flashed a smile that made his eyes wrinkle. "Look at this crowd. Lunch must be ready, huh?"

Roshin passed the older man a multi-tool Swiss-army-knife thing, and he pocketed it.

Across the room, Ceely came flying through the swinging doors from the kitchen, panting. Her stance was still defensive, she held a lethal looking paring knife already coated with blood.

My wheezing turned to coughing. My throat burned and crinkled like tissue paper. And from where I was still sprawled out, I could see a section of the ceiling missing in the hallway, it was propped against a wall, giving a clear view up into the ductwork. Perry must have boosted Roshin up to crawl through.

Hands on me made me flinch. I began to scramble back on the floor before I had even whipped around to look. Roshin was the one crouching, holding his hands up.

"It's alright, Jacob. I was just helping you up."

"Oh-." My voice came out a croak. I nodded, taking the slender brown hand that he once again offered me. My heart was still racing, I was wobbly as he pulled me to my feet and steadied me. Unwilling to be rude even in pain as I was, I forced out, "Thank you."

JJ lumbered out of the kitchen. He held a white dish towel to a gash in his forearm, had damp hair and a scalded red face. He was glowering.

Perry looked them over, his face was blank. "Helping with lunch, gentlemen? What are we having?"

I opened my mouth to speak, but was seized by another coughing fit. I didn't understand, how could Perry be so obtuse? Thinking we had left the door locked on accident, that might be one thing, but seeing all of the disarray, and Ceely holding the knife... No. He did know what had just happened. He had to. He was choosing not to acknowledge it, just as Roshin had played cool when he dropped in on Colson strangling me.

They had come to some agreement and Ceely and I were being asked without words to go along. I didn't understand it. I wanted to run from that room and straight to the Captain's quarters, or to find him on deck, demand that the two men be thrown in the brig to await prosecution... But I also didn't want to realize that I had made the wrong move when I didn't have all of the facts. I looked to Ceely.

She answered Perry's question for the two men, wiping blood off the paring knife on her apron. "Chicken salad, collard greens and fruit cocktail."

"Sounds delicious," Perry said. "It's about that time, need help bringing it out?"

"Sure."

They went into the kitchen together and each came out carrying a hotel tray. Roshin moved to the steam table to turn one of the warmers on for the collard greens, and then two more men from the crew came in, chatting. They made a beeline for coffee, while the fruit cocktail, plates and silverware were brought out. JJ and Colson both went to get coffee, still stiff and staring at me. Wondering would I be the weak link in the chain? More men of the crew came down from the deck, and suddenly lunch was in full swing around me, and I, still standing in the center of the room, rubbing my sore throat.

Ceely appeared with an icepack for me. Her gentle hand on my back guided me to the serving bar. "Something to eat, Jacob? Maybe something warm would be good for that sore throat."

"You're going to pretend nothing happened?" My voice was still rough.

"Come sit down."

She had built us two plates and carried mine for me. She did not sit us near Perry and Roshin, instead going to an empty table. "Think about it, Jacob. Nothing really happened. -A few cuts and bruises, sure," she tacked on the amendment when I opened my mouth to object, then rushed on. "But those will heal. If we blow this out of proportion, nobody wins. Not me, not you, not the Captain, not the company or the government."

"Well, it's not just about winning. It's about protecting the company."

"From what? Lawsuits? Lost time? Lost profit? We do that by moving forward."

I looked behind me at Perry and Roshin, who had two others now sitting at their table. They were each watching me, and neither pretended not to have been. I turned back to Ceely. "You're worried the Captain won't let you continue on, if he knows about the incident."

"Near-incident," she replied. "And remember, I'm not the one who left the door unlocked, Jacob. That detail will have to go in your report, if you file one. With nearly half the crew involved, the entire mission might get scrubbed, the Captain might be demoted or even court-martialed. And you might never see another job outside of a cubicle. But of course, it's up to your discretion…"

She started to eat her food and looked completely unphased by the 'near-incident'. I searched the lines of her face, and I distantly hoped that someday I would have the same ability to compartmentalize. What a tough old bird. Stabbed one assailant scalded him, might have made it out fine if Perry and Roshin hadn't shown up. Probably would have left me on the floor, but who could blame her?

Maybe I should trust in her wisdom and incredible resolve. I had frozen, when last I needed to decide what to do. I had wound up useless, almost unconscious, while she led that man on a chase around the kitchen, fought him off.

Ceely's eyes opened wider, focused on something over my shoulder, and I whipped around to look.

The Captain walked in the galley's door, scanned the room. He headed for coffee first, he took it black. Then he made himself a plate and made his way over to us. And as his steps approached, my back straightened on its own. He slid right in next to me, as I hoped and feared he would.

"Afternoon," he said.

"Hello."

"Good afternoon, Captain," I said.

"Lunch looks good. Didn't have any trouble?"

100

"None," Ceely breezed.

I said nothing, took a bite and chewed, mulling over all the things that would come of speaking up. In the end, I worked my way through my plate, while the Captain and Ceely made small talk, their energy strangely false, him almost combative toward her.

"Finding everything alright?"

"It's a big kitchen, but I managed."

"And your room?"

"It's cozy. There's nothing I can't find, in there." She had a pleasant smile for him.

"You must feel... confined."

"Well, I would like to see more of the ship."

"I'm sure you would." The Captain shut down the conversation for a minute. We all chewed in heavy silence.

She tried again. "Could you or one of your men find the time to show me around? Or at least let me check on my sub."

The Captain scooped up the last of his fruit cocktail, popped it into his mouth, chewed and made her wait for his reply. She watched his angular jaw moving, head down, looking up from under her lashes, and her eyes were dark and unflinching. She looked to me like she was simmering with indignation. More than indignation. Rage. I suddenly felt very uncomfortable to be sitting near the two of them. Then Ceely took a breath, blinked, and looked over at me, then down. Her face had smoothed out, she flashed a tiny smile my way. The tension left the air around the table.

I wondered, had I just seen through a crack in a careful façade? Or had I just misinterpreted? There could be a dozen explanations for that look; perhaps the stress of the recent attack had gotten to her more than she was letting on, had sent her into a numb place or a panicked place for that second and fight or flight was reading to me like anger... Maybe her head was hurting, or her hip. My mother always became irritable when her arthritis acted up... It had to be one of those. They all made more sense than a graceful, grey-haired woman of Ceely's age still smoldering that way. That would sure be something.

The Captain finally answered. "I guess even inmates get yard time."

I felt relieved. I knew that Ceely would be safe with the Captain for whatever time they spent together. And maybe once I made it back to my office, locked myself in, I would feel safe, too. For a few minutes the two of them finished their lunches in silence. I hardly ate because my throat was sore, and my stomach was still uneasy.

When the Captain stood, picking up his tray, Ceely did the same and held out her hand.

"Let me get that for you. Finished Jacob?"

I nodded, and she stacked the trays, taking them to the wash bin. The Captain watched her go, not taking his eyes off of her even as he addressed me.

"I need you to come with us, Jacob. I'm sorry if it's an imposition."

My heart sank. I couldn't help it, I scoffed. "What for? Protection?"

He blinked, glanced over, then back. "Exactly. She's not here just for the work."

"You think she's scheming to claim some sort of abuse, and sue the company?" I said it slowly, knowing it was not correct.

"I don't know if that's it, but we need to protect ourselves as best we can. Would you be here, just for the work? Just because you had nowhere else to be?"

"No."

"Nobody would."

"Maybe Perry." The older man had met Ceely at the wash bin, said something, then left the galley with his usual unbothered smile.

"Maybe Perry," The Captain conceded.

Ceely rejoined us. "Ready?"

Down, into the lowest level of the ship. I had never ventured so low before; the machinery held little interest for me. The ductwork, pipes overhead. Darker than the halls on the other levels, even with bulbs attached to the metal walls at even intervals. We meandered around a massive furnace unit, cold and dusty, and past the locked door to the engine room.

In the back nook -where the ship's massive, metal walls curved toward the aft, and gargantuan, rusted bolts held two huge sheets in place- sat Ceely's sub.

There were hydraulics and motors for a pair of mechanical arms on either side of the closed porthole door, another small vessel meant for unmanned, underwater rig repairs nearby, but it was all cold metal. The sub's sunny yellow paint made it stand out, look lonely among them.

Ceely's face looked empathetic, as though she thought the same way I did. She traced a hand along the sub's side. She was sorry to have left it, even for a day, I could tell. It had to be like a friend to her, after so many years on board.

"Perfectly safe. Just how you left it."

"You really haven't gone onboard? You or your men? Not even to search?" Her question was directed at the Captain.

"Just a scan for harmful materials that the ship's computer ran as you docked. It would be a breach of policy and of the law for any of my men to trespass on your vessel, as I said."

"There are cameras," I added. "All over the hold."

Ceely nodded. "I'd like to power up the engines, perform a quick systems check."

The Captain nodded.

She reached up to get a grip on the manhole cover, lifted one foot up on her sub's starboard side, and puffed out a big breath as though she was going to haul herself up. I had enough time to doubt that she could make it before the Captain hurried to her side.

"Here."

He cupped his hands, let her put the toe of her work boot into them, and then grunted as he heaved her most of the way up. She only had to swing one leg over the submarine's big tube of a body and then, balancing -and the Captain and I surely feeling the same trepidation at seeing her fragile, old body so high up- she opened the hatch and climbed down inside.

The submarine's engine roared to life a minute later. I had never been particularly good with machines, but even I could tell that its whir was not healthy. The thing bogged down and its shaking became more pronounced but then it smoothed out again.

I found myself circling the sub, while the Captain just stood with his arms crossed. The propellors whipped up dust, the rudder shifted as Ceely no doubt directed it to. I hurried to the front where I could see her through the wide glass window. She did not notice me, taking notes on a little pad as she manipulated controls. Even when she looked up, it was to take stock of the submarine's mechanical arms. Both moved left to right, up and down, but only one could still grab with its two prongs. The other grinded and then sparked, and moved no more.

Ceely shook her head. Took more notes. Watching her, I felt strangely moved. She had to have a wild passion for the machine, to live in solitude out on the ocean the way that she had. I had never found such an interest in anything; I only found joy in living between the lines, thrived on conformity, excelled at normalcy. I felt okay about it except for in the rare moment when I met a true wild person. And I was surrounded by primitive, wild people on the 'Last Chance'. It made me feel inadequate.

Burning in the sensation, I tapped on the glass. Ceely started like a deer in headlights, an animal in an enclosure. Her hands even shot to the steering console of the sub's, like she was ready to take evasive action.

I put my own hands up immediately. "I'm so sorry, I didn't mean to startle you."

Remembering where she was, she rubbed a liver-spotted hand over her heart, surely pounding. "It's not your fault."

"Your sub is incredible. I only wanted to ask if I could come aboard?"

"There's no room." Her answer so sudden and sharp wounded me as efficiently as a knife would. She seemed to see it on my face, even though I tried to shake it off. "I'm sorry, Jacob. It's nothing personal. My sub is just very personal to me. It's private."

"Of course... no worries."

The Captain furrowed his brow, deep in thought, and said nothing.

Chapter Four

With Ceely deposited back in the galley -and the Captain checking the handle to ensure it was locked behind us, a wiser man than I- I was finally free to return to my office. It was a bit too warm, but familiar and with a lock of its own. Finally exhaling the day's stress, shivers broke out all over my body. The tears swam up before I realized they were coming, and I let them come for just a minute.

I felt like the smallest child on the block again, living in the smallest house, with no muscle and no status to protect me. My father was a clerk, same as me, although I had already risen higher than he ever had, already made two or three times as much for my salary as he must have. I lived in a nicer apartment -at least when I wasn't stationed on a Hellish, brutish oil tanker in the middle of the Pacific. If I ever adopted children, they would have an easier time growing up. More opportunities, too. They would be shoulder to shoulder with the sons and daughters of diplomats and businessmen, not rail workers, factory workers, dockworkers, day workers of all sorts.

Maybe their other father ought to be someone stronger than me. Just in case any disputes arose from the playground. Children did need discipline to really flourish, and I would probably be too soft on them. So my partner would need to have a steady, firm hand to help guide our kids... someone like the Captain. Of course I thought of him first, as I tended to since meeting him. But then I thought, no. His gracious nod as we went our separate ways earlier did not make me feel as though I was glowing, the way that those odd moments of appreciation once had. I supposed my attraction to him was a flash in the pan, as they always were. Someone strong, though. Someone strong and kind, if such a person could exist in this hard world...

I dried my face. Enough of that weakness. It was not fair what had happened, but it served a purpose. I would be a shoe in for advancement in the company, once my tour here was over. If I could just hang on that long. I could. I must.

A knock on my door made my skin jump. My heart started pounding in my chest, blood rushed to my legs. I could pretend that I wasn't in. But I would feel like a coward, and whoever was knocking could probably see light under the door.

"Who is it?"

"Roshin." The quiet reply though the door.

My heart went on beating, but I found myself on my feet, crossing the room. I felt sure he would be reasonable, unlike Ceely and Perry, he would commiserate with me on how insane the events in the galley were in his own, quiet way.

I opened the door and he stood alone in the hall, holding a steaming mug.

"May I come in?"

I nodded, stepping back, shutting and locking the door behind him. The sound of the lock clicking into place made muscles twitch in his face and neck, his eyes did a quick scan of the simple room behind and all around him. Definitely a convict, but not like JJ and those others.

We stood awkwardly for a moment.

He held out the mug. "It's orange blossom tea with fresh mint and a spoonful of honey. For your throat."

My throat clenched painfully on cue. I'm sure I winced. I reached out and took the mug, staring at it, unsure if I should accept. My mind said *drugged, poisoned.* Then it said *idiot, fool.*

"Thank you... Orange blossom tea?" I knew there was no such thing in the kitchen. I had gone over the inventory before our departure.

"From my own supply. I never go anywhere without a tin of it."

I felt color rise in my cheeks. I lifted the steaming mug, hoping the warmth would disguise the blush, gave it a blow and took a sip. Orange and honey and strong tea, with the mint covering just a bit of the aftertaste. Not too bitter. "It's lovely."

"Yes…" Roshin looked out the small porthole window in the office's outside wall for a long moment. The air felt heavy between us. The older man with the tunnel eyes which had seen too much seemed to be weighing something, hesitating. His lips pressed into a worried line. He had nice lips. When he spoke again it was in his usual soft-spoken tone, but the careful way he laid his words out -like terra cotta bricks on a long road- kept me tuned in. I was on edge at first, then finally, beginning to realize that my mistrust was misplaced, I was able to sink into the story.

"I was born in Syria, and lived there for the first five years of my life. My mother was a homemaker, my father worked odd jobs, so it was hard for them to provide. We had to go where the work was, and there were never benefits or room for advancement. Pakistan, Turkey, Israel for a year or two each. Entry level positions, and he was often replaced by automation or let go in favor of younger workers when policy would mean that he was coming up on a raise. One year we lived in England, where my father had a promising position… But the gloomy weather, there, the rising Nationalism of the English people, their hostility all left my mother unlike herself. She was lonely, never feeling very well. She missed her family in Syria, she missed the sun and heat of her home, and any place that the

110

people looked like her, and would extend a simple courtesy, or even just a smile.

"So for her sake, we returned to the town where I was born. My mother's light, her warmth was what the rest of us all needed, you see. It was worth it to live more simply, to see her happy again. I think that love my family had for each other was ultimately our undoing, but I wouldn't trade the life I've lived for anyone else's…"

He paused, he had been looking anywhere else other than at me. He looked out the window, up at the ceiling, down at the floor. With his face still angled down, he looked up with his tunnel eyes and checked that I was listening, that he was not making a mistake, being met with hostility.

I nodded, holding the blue mug of orange tea in both hands. "My mother was a homemaker, too. My father struggled to provide, too… But I can't imagine moving so many times."

Nodding in turn, Roshin rung his hands a moment. "I think it's why I get anxious if I stay in one place too long… that, and the other, of which I'm sure you have some idea."

I took a deep breath, already feeling ashamed. Who was I to want to know everything about a stranger? Did I think myself God? I was stupid to think that knowing the redacted words on the page describing him could mean knowing him.

"I had an older brother, Mahir. He began working when he was only fifteen, to help support the family, and because he liked the freedom that a little pocket money gave him, at first. He was smart with machines, the way that I was smart with mathematics and poetry. There was hardly anything that he couldn't fix. Everything was pleasant for a few years...

"My father was killed on July eighteenth, the year that I was to go to University in Cairo. It was a terrible thing. He was working in a warehouse, the heat would often rise above a hundred degrees. He was in his fifties by then and shifts were long. A person had to be moving constantly to meet their productivity quotas, if they missed even one, they would be dismissed without any severance. I found out after the fact, from one of his coworkers, he had asked the overseer for a break when he grew dizzy. His request was denied, and he dropped dead on that warehouse floor among the latest electronics. Such a stupid, cruel thing."

"-I'm sorry," I said, an automatic response but also feeling deeply hurt for him. I was sure that if it had been my own father, I would be a much different, harder person.

Roshin nodded, hardly noticing me. He was miles and years away. "My family was devastated, of course. My mother's light extinguished... My brother grew scared of the machines he climbed inside to make his money, sure that he would die on the job, too, crushed. I felt like I was adrift, I couldn't imagine leaving my

112

family to go to Egypt, or how I would focus on my studies if I did. I planned to take up the task of supporting my mother and brother, but she wouldn't hear of it. My scholarship could not be guaranteed, if I deferred by even a semester, and she wanted me to make something of myself, not end up fighting for opportunities for back-breaking labor like my father.

"The same way that she was the warmth of our family, her will could be as cold as iron. She ordered me off to school, and she ordered Mahir back to work. He was the man of the house, now, she said, and I was the family's future, our only chance at prosperity. I went to school, and despite my listlessness and sadness, I did well in my courses.

"When I first came home, on a break, my mother and brother seemed tired, but mostly themselves. Mother had started cleaning houses to make money... I told her all about school, and she was delighted to hear it, she lit up the way that she used to, but that week left me feeling even emptier. I felt guilty. I lived in a small dormitory, but honestly, my life was better than the one I had left behind. I was working hard, but much less troubled than Mahir, he was only twenty-three years old and his hair was going grey. He hardly slept, started drinking. I started to dread going home, to see my family wasting away. I stayed on campus over my next break, made an excuse. If I hadn't, things probably would have been different..."

I didn't know yet what he felt responsible for, but I already felt the need to defend him from himself. "Everyone needs a break, sometimes."

"People have less responsibility to their families in the Western world. I don't mean to offend you. It's neither better or worse... better for the children, more fair to them, maybe, but that lack of care for others bleeds into the rest of the world, into corporate policy. I wanted to do better. I went home for my next break, they looked even worse. I skipped another. I completed my second year at University. I went home for the last time after working the summer in Cairo, before the start of my third year."

The fact that he said 'the last time' did not escape me; it sent a pang through me. I was beginning to grow afraid of the outcome of the story. "What did you study?"

"Physics..."

"I took a physics course," I said. "I enjoyed it. So logical."

Roshin nodded. "The last time I went home, my mother was still tired and unhappy, but my brother looked clearer, clean shaved, much more optimistic. He left every night, picked up by friends. I worried he might be on drugs, but my mother told me I was wrong, to let it go, he probably just had a girlfriend." Shaking his head, then, pinching his eyes shut he huffed a big breath. "They were anarchists. They blew up the Amazon warehouse where my father died. I was back in school by then, I saw it on the news and when I realized it was the same warehouse, I put the pieces together. They tried to evacuate the workers but two people did die in the blast. Security.

"Two men in suits came and pulled me from my class. I was believed to have been a co-conspirator. I hardly saw sunlight again for six years before it was determined I was no threat to anyone. On the day I was released I learned that my mother and brother were both dead, I was the last of us. I was nobody's hope or future prosperity anymore. I had nothing... I didn't take the first job I could get, I waited for something dangerous. Bank security, abortion clinic security, armored transport, fishing boats, here. Feeding the beast, the entire time, waiting to be ground between its gears..."

He trailed off. Glanced up at me.

"I'm so sorry," I said. My voice was rough, there was a knot in my throat worse than when I'd had the life nearly strangled out of me, earlier. "Just so sorry. I read your file," I found myself admitting it, and suddenly the warm mug was shaking in my hand. I reached over and set it down on my desk. "I saw passages redacted, and I inquired to my boss whether they could be un-redacted. It wasn't my place, I had no right."

"You wanted to know about me." Roshin shrugged, strangely cavalier. "I wanted you to know about me, it's why I told you. If you trust what I told you, then it should be a weight off both our shoulders."

115

"I do…"

He started for the door, unlocked it and opened it, but didn't go through. He didn't look back. "I hope the tea helps your throat hurt less. My mother used to make it for us, whenever we were sick."

He left and shut the door behind him.

I reached over and locked it, exhaling and shivering. My hands found the mug, I drank a big gulp and it had gone lukewarm but it did help me feel steadier. I moved to my computer. Pulling up my company portal, I sent a message to Stephen Scott asking him to disregard my last message. I no longer wished to see what was under that black ink, to read what anyone else had written about Roshin. Whatever they had said could not hold a candle to the real thing, couldn't paint half the picture.

Chapter Five

I was the second one to dinner, that night. Perry was already helping Ceely to bring out steaming pans of beef and broccoli and Lo Mein noodles. Skirting past them to head back into the kitchen, I washed Roshin's blue mug in the sink before going out and fixing a plate. By then, Ceely was sitting on her own, sipping coffee, and perusing what I could clearly see were schematics on the handheld device I'd lent her.

I stopped and surveyed the empty tables. I felt uncomfortable at the thought of sitting with Ceely, I never knew what I was going to get with her. But then, if I sat with her, Roshin was more likely to come and sit with us, it would be less noticeable. The Captain, too, might end up gracing us with his presence again... But the back of my neck prickled with discomfort at the thought of going over, being asked for space.

She felt my eyes on her and looked up. Waved me over.

Breathing a sigh of relief, I went. "Cracking the books?"

"...Yes. I'd like to know more about Carius Industries. How and when it was founded, its mission statement. Do you have access to some sort of company history, or recruitment video?"

"Certainly." I held out my hand and accepted the device. "I just assumed it wouldn't interest you, that you'd rather get down to brass tacks."

"Normally you would be right, but I have a hunch about where some of this technology came from."

While I searched files, I found myself wondering if this could have something to do with why she was really here. If the Captain were right and she had some ulterior motive, maybe she would need to know more about the company. Probably I should tell him, just to keep him up to speed. Maybe she needed to be kept away from the machines.

"How is your throat?"

I blinked. "Fine, thank you. Still sore, but I can speak."

"Good... I didn't thank you, for not running away... or stepping aside, earlier."

I felt my cheeks warm. "I was no help to you. Not really."

"You bought me a few seconds I needed. If both of them had chased me into the kitchen, they would have caught me."

118

Her voice stayed the same calm and level tone that it always did. Grounded and maternal. I nodded my acceptance, and I did feel a bit proud.

"Here's a welcome video Carius shows most new recruits."

The video started to play, I could hear it but my attention was elsewhere as I saw Roshin enter the galley with a few others. His eyes found me, my heart beat became pronounced in my chest.

"Hello and welcome to Carius Industries. Here, you'll be a part of a dynamic team from all walks of life dedicated to providing the things this world needs. Carius is at the forefront of nuclear and wind-powered technologies-."

He was at the serving bar, had filled his tray. His eyes found me. He looked away and walked straight past me, keeping his head down until he was situated at the table closest to the door, and I could only stare at his back, feeling lost. Was I not receptive enough, earlier? Did I not say the right thing? Maybe he was just feeling as confused as I was. Maybe, like chess, he had made his move and now it was my turn. But I didn't know how to make those kind of moves.

Ceely tapped the screen to pause the video. "It's what I thought. Carius acquired Jordan-Dorian, the company for which I was the chief mechanical engineer back in 2023."

It reminded me of my earlier suspicions, set the back of my neck to prickling again. "What?"

"These engines in the flight rigs, I recognized them right away, they're adapted from my design. I'm guessing Jordan-Dorian went under when I dropped off the map."

I blinked. Turned it over in my mind. "If that's true, then... Assuming you did even the basic due diligence when you signed your contract with your old company, then you'd have a claim for thirty years of lost dividends, with profits in the trillions."

"It's true. And I always do my due diligence. But I don't care about any dividends, it also makes me the perfect person to be servicing the engines in the event any repairs need to be made."

Her excitement was limited, much less powerful than mine would be if I found out that I was essentially a millionaire. There was only a cool satisfaction evident in the purse of her lips, the tiny smile as she shook her head and sipped coffee.

The Captain would need to hear about it. If Ceely had all the money a person could ever need waiting to be collected with some comparatively light paperwork and litigation, then that cut her possible sinister intentions down to next to nothing. I sat back and wondered if she was just a person that I -or the Captain, or the world- would never understand. Some people would never pour themselves out to you. Maybe I needed to focus my energy elsewhere, as uncomfortable as the not-knowing made me.

"How's the food?"

I hadn't even tasted it. I quickly took a bite of broccoli, mumbled approvingly, and nodded. Notes of soy, ginger, garlic, sesame seeds. She cooked the same way that she seemingly built, efficiently.

The Captain walked into the room with the rest of the crew, going for coffee, making his way around and making small talk or checking in with Roshin, Perry, JJ while the other men went through the line collecting food. JJ was sitting with his co-conspirators, eating, and as soon as the Captain stepped away, his eyes locked on Ceely. She sipped more coffee and stared right back at him, undaunted. He broke the gaze first, smirking.

It put me on the edge of my seat, keeping my eyes down after that. When the Captain slid in across from us, he cut off the men's view of her and my entire body relaxed in his presence.

"Captain. How are things?"

"Operational."

Ceely said, "I hope you like Chinese."

He replied in coarse Mandarin that yes, he did. She nodded, seeming to get the idea.

I smiled, wondered if I was still up to the task of conducting a conversation in the language, then decided that I would have to be quite full of myself to make that leap, and besides, it would presumably exclude Ceely. I stuck to English.

"We've just discovered something interesting. Apparently the company which Ceely last worked for -

as their chief engineer- was acquired by Carius when the company was still in its infancy."

She was not bashful, nor prideful. "The engines which carry your flight rigs are based largely on my design."

He was intrigued, but it eased his suspicions none, I could tell. "That is interesting. And you had no idea of this, the last time that you resupplied, set foot on land, or ventured out on your submarine, or wound up here?"

"No. It's a coincidence."

He nodded, pushed his plate aside so that there was nothing between them but the empty table. He folded his hands on top of it, leaned forward. "I don't think that you've lied to me yet, Captain Bennett, I tend to have a good eye for that. But I do know when I'm not being told the whole truth, and you've been holding something back from me since the moment we met. I don't trust you, and whatever it is that you're doing here, I'm not going to let you bring any harm to the ship, the crew, or the company."

I felt sweat break out all over my body; I hadn't been expecting to suddenly be witnessing something so hostile and forthright over dinner, with the crew all around. The Captain had kept his voice low to prevent anyone overhearing; part of his balancing act of holding the crew's respect and obedience. They couldn't know that anything was amiss. The beef I was chewing became lodged in my throat. Coughing, I tried to dislodge it.

122

Pursing her lips, nodding, Ceely shrugged. "You can keep as close an eye on me as you want, Captain. I have nothing to hide." She sipped coffee, seemed to notice me coughing, and gave me a pat on the back.

By then, I was breathing again.

The Captain relaxed, starting on his dinner. "We might reach the drilling site tomorrow, or early the next day. You'll get to see your design in action."

"I hadn't intended for my work to help streamline the harvesting of fossil fuels. I had hoped it would be a prototype toward replacing them. Maybe even lead to safer and further space travel."

He shook his head. "The world will always need oil. We'll just have to dig deeper and sacrifice more to get it."

"And wake up more monsters," Ceely murmured, and I had to look over, her voice was softer than usual, sadder. The Captain noticed it, too. She shook it off. "Is it because of the creature that they came up with this flight rig?"

"Yes, to get it out in a hurry and to eliminate cost and risk of setting up and dismantling a drilling platform."

I chimed in, "And to evade certain laws about construction in international waters."

"And to keep ahead of environmental activists."

"Right…" It didn't sit well with her. "In the event of an attack the company flies the rig out, and leaves the crew to the beast or, presumably, any other threat?"

The Captain answered. "The flight rig is a trillion-dollar piece of equipment. We represent about seven or eight hundred thousand in value. Settlements, lost labor, media damage control…"

"Eight hundred and twelve thousand dollars," I corrected him. "And most of that is the value of the ship."

"Of course it is." Ceely was deeply, surprisingly perturbed.

"The food is good."

"It is…"

"Thank you."

I wondered if I should go over and give Roshin his mug back, or if it would be some huge spectacle, embarrass him, put us both on the chopping block. The men are too tough, small-minded, probably giving any hint of closeness between us is too dangerous. But it would be rude to keep it. And if he was waiting for me to make the next move, returning his mug would be the best thing I could come up with… I stared at the thing, and at him, deep in thought while Ceely and the Captain had another exchange.

"Would I be able to collect some tools after dinner, to start working on the reconditioning of my sub?"

He only nodded. Then looked at me.

"Want me to come along?"

"I don't think that's necessary." It seemed the Captain had figured out the financial implications of Ceely's design being used in the rigs. His suspicions of her making some accusation against him to sue the company were gone. But he looked at me again. I didn't know why.

I kept my head down and focused on my food, thinking the whole time about my mug conundrum. Would returning it make me look like I *didn't* care? Maybe he was alright with me keeping it... No, I couldn't assume that.

I have to just do it, I realized, *without thinking about it.* Or I would never riddle out the correct answer, never work up the courage. I had wasted too many minutes wondering and had failed to eat my food before it got cold. Roshin did not waste time, as a general rule. He had finished his small meal and stood, heading to the dish bins.

I flew to my feet. Knowing there were eyes on me, at least the Captain's and Ceely's, my face was aflame. I caught him under the door's archway.

"Here," I thrust the mug at him. It shook visibly for the entire two seconds it took for him to recognize me, and reach up, and take it. His finger touched mine. My skin tingled.

"Did it help?"

"Very much. Thank you."

"Of course."

"I'll see you around."

"Yes. Goodnight."

"Goodnight." My face was smiling, though I was trying to hold my smile back. And as Roshin turned out of my view, and down the empty corridor, I thought that I saw his lips react, too. It was not a smile, just a slight tightening that made a crease appear at the corners.

I turned back into the galley, heart pounding and more than a few pairs of eyes on me. I hurried to my seat. The Captain kept focused on his meal, but I knew from all my time observing him that he would have noticed the exchange, calculated possibilities. I knew the risk assessment, myself.

There were hard men around. And hard men did not like soft men like me. The Captain was probably thinking that here was another crew member in danger, and making a spectacle of himself, and that was just great. His heavy sigh, small head shake confirmed it.

I didn't care. I had hardly felt so alive in all my life, so seen. And, to think, I'd had to come to this God forsaken place to find myself.

I hardly slept a wink.

The next morning, I got up early and showered and shaved, and checked my messages, still sitting on my bunk.

Scott apologized for not getting back to me sooner on my request for Roshin's records, and was glad that I had closed the matter on my own. Lucille Bennett was a tricky matter, and would require some favors from higher up to reintroduce her to the IRS and Social Security offices. She would need to submit to a blood test to prove that she was who she said she was, but if that turned out to be the case, she was a welcome addition to the company and arbitration should be begun to settle the matter of her lost dividends.

In a post-statement, Scott mentioned how incredible it was to deal with the challenges of having someone who was legally declared dead declared undead again. It was not the first time a person had been wrongly assumed to be a casualty of the creature (C.O.C.) but that he never thought he would get to handle one. The head clerk was as much a nerd as the rest of us, it seemed.

I saved documents which needed Ceely's signature, and headed for breakfast. Perry was there, as he had been at dinner. Breakfast was a square of a baked oat bar with cinnamon, cranberries and little chips of chocolate, along with crispy bacon. I collected some, and coffee, and joined Ceely at a table. She picked small pieces off of her oat square.

"Can't taste the orange zest," she murmured, disappointed.

I bit a corner. "I think it's yummy."

She nodded her thanks. She had schematics out again.

"I've got word from my superiors. They sent me some applications you need to sign to restore your status as one of the living, and an employment contract, they're interested in arbitration and settling what they legally owe you. I'd expect something along the lines of a yearly stipend, more of a generous wage for your continued work with the company than a lump sum."

"I told you I don't care about that. They can pay me what they want to."

"I know, but don't be rash. It's your money, not the company's. You could give it away if you wanted."

"True."

"They also need a blood sample, to confirm your identity. The sooner, the better to get the ball rolling."

"Fine. Who's the medical officer on the ship?"

"Officially, that position doesn't exist. The Captain has the most medical training. Perry had some when he was in the army, and I'm CPR certified, myself."

Perry was standing at the window, looking out, sipping coffee with the sun on his face.

Ceely called to him. "Perry? Can you do a blood draw?"

He seemed to have forgotten that we were there. Smiling apologetically, he answered, "Needles freak me out."

"The Captain, then. Unless you'd like to take a stab at me?"

I shook my head.

"I'm sure for verification purposes, they won't want me doing it myself."

"Could you?"

"How hard can it be? I had two children, and needles in my spine with each one. Not to mention my cervix scraped every year since I was nineteen."

I tried to huff in a good-natured way, but it made swallowing my next bite a bit difficult.

Roshin came in after a few other men had, and sat alone. I was disappointed, but then, it was early in the day. Perry scanned the room and seemed pleased with the array of faces -no doubt in terms of the protection that their presence offered Ceely- and left the galley. Probably going to sit on the bow with his pear or orange or apple.

The Captain did not arrive to eat breakfast with us. When one single man among the last group of men left in the galley stood up, the others all began to rise, too. They seemed to be aware of the concern we all had for Ceely -that the Captain did not wish for her to be left alone- so they all went at once. I went, too, and found him up on the deck. It was a humid morning, almost completely windless. The grey seas around the tanker were calm except for the spray of salty droplets as the bow cut through the water, and the choppy wake left behind us. I hadn't been up on deck since Ceely approached in her sub and the alarms went off. Had it really been only a day and a half ago? And still the storm that seemed to be threatening us had not materialized.

Men were on hands and knees scrubbing the deck. One was being strapped into a harness and climbing over the edge to scrape barnacles off of the sides with another man spotting him. Perry was in the gunner's turret doing systems checks. The Captain was in the control room with JJ.

My stomach churned at the sight of them together. I wondered again if I was doing the right thing keeping my mouth shut. I was letting the Captain be bamboozled, after all. And while I didn't always like him, I did always respect him.

JJ stepped out as I was stepping in. He bumped my shoulder with his own, not aggressive enough to knock me around but enough that I knew it was intentional. The Captain noticed and his eyes narrowed as he watched the older man go, but he said nothing about it. "What is it?"

"The company requires a blood test to confirm Ceely's identity."

"And I'm the only one who knows how to work a needle." He stated it plainly, as though it was fact.

It took a minute, but I realized he was making a joke. Plenty of the men must have experience with drugs, all of them having some kind of criminal background the way that they did. Probably not Roshin.

I tipped my head, tried to chuckle but the sound came out tense, dry. I wondered if the joke were not deeper, darker than I realized. Had the Captain once stuck needles in those immaculate arms? Or did he just mean that he was covered in tattoos?

Shaking his head at me or maybe at himself, he stepped out of the control room.

I hurried after; the Captain never strolled, always moved with purpose. "Should I come?"

"Yes."

Down we went, and I sucked in a last lungful of air. It was not clear air, exactly, not like the filtered stuff back at my office on the mainland. It had a smog to it, an acrid taste. But it was not the confined air below deck, stale.

The galley was locked. Ceely came and looked through the round window at us. She opened the door.

"Time for my checkup?"

The Captain tipped his head.

The med bay was a room and bathroom in the same block as our crew quarters, the same size. It had a bed, no dresser, just a first aid kit hanging on the wall and a locked metal cabinet beside it. A computer and small work station on the back wall.

The Captain kept a few keys in his pocket, probably all for the ship. They were attached to a chain that also hooked onto his belt. I frowned at that; I had thought he carried a master key which could open any lock on the ship. Maybe a few locks were thought to be important enough to warrant their own key. He found the right one as I was still stepping inside, and waited for me to close the door and lock it before opening the cabinet.

There were bandages, surgical instruments, IV bags and tubes, syringes and artificial skin grafts in shiny bags. The top shelf held the medications, only a few types. Some liquid and some pill form, antibiotics and probably narcotics, too.

Ceely sat on the bed, rolled her sleeve up.

The Captain assembled tools, washed his hands, put on gloves. A small vial, a small needle, an alcohol swab. Neither of them spoke as he wrapped a rubber tube around her arm as a tourniquet. He wiped the skin with the cleanser in a circle around the inside of her arm. I could see the blue veins standing out on her milky skin. His hands were not shaking -as mine surely would have been- as he opened the needle's package, knelt in front of her, and ran a fingertip over her veins as they became engorged.

I leaned against the door and watched, silent, still, feeling like I was becoming scenery, invisible. I didn't know if it was who I was -a clerk- or who the two of them were: self-possessed, secure, locked in contention because of his mistrust and her ulterior motives.

"Have you done this before?"

"Twice. Ready?"

"If you are."

He was focused, tongue between his teeth, lips parted slightly. He pushed the needle in and her face reacted infinitesimally. Blood blossomed into the end of the needle, he hooked the small vial up in a smooth motion and it started to fill, the red blood surging with beats of her heart.

"Very brave," he said. The vial was full, disconnected, sealed and set on the gleaming metal tray wheeled up nearby. The needle slid out of her flesh, a dot of blood remaining at the mouth of the small puncture. He taped a cotton ball down onto the crook of her arm.

"You too. Well done."

"I don't have any lollipops for you."

"How about a Vicodin?"

"Sure, they won't miss one." He pulled his gloves off, stretched them taught and shot them into the trashcan.

I was captivated, watching the two of them.

He was so professional, so aloof, but so careful. He would not poke the woman without being sure that she was ready, praising her for her braveness. A suspicious and unbending man, but still a gentleman, still sprinkling in his dry humor.

And her. Brave, or just used to pain, not willing to let him see her flinch. Maternal in her offer of praise, reciprocal of his own, but still trying to keep him on his toes with that request for Vicodin. I couldn't know if she were trying to mirror him or if they were just so much alike.

He went to the computer on the back wall, entered a security code, then positioned the vial into a special compartment. It punctured through the top, whirred as it analyzed, then showed the results all in seconds.

"Lucille Amelia Bennett. In the flesh."

"The one and only." She rubbed her arm. "I'm sure I can make it back to the galley from here-."

"No." The word was cold and hard as iron. He was busy disposing of the remnants of the sample. "You'll wait while I disinfect, then I'll walk you back, myself. Jacob, you can go."

I had forgotten that I was there. I nodded and went. "Yes, Sir."

Chapter Six

There was very little that I actually had to do, so I found myself pulling up the ship's security system, watching the hall outside of the med bay. The Captain and Ceely exited not five minutes after I had, and I followed them to the galley. He did not leave her at the door, instead leading her inside and back to the kitchen, checking inside for villains, I was sure. Once satisfied, he did go, and she walked with him to the door. They said something, and I wished the cameras picked up sound, or that I could read lips.

With the door closed, the Captain checked the handle to ensure that it was locked. Then he headed up the hallway, up the stairs, out of frame. I was touched by his concern for her, even though he did not trust her or want her on his ship.

Humoring a hunch, I went back in the camera's memory, to dinner. I had left before most, I had not known how the meal had ended. As I suspected, the

Captain had stayed until the last crewman had left, then had helped Ceely to bring back the serving trays and pans, and they had washed dishes together without much conversation. Then he had walked her to her room. And just like he had, moments ago, he had ensured the door was locked before leaving her.

I let the video play even as he left the frame, thinking. He must have asked Perry to take the day shift, said that he would take the night. It truly was inconveniencing him to have her onboard. I felt my respect for him grow. My bosses back home would have delegated the extra work to anybody else, not lifted a finger, let alone gotten their hands dirty.

Movement in the frame caught my attention. The door to Ceely's room had opened. Her grey head poked out. She looked both ways, then went down the hall, alone. To the stairs leading down to the ship's lowest level, where the engine room, her submarine, the unmanned repair sub, and many other things were. Just the sight of it made my heart start to pound.

It was worry for her, at first. I reminded myself I had seen her just minutes ago; the video was old. She was fine.

There were cameras down below, and I fiddled with the system until I found the one which showed her entering the engine room. I had no view inside, could only wait for her to reemerge with an armful of things. Seemingly random bits and bobs I could only make out some of. I saw metal wire on a spool, some little tools and a white box that contained I knew not what, sturdy gloves, what I thought to be a torch of some kind...

The engine room contained all kinds of extra supplies. Anything an engineer could need to fix an engine, or really any component of the ship that could break. There was even a massive, spare propellor.

I knew that the Captain had taken Ceely down to collect some tools and supplies needed to begin tuning up her ship. Why feel the need to sneak back down, and help herself -putting herself in serious danger- if she was not hiding something sinister?

She was doing it right up the hall from where I laid my head at night! The Captain needed to be shown... I had little doubt he would take swift action, was only unsure as to whether Ceely would be immediately exiled from the ship, her sub flagged for collection and her wanted for questioning, or be thrown in the brig to await trial. Maybe they would send her back on the first flight rig to come out to us.

I would probably be commended.

I could unravel the whole thing, her plot, and probably impress even the Captain. If I were brave enough to go snooping. Her room would be unlocked, they could only be locked from the inside or by the Captain's master key from the outside. Her submarine would be unguarded. I knew which one appealed to me more. It was a breach of the law, of ethics, and of company policy, too...

But to make an omelet, one must break a few eggs.

The Captain would go below deck, search the submarine himself, if he knew her to be sneaking around, if he had even an inkling that the ship and crew were in real peril. He would consider it not only his right, but his duty.

I found my feet. In the largest compartment of my desk, I had a kit in case of emergencies. Tsunami, creature attack, plain old power outage. I collected the flashlight and gave it a test, on off, on off. My feet carried me to my door. My hand rested on the knob.

Everyone would be impressed with me. Nobody would be cross. Roshin would have a reason to come to me again, to offer praise, to hear the thrilling story. Puffing up my chest as big as I could, I launched myself into the hallway, and my legs wobbled as I went, but I did go, almost fell on the stairs down but caught myself with a grip on the railing.

The engines were working, a constant thrum of noise not very loud out in the main cavern of the ship's bowels, but enough that my movements were largely silent. It smelled of cleaning chemicals -probably the floor had been cleaned recently- and it smelled of combustion, too. There was nobody below that I could see. Still, I felt the eyes on me of the camera system. I hurried to the back of the room where Ceely's yellow submarine was dry-docked.

It loomed above, rusting in a few places where plates were welded together, more intimidating than it had been in my mind. She had gotten a boost up. I could probably haul myself halfway up and scramble the rest, but my nice leather shoes would not help me much, their flat soles…

There was a table not far away. I gave it a pull, and it hardly budged. The thing must weigh almost a hundred pounds. Of course. The company couldn't have equipment sliding around with the rocking of the ship in harsher weather. I dragged it, its legs shrieking on the metal floor the entire way and my ears aching from it, my entire being sure that the hellish sound would bring some curious passerby down on me. By the time I got it in place, my heart was pounding harder than it ever had. I was damp under the arms.

My legs felt like jelly as I mounted the table, then stood. I had to catch my breath, scan the room one more time. A small part of me was hoping I would be discovered. Marched before the Captain before I could commit this justified crime. Surely, they would respect me just for trying...

But there was still nobody. The Captain ran a tight ship; everyone was where they were supposed to be, keeping busy. Everyone except for me.

Not allowing myself another second of doubt, I jumped and swung one leg over the huge arch of the submarine's round body. Although the thing didn't budge a single centimeter, I still felt unsteady. I thought of the mechanical bull friends from college had ridden at a western-themed bar… I had been too bashful. If they could see me, now!

The handle of the hatch twisted with a small squeak, opened easily enough, and then I was climbing down into the cool dark with the lit flashlight clenched between my teeth. I whipped my head each way to ensure that there was nobody and no-thing waiting in the dark corners of the sub to grab me and drag me down. It was just an empty tube.

The only things taking up space were the ripped old office chair welded at the legs to the floor, a refrigerator for provisions, the small console opened at the vertical panel underneath the simple controls, and wires sticking out. That didn't surprise me. She had said that she needed to work on reconditioning the ship, tuning it up. Probably that was half of the truth, at least.

Still, I needed to check it out. I got down on my hands and knees, and shining the light, I stuck my whole head inside the console. There were no sticks of dynamite, no bricks of C-4, which I thought I would surely recognize. I wasn't surprised; it wasn't what I was expecting to find anyway. I didn't think that Ceely had violent intentions, and neither did the Captain… we just believed she could be hiding something which could turn out to be dangerous.

Electronics were not my forte, and I soon decided that if there were anything wrong with the wiring or mechanical components in front of me, I would never know it. I stood up and studied the controls more closely. A steering column. The two joysticks which controlled the ship's mechanical arms, and a switch on each one which probably launched the harpoons which had once been mounted there.

There was another access panel in the back which lead to the single engine. I would have to check there, too, see if anything was tucked away in the corners, or could there be something *inside* of the engine itself? Perry had already investigated the ship at a glance, read for chemicals, and found nothing. It didn't make sense.

I started toward the other end of the ship and my hand reached out automatically to trace the top of the white refrigerator unit. I stopped. Empty, probably, a too conspicuous place to hide anything, and she had been out of provisions and starving when we found her. But if I couldn't exactly feel it running, I could sense the energy coming off of it, the hum in my ears was that unit going, not the ship's engine anymore. Keep the sub hooked up to the ship's power, that had been one of Ceely's requirements when securing her position with the Captain. 'Pay me what you want, but keep my sub hooked up to your grid' she had said.

Maybe she was spiriting away provisions already, and that was all...

I felt dread sitting heavy in my stomach. What if there was something inside? What if it was some sort of trap on a weighted trigger, and the moment I opened the refrigerated chest's lid, I was pierced with projectiles, sprayed with acid?

But that was ridiculous. Ceely was a woman, probably seventy-years-old, not an ancient pharaoh protecting his treasures from beyond the grave. Whatever she was hiding, she would need access to it, too, eventually. I tucked the flashlight between my lips again.

I got both hands on the lid and heaved it open impulsively. Leaning on the edge, bending over to peer down in, the lights illuminated *something* inside, pale beige and rippled in texture, a tangled mess that I squinted and leaned closer to decipher. And as my eyes roamed, the beam of light from the flashlight in my mouth roamed, too, and fell on something that gave me a start, for it almost looked like a face. My skin taught, my heart racing, I looked again, and when I realized that it was in fact a face, sunken and shriveled but a human face, the yelp that escaped from me echoed around the sub and knocked my legs clean out from under me.

I hit the floor of the submarine with a thud. Pain flared. I scrambled and banged my head on the round side of the tube, and there was more pain, enough to scramble my already wheeling mind. I didn't know anything except that there were bodies in that ice chest - a freezer, not a refrigerator- I needed to get away from. I shoved myself to my feet and snagged the lid, dragging it closed. I had dropped the flashlight inside with the bodies, it was dead to me.

In the dark I stumbled to the other wall, finding the ladder with only my hands and starting to pull myself up. My foot slipped off the first rung and my stomach lurched as I fell, then I was going up again and my head poked out of the suddenly claustrophobic tube and its foully tainted air. It didn't actually reek, that was just my body reacting to the horrible truth of death so close, my breakfast rising back up my throat. I choked and clenched and slid down the side of the submarine, hit the table going fast and toppled it over as I flung myself away.

My eyes were prickling, seeping, I hadn't actually puked but was dangerously close, my guts curling and coiling around themselves. I was banged up all over, but I found my feet and ran, steps getting longer, more confident, I made the stairs and went up.

The Captain.

Another flight of stairs to gain the upper deck. The open air helped calm my nausea just a bit, I felt pierced by the daylight and became aware of the rocking of the ship, the sweat warm and itchy all over my body. Several crewmen were around and noticed my sudden appearance.

Roshin was one of them. "Jacob?"

"The Captain?"

"Went below. Probably in his office."

And back down I went. I was sure I would not feel another moment's peace, but if it were possible, it would be getting this responsibility off my chest, unburdening myself to the Captain. The moments leading to his office were a fervor, then I was pounding on the door.

After a moment, he appeared. His eyes took me in, he processed the state of me in only a moment. "What is it?" He swept me inside, closed the door.

"I- I was looking at security camera footage, earlier." I froze, unsure how to tell him that I had been watching him and Ceely together, not really sure what had possessed me and definitely not knowing how to put it to words.

He guided me to a chair opposite his, and pulled the bottle of whiskey and one glass out of a lower desk drawer, pouring me a generous portion. I could not turn it down, didn't want to. I had never liked the drink, but then, I had never been in such a state before. I threw the liquor back and swallowed, gasping at the burn that sprung up the back of my throat.

"-God…" I slumped back in the chair. My exhausted and damp body suddenly felt like it weighed a thousand pounds.

The Captain's face was stern and inquisitive. He was leaning forward. "Go on."

Part Three
The Captain

Chapter One

"I was watching Ceely on the security camera, the footage from last night. I only wanted to know how she got to her room, saw you drop her off, there. But then, once you were gone, she went out again. She went down to the engine room and retrieved some things, tools, supplies. I don't really know what came over me, but I felt suspicious and I went to investigate. I went inside the submarine. In the freezer, the deep-freezer, ice chest thing-."

"-What?"

"Bodies. Two of them. Small ones, tangled up together. Not fresh, old. Frozen."

"Bodies?"

"Yes. Human bodies."

I sit back, perplexed, unsure what to make of it. My mind turns down several avenues. First, I take in the sight of Jacob, red hair damp on his crown, skin even paler than usual. He has had a fright, but he is of a more delicate constitution than most of the crew. He could be mistaken, overreacting. Secondly, whether the information is sound or not, it has been acquired through illegal means. It would not hold up in court, if this were America, if Ceely were on trial...

But it's not America. There are no trials out here. We are ruled by different laws, older ones, more brutal. If there are bodies -small, frozen bodies- in that submarine which I allowed to be brought onboard my ship, then my response will have to be swift and hard to have any hope of keeping order, my paycheck, my current position and ongoing employment.

Jacob waits patiently for my deliberation.

"I'll have to investigate this myself and give Ceely a chance to explain before I proceed with any course of action. Return to your office and do nothing until we speak again."

He looks deflated. "Is that all?"

I know that he wants praise. "What else?"

He goes, not saying another word or looking back.

I sit back, take the bottle of whiskey in my hand, and hold it up to the light. The hundred intricate points of glass on the finely made bottle catch the light, channels between them carry rainbows to reflect on the tattooed skin of my thumb. I imagine taking a drink of the amber liquid. I can practically feel it burning its way down my throat, warming my stomach, sending the tingle up my spine and all the way out to my fingertips. Just pretending has to be enough.

I have to face this stone-cold sober. I have a responsibility to never be impaired while I am on this ship. I could need to react to crisis at a moment's notice. Everything depends on it, not just my safety and the safety of the crew, but my paycheck, advancement, stability.

I have to confront Ceely.

I put the bottle away. I should go and confirm the presence of the bodies myself, but I trust Jacob, despite myself, and it would be against policy, and it's not something that I want to see. There is an intercom on the ship that I have seldom used. I don't want to go and collect Ceely, I feel like it would weaken my position. I want her to report to me, hope that it will put her on edge like a child being summoned to the principal's office. I want her to do it safely, though.

I activate the intercom.

"Perry and Ceely, come to my office." He is intuitive and helpful, he will know to go and escort her. She is intelligent and putting on a front of compliance. She will wait to be collected.

Bodies. Two small bodies. In a chest freezer. Did she kill them herself? I don't doubt she is capable. Most people are, if you back them into a corner.

In the middle of the ocean, on her own for decades, rarely touching land or encountering another person. Is it because of the murder and guilt and self-exile, and did it drive her to madness? Or did the madness come first? She could have tossed those bodies overboard at any time, and there would be no identifying or incriminating evidence left on them in a day. Sink them with stones or weights to be sure of it. Why is she carrying them around?

Probably because she can't let them go. Guilt and love are maybe the two most enduring things in the world, with guilt having the edge if they were in a cage match. I certainly don't want to meet mine in a dark alley. Guilt or love had to be what kept those bodies on Ceely's sub. Smart money on guilt.

I imagine her sleeping next to them everything night, for years, and feel a vague sense of nausea along with a specific tug of pity. It is all that I can picture in the moment she knocks and enters.

Perry sticks his head in. "Was that all you needed, Captain?"

I realize that he checked Ceely's submarine out. Of course he would have looked inside the freezer, seen the bodies. And he said nothing to me. I stand, cross to him, and guide Ceely into my office, stepping past her into the hallway.

"Wait inside, please." I shut the door. Cross my arms, and address Perry. "You inspected her submarine."

"Mm-hm." His eyes look away, he seems to know where I'm going.

"The bodies. You didn't think they were worth mentioning?"

He inhales, folds his arms over his chest and leans on the white wall. He's considering whether to lie to me, I think. Blame it on getting old, it slipped his mind, or his eyesight failed him and he mistook those corpses for driftwood, dried fish, hide of some sea beast collected to make purses out of.

Then he puffs out the big breath he was holding. "It was shocking, at first. No sign of trauma, though. Didn't seem like a murder most foul... Disfigured but by the elements, by nature. Old bodies, in terms of exposure. Physically young, though. Either that, or they were little people... More likely that they were kids, and call me sexist but a woman who appears sane doesn't carry around two kids' bodies if they're strangers to her. Either way, it doesn't equate to her being dangerous, not in my mind. Worst case scenario, someone hired her to go find those bodies, she's a scavenger. Which all implies that she told the truth and stumbled onto us by accident, not that she came to sabotage."

"Contaminants."

"I don't think so, not with the bodies in that state."

"So you made a judgement call that wasn't yours to make."

"Well…" Perry nods in acceptance. "I'm sorry, I let you down, I guess, but I just didn't see it that way at the time. I saw it as none of my business. Or -respectfully- none of yours, Captain."

I'm simmering, I know there's nothing I can say that will help get rid of the feeling. I'm mad at him, but I'm mad at myself, too, for trusting him. I'm mad that the strange code of criminals no longer includes me; that I have become the authority they feel the need to protect each other from. Mostly I'm angry that I have one less person I can call on, it really does all have to fall on me.

"Dismissed."

"Thank you." He goes.

Ceely lingers in the entryway until I gesture for her to take the seat opposite me. Closed in the quiet room with her, I feel a strange fear. I do not know what is coming, do not think that she will leap across the desk and stab a pen into my eye socket, but I know that whatever is coming will be hard to reckon with.

As it is, I do not know how to start. I stare at her, study her face, her eyes and mouth giving away that she suspects what I know. I hope she will speak first, but she does not. We sit in silence for a full minute. It must be as prickly for her as it is for me. But she endures.

I try to begin, say her name. "Ceely." I sigh, rub the back of my neck, trying to work the tension out. "Did you bring dead bodies on my ship?"

Blinking, taking a deep breath, she sits back in her chair. It is not the easy, posturing slouch of a person about to be sentenced to life in prison, just an exhausted woman with her best days behind her hardly able to hold herself upright any longer. She may even be a bit relieved not to have to hide anymore. "Yes."

"Why?"

The word comes out of me sounding weak. I sit up straighter and cross my arms to make up for it. I realize I am a little afraid of what her answer will be. We have not spent much time together during which she has not been lying by omission. But when proximity was necessary and unavoidable -when I was sticking her with that needle, when we were washing dishes together- when I set my inquisitiveness aside and just made conversation, I found her so easy to be around. I maybe even admire her. How can I not? She is blisteringly quick witted, fearless, so strong but still warm.

She looks at me. Her mouth pinches, wrinkling at the corners. Looks away and shakes her head, almost as if she is going to say that she does not know, but that will never work. Then I realize she is just at a loss, her eyes are blinking fast as they start to shine, she clears her throat and I can tell from the sound that there's a knot in it.

I brace myself.

When she looks back at me, her face is wide open, unguarded, like an open book. I know that she is going to tell me the truth. I feel stunned by it, the clarity with which I suddenly see her; I feel honored that she is letting me. I feel afraid.

"It's a strange story. I don't want you to think that I'm insane, but I guess that ship has sailed."

I get out the whiskey and pour her a glass. Follow its path as she drinks it down her long, white throat. I'm still craving it. I wait.

"I was living in Los Angeles when the creature emerged. I was in Montana on business, working for the company that Carius eventually absorbed. My two girls were at home. Astrid and Josie are their names. They drowned that day."

Love. Maybe a little guilt, too. I feel a pit in my stomach. Knowing that nothing I can say will help, I nod to show that I am hearing her, that I understand, that she can go on.

"I couldn't leave them down there. So I built my submarine at a friend's farm, in about a week. The coast was on lockdown, being patrolled, but I made it past them, got my girls. Then the creature showed up. It was attracted to my movements, curious, or maybe it just wanted to eat my daughters like it ate so many other people. I was prepared for that. I was hoping that it would come." She smiles a rueful little smile as she says it. "I wanted to kill it. And if it killed me, too, good... I shot it twice with harpoons. A storm whipped up out of nowhere. I know now that it was the creature's defense mechanism, and when the submarine and I were struck by lightning, I blacked out."

I pour her another drink. I can tell that she needs it. She wipes a tear and then takes just a sip.

153

"I woke up not far from where we found each other, and the storm and the creature were gone. I had white hair, and wrinkles. I was thirty years older, and I hadn't lived them. They were just gone."

It sends a chill down my spine. The seconds tick by.

"Do you believe me?"

I nod, look away from her because it's hard to think straight looking into her shiny, brown eyes. I can hardly stop myself from picturing her as a younger woman; not a girl but a mature, filled out woman about my age who has two young children and just the beginning of laugh lines around her eyes. How gorgeous she must have been. I can see that version of her through the white hair and wrinkles, when I look at her next.

"I'm sorry," I say.

The glass shakes in her hands as she lifts it and drinks the rest. She nods, trying to be brave. "It's them in the freezer. You guessed that by now."

"We can hold a service and bury them at sea-."

"-No."

"Or send them on the next flight rig for burial or cremation, whatever you prefer."

"No, you can't."

"You should go with them. I understand that it's hard, but I can't have them on my ship."

"No, you don't understand. The shock sent me forward in time, it changed my body and it changed theirs, too, sort of mummified them -I don't believe they have any rotting tissue which could cause any kind

154

of outbreak on your ship- and I have no reason to believe that it will, but, there's a chance that if I encounter the creature again, it could send me back. It could send all of us back, change their bodies back. I know that it sounds crazy. But if there's even a small chance that it could work, I have to keep trying." By the end, her voice has come unraveled, the knot in her throat is back, her tears are falling freely down her sun spotted cheeks.

My voice is small so that it will not carry a tremor. "I can't have dead bodies on my ship."

Her face goes blank. She stands. "If that's your decision, then I'll take my girls and go."

"Hold on." I shoot to my feet and fly across the room, cutting her off at the door, slamming it shut as she tries to open it. "I can't let you do that."

"You can't stop me."

"You signed a contract, you would be AWOL, Ceely-they don't take kindly to that."

She puts a hand on my chest and tries to push me back, still pulling on the door. "-Do you really think I care about the law anymore!?"

"I'm the Captain of this ship."

"I don't give a damn, get out of my way!"

"No!" I grab her by the arms and turn her to face me. I have lost my composure, and she is shocked by it, looking at me warily. "I can't let you leave, Ceely. I'm responsible for you, now. It would be suicide."

She tries to pull away, pushing against my chest, twisting in my grip, but I hold firm, tugging her back. My heart is pounding, I'm at a loss as to what to say or do or how we got here as she stops struggling, teeth clenched and scowling at me, seething. I look between her angry mouth and her shining eyes, not really understanding myself in that moment or why I can't let her go, and she puts it together a second before I do. She recognizes the strange prickle between us.

She blinks, scoffs, starts to say, "What are you thinking?"

But I shut her up before she can get it out, I kiss her hard so that I don't have to hear her disbelief, her derision. It makes every drop of blood in me light up, it careens through my veins and not an insignificant amount heads south. As blasphemously erotic as that moment is, my hands pry themselves loose of her soft arms in the same instant. I could never hold a woman close to me against her will, even as desperate as I am.

Ceely stiffens in that first moment, but she does not pull away.

Vindicated, I bring my hands up to push her hair back behind her ears, cup her face and lift it, exposing more of her. I slide my body closer as I deepen the kiss. She reacts infinitesimally at first, lips fitting to mine as though unsure, or insecure, but her hands are still on my chest and I feel them twist the front of my shirt. My eyes have already closed to revel in the fireworks exploding behind their lids, but I steal a glance and find

156

hers closed, too. She opens her mouth and my head spins, my step forward and her step back are both wobbly stumbles that land us in a tangle of limbs against the wall.

We are hip to hip and I'm straining against her for the friction, already hard and wanting to get inside her, but I can't take her hot, inviting mouth and her fingers threading into the front of my pants at face value. I break the kiss, gasping.

"You don't have to."

Eyes fluttering open, a bit dazed, she demands, "Have to?"

"I'm the Captain, it's against policy, it could be considered coercive-."

"-Shut up," she orders.

"Yes Ma'am."

I kiss her again, never so obsessed with a pair of lips in my life, bizarrely riveted and content enough to spend hours or days there. Hip to hip and touching the warm skin at the small of her back, eliciting a tiny moan in her throat that echoes through me like judgement day trumpets. It's going to be the end of me. She explores my chest with her hands roaming under my shirt. Grows impatient.

"You have a bed?"

"Through there."

"Let's go."

"Are you sure?"

She drags me by a belt loop instead of answering. I am briefly embarrassed by the utilitarian setup of dresser and neatly tucked twin bed, as simple as the crew quarters. Only a few stacks of books indicate that anybody spends their nights there.

Ceely takes control, pushing me down on the firm mattress and climbing on top. I let myself be swept along, as nervous and pliant as I was the very first time, all my years of experience having gone out the window.

This is a woman, the thought keeps resurfacing as she does what she wants to on top of me, whenever she changes the angle of her movements, finds what she likes and gives me a crumb of a sigh or hum to show her pleasure. I touch skin that is laced with stretch marks, starting to droop, a soft store of extra weight. I run my tongue over blue veins showing through the thin, pale skin around her pink areolas and feel thrilled.

All pretense and shyness have been stripped away. No makeup, no perfume, just a body over me in the plain light from the small window, strangely erotic in her physical fragility, but so strong and unbothered by any tedious insecurities and that is what ultimately makes me so reverent of her. No one has ever let me see them like this, let me bury my face in a mix of brown and grey hair between her legs as soon as I remember myself and that I have something to prove. I put her on her back and hold her hips down with one of my arms across them, my fingers tracing different patterns along her inner and outer labia, circling around her clitoris, exploring until she is giving me delicious moans to show what she likes most, and doing it again, again, forgetting that I am a person for the seconds that she arches and cries out and I feel her walls close around my finger. I don't know how we got from the hard woman I met a few days ago to this soft, sensual woman with needs, but I feel a swell of pride that I'm the one giving her what she needs.

Am I a man, or is this all I was born to do? I am a man, I remember because my cock is throbbing, needs to be touched. Ceely urges me to lay over her, wrapping a hand around it and guiding it back in.

I push my own desires to the back of my mind, relishing in the feeling of her stretching around me for only a moment. Then I am back to lavishing kisses on her face, neck, breasts. My hands glide over any spot that has made her shiver already, releasing energy stored up there again. I want every part of her involved, captivated, tamed. Men can race toward orgasm, while women must be coaxed.

I'll do anything to make sure that it happens again, even manage to hold off until she is ready. Her hot, rippling flesh squeezing around me and the torturous wait make the feeling of spilling inside her seem like it may be the last thing that I ever feel, like all of my life is draining out of me, I'm melting into her and we may never be able to be truly separated again. *Succubus*, I think. But the noises she makes remind me again, *this is a woman.*

I don't want the feeling of triumph to fade, pull her close to me and hold her tight. Her grey head rests on my tattooed chest, she seems less fierce than before. Her softness lets me feel like the strong one, and I'm grateful as I try to piece myself back together, remembering who I am. I am Caesar Alvarado, captain of the USS *Baton Rouge*. I am responsible for the mission and the crew, and this woman has jeopardized all of that. It is also true that I cannot let her leave.

She will die out there, all alone, and I will sulk through the rest of my life, unhappy even if I land a decent commission and can take care of my moms in their golden years.

Less important but still suddenly preying on my mind is the fact that if the men find out I have slept with Ceely, I will lose a good portion of their respect, of my hold on them.

And Jacob. He is not going to want to let it go, this thing with the bodies. I can threaten him. He did go against policy and break the law, going onto Ceely's submarine. It would probably be only half as effective as appealing to his kind heart and asking him nicely. But of course, I don't want to do that.

Looking down at Ceely's soft, sleeping face, I know I cannot force her to jettison the bodies. Not if it means that I will driver her away. I feel content, laying there. Though I know I can't stay there for long.

I gently rock her awake. We've been laying for probably a half an hour by then. I have tried to come up with something to say -the right thing to say- but all that I've got is: "We can't stay here."

Blinking, dazed, she nods. "We've got work to do. Of course."

She sits up, her breasts droop in a natural way lower on her chest. I force myself to look away as she dresses, focus on pulling my own clothes back on.

"I won't force you to do anything you're not ready for. I know that I couldn't… it wouldn't feel right, even if I could, even though I don't believe…" I shake my head. "It doesn't feel right to leave them in a chest freezer, either… None of this feels right. Except that." I tip my head back to the bed, her pretty lips turn up at the corners in understanding, in agreement. They wrinkle as they do.

I feel the thrill again. This is odd, but I like it. It feels undeniable. As we move through my sleeping quarters into my office, my hand is magnetically drawn to Ceely's lower back. As we stop at the door, I give her a decisive kiss.

"It was fun," she says.

I think she's telling me she doesn't expect it to happen again. Dismissing herself. I catch her arm as she tries to go.

"I'm walking you to the kitchen," I remind her.

As soon as we step out into the hall, she puts distance between us. There are no more touches; she understands that it is too dangerous, that my position is too tenuous. She is mature enough not to demand that I claim her publicly, put her above all else. She has bigger fish to fry. For a minute I am pleased with the easiness of it, the lack of drama. Then I wonder whether she would ever publicly claim me, put me above all else. I am disturbed by the swapping of roles. Instead of having to tolerate the changing mind and insecurities of a lovestruck girl, am I to become the insecure one?

I can't let that happen, or she will react the way that I always have; with regret and distancing myself.

If I can keep myself calm, level headed, then maybe we can be good for each other. Make each other's lives easier, fuller, be strong and secure and take on anything in the world.

It's a pipe dream, probably. But it's just about all that I've got in this God forsaken place. So I'll let myself get carried away in my mind, keep my feet moving, check that the kitchen is empty and safe before leaving Ceely there. I hear the lock click into place, standing in the hallway. I check it anyway. When I turn away, Jacob is there, arms crossed.

I start to head for the stairs, to go up on the deck and check on the bulk of the crew. "You're not going to report the bodies. Don't say anything about it to anyone-."

"-What? Do nothing?"

"Nothing. Not a word to anyone, even Roshin, do you understand?"

He has been keeping pace with me, and it makes him miss a step as we climb the stairs. He stumbles,

162

catches himself on the railing. "Do nothing about an insane person on the ship!?"

"She's not insane." I turn to face him, stopping us in the mouth of the upper deck. The door I had opened falls closed on us, cutting us off in the cool, artificial air with the warm, smoggy, briny sea air washing over us for a moment. "She's not insane. She explained it all to me, and I'm handling it the best way that I know how to, because that's my responsibility. You should worry about yours."

He blinks. He is wounded by my dissection of him, the dismissal of Roshin, the characterization of himself as a busybody, but mostly, I think he is perturbed by my lack of effectiveness. He idolized me, and that shine is gone, now. It can make a person feel stupid, believing in someone. I know. I learned that one young, and Jacob should damn well know better by now.

He doesn't say anything.

I restate my final point, just so there's no misinterpretation. "Leave it alone. Go back to work. That's an order."

He goes, a kicked dog. I hate to do it, it doesn't feel good, but I don't have much choice. I'm out on a limb for Ceely, now.

Chapter Two

I skip lunch as I often do, feeling that my head is clearer, my decision-making sharper when I am hungry. I've thought that since I was a child. I liked the tenacity, the inventiveness that arose in me when I didn't know where my next meal was coming from. If I was the smartest kid on the street, if I hustled, then I got to eat. So I was always the smartest kid on the street, always thought a few steps ahead, brought groceries home when I could and learned to cook, to feed my mom, too.

I stay up on deck as the men go below. I update our approximate position with a sextant on my paper map, paranoid that the GPS equipment could go out. Both the old-fashioned way and the modern grid show that we will reach our destination tomorrow, early or mid-morning.

By dinnertime my will is weak. Hungry and a bit anxious, I lead the men all down. They line up to fill trays with lemon baked chicken, mashed potatoes and buttery garlic green beans. I wander over to Ceely at the coffee station.

"You don't sleep much, do you?"

It triggers a yawn that she hides in the blue mug. "Forgot how. Happens when you get old."

"Have you eaten?"

She shakes her head. We meander over together and end up sitting alone at a far table. Jacob goes to sit at a table with Roshin and a few others, but not before looking over at us. Ceely notices.

"He doesn't like me anymore. I hurt his feelings yesterday."

"I hurt his feelings today," I say, meaning to take the blame. Then I realize that she has a right to know. "He saw you going down below on a security camera. He went inside your submarine and he was the one who found the bodies."

She blinks. "I never would have thought he had it in him."

"Big week for the kid." I realize she and I still haven't discussed what she took from the engine room or why she felt like she had to sneak down there, endangering herself instead of just asking.

She beats me to addressing it. "There are some things you think you might want to know about me. I know. It's your job to know these things. But you're not entitled to every detail about me, just because you're the captain of this ship. Everyone needs their privacy.

165

It's actually better that you don't know, that you trust me enough not to ask. Can you do that?"

I feel uneasy, knowing that I don't know everything. But the way that she says it makes me realize that there is truth in it. We are entitled to our separate lives, even though there is nothing I wouldn't want to tell her. I can understand that she is different. Women need mystery, think it creates allure.

And if she tells me the honest truth and lays all her great designs out in front of me, if they are in direct conflict of interest with the company's regulations - with the wellbeing of the crew, the mission, and my career- then I'll have an impossible decision to make. She is trying to spare me that, keeping me blissfully ignorant. So I nod my acceptance in the end.

"Good. How's the food?"

The chicken is a bit dry, but thick pieces like this can be hard to keep moist while ensuring a proper cook all the way through. The seasoning and lemon are good enough to make up for it.

"Delicious," I say.

"No it's not. It's dry."

"You're harder on yourself than anyone else is. You don't know how bad we were eating before you showed up. Better food in prison." I'm nervous as soon as it leaves my mouth, but it hardly fazes her.

"Oh? How long were you in for?"

"Two years."

She finishes chewing a bite. "And what landed you there? Or is that something better left unsaid?"

She's giving me the same window that she asked for. I don't have to answer. But I want to. "Dealing drugs."

"What kind?"

"All kinds, since I was nine or ten. I needed the money, for food and to keep the lights on. I didn't want social services stepping in and taking me from my mom, although it ended up happening anyway... I never used."

"I thought not. You don't seem like the type. But your mother did?"

"Mm-hm. We were living in California, too, when the creature came up. We weren't hurt, but she lost friends, her job, our home. She was never really the same again."

"That's too bad. I'm sorry you had to go through that so young."

"It wasn't all bad... The rest of the world tells us to cover up our culture to be liked by the white bosses, to get anywhere. It's lonely and it's dehumanizing. Then you find something like a family, that never tries to smooth out your rough spots or hide who you are? You'd die to hang onto that. Especially when you're a dumb kid."

Ceely nods. She looks like she's thinking it over, trying to understand, so she says nothing. We finish our dinner in comfortable silence, and when the rest of the

167

men have gone, we bring dishes back. She washed and I rinse and stack, with a radio tuned to an oldies station. Ceely hums along with a few that she knows. It's a deep and rich sound, not girlish. I can feel it reverberate in my own chest as clearly as if it were me making the sound.

It's almost too pleasant a way to spend an evening, at least on a doomed oil tanker crewed by the damned in the middle of a monster infested ocean, selling our lives for some corporation's bottom-line, to the tune of wild profits we'll never see, can't even dream of.

When we finish, I ask, "Spending the night with me?"

She blinks, her lips purse as she considers, then she shakes her grey head. "Not this time."

It stings for a moment. I try to keep it from showing. Nod. "I'll walk you back to your room, then."

We go and she quickly tells me goodnight before shutting the door. I hear the lock click into place and my heart sinks. I guess I had been hoping she would change her mind and invite me in. I double check the knob for security, then lean my burning forehead against the cold metal of the door, and walk through what I am feeling.

I can't carry this disappointment around with me, and certainly not this feeling of expectation -almost entitlement- that has sprung up without me noticing. I will not be like some fiendish crackhead stealing car stereos on the street, some young hotshot breaking down his woman's door after she closes it on him. I cannot. There are plenty like that, already. It's okay to want, it's human. But not to need, never to demand. I repeat it in my mind as I walk to my quarters.

To be a great man, a wise man, you've got to constantly humble yourself. That's what the wisest of my father-figures had taught me. K was always imparting wisdom, the smartest guy on the block. Always thinking two steps ahead. He had to be, with a name like Kevin. He taught me to play chess.

K died too young, but he went out on top, and it used to be the most I could hope for, for myself. Now I take those grains of wisdom and apply them every day. It's all mostly the same, on the streets of California, or in prison, or in international waters.

In bed the sheets still smell like Ceely and it makes me hard instantly. I could masturbate, but feel it would be a mistake to reinforce her power over me with that kind of physical response, so I repeat a mantra in my mind of my duties to myself, to the crew, to the company, to the country, until my yearning has subsided.

When, finally, I sleep, it is deep and dreamless. I am not rousted by alarms or nightmares of them; the ship is not under attack, there is no hurricane or tidal wave or destructive, enraged creature from the deep screaming toward us. I don't know if it's the day's activities sapping my strength that allow for such rest or if it's that the sirens did go off, that I did rise to meet the situation to the best of my own abilities, and all that came of it was her.

In the morning, I feel elastic and strong as I first stretch every muscle out on the bed. The sun streams in my porthole window. It rises so early this close to the equator, it's only quarter-past five.

I think of Ceely as I stand in a cool shower -always cool, it's for waking up my mind, not to dull my libido- and by the time I'm dressed and ready to face the day, I've convinced myself that she will have disobeyed me and snuck out again. She will have gone to the engine room to take more tools and supplies, and maybe met with one of the several crewmen who is a truly violent opportunistic sadist.

I move briskly to Jacob's office and knock, but he's not up yet, so I let myself in. I don't sit at his desk, just bend forward as I wake the computer and open the surveillance system.

First, I check the kitchen, and to my great surprise there she is. She's wearing her grey hair pulled back, a white apron over the crew-issued navy-blue coveralls she wears. She's whisking what must be three dozen eggs in a huge bowl, with a deeply focused and also far off look on her pretty face, which is not bruised or harmed in any way. A strand of her hair has come loose and sticks to her temple. It must be hot in the kitchen, ovens preheating to cook whatever breakfast casserole she is concocting.

170

I won't eat it. I usually just have a protein bar to get my metabolism going, and besides, I hate eggs. One of our nosy, do-gooder neighbors was always bringing them over, inviting me to come and collect them with her from her chicken coop. She would explain how to tell if they had gone bad, teach me how if they were left unwashed, a protective coating on the shell would keep them fresh much longer than if they were washed, and no need to refrigerate them. She knew that the power was off half the time, at our house, and that food was scarce if mom was having a rough week.

I got so sick of eating eggs that I finally went out and did my first drug deal.

So Ceely is safe; that part of my suspicion is wrong, and my muscles relax all over my body. I puff out a big breath and hit rewind. Video reverses all over the screen; on deck, in hallways, in the med bay and down in the ship's bowels.

No one in our out for most of the night. There's midnight gone, eleven. Ten-forty-two, she walks by the camera in a blur. I jam a finger down on the key to freeze it, then press play and watch her go at a normal speed, from the hallway in one frame to the lower deck in the next. She walks right past the engine room, though.

I search viewpoints and there she is, climbing into her submarine, closing the hatch. Staying there all night, on the cold floor next to the cold bodies in the ice chest. I shut my eyes and live in the sadness the image

171

conjures for a few long seconds. I need to get her to come sleep with me, tonight. She has obviously forgotten how to feel warm and comfortable and safe somewhere, and I need to remind her. It won't do.

The door opens and Jacob jumps halfway out of his skin when he sees me. His hand shoots up over his heart. "God!"

"Sorry. Come here." I jerk my head to accentuate the statement. I have realized I don't want to make an enemy of him. He could be a problem. He has friends high up and he has access to things that even I don't. Not to mention he jumps to hurry over, always eager to obey me. It seems I'm forgiven without having to offer any explanation for my harshness, but I still do.

"What's this? She was sneaking around again?"

"Going places she shouldn't, disobeying my direct order, yes..." I rewind and let him watch her walk through the bay and climb up into her submarine.

He shivers.

I say, "The bodies are her daughters'. They were killed when the creature emerged, thirty years ago. She built the sub to go down and get them, she shot that thing while she was down there. And somehow, the thing whipped up a storm and she blacked out. When she woke up, she was thirty years later, thirty years older, her children's bodies changed, too. And now she thinks that there's a chance she could create the same reaction as before -or an opposite one- that might move her backward and let her save their lives. Only if she keeps them close, in range of the creature and its storm."

Jacob's mouth has dropped open. He is staring, processing, he finally shakes his head. His tone is skeptical. "Moved through time? As some sort of defense mechanism? You really believe this?"

"Yes. She wasn't lying when she told it to me. I'm sure of it." My resolute belief shakes his own.

He clearly thinks me to be a good judge of these things, probably better than himself.

"Even if it's true, that doesn't mean that it can send her back, or that it will, or *reanimate* the bodies, or that it won't just kill her instead."

"I know."

"In fact, if she attacks it while in range of the ship, it could kill all of us-."

"-I know-."

"Or move all of us through time!" He's a bit hysterical, laughs as he says it, waves a hand and wheels around.

"I know. I won't let that happen. Do you trust me that much?"

He is already nodding.

"I also can't jettison the bodies, I can't do that to her, and I can't let her run off chasing that thing again. She'll die out there, all alone. I don't want that to happen, I don't think that you do, either. Because you see what I do. She's a good person who's been through something unimaginable, and it messed her up. Like it

173

would anyone. I think with a little time, and a little bit of compassion, we can save what's left of her life."

Face grim, eyes big and a little moist, he nods. "Alright."

"I'll leave you to it, then."

I try to go, but he stops me when my hand is on the doorknob.

His voice squeaks, uncharacteristically tight. "Captain?"

"Yes?"

Clearing his throat, he goes on. "A communication came through, late last night, from my superior. There's a man named James Bender who is requesting permission to communicate with Ceely. Some old acquaintance."

It puts me on edge. Old acquaintance, or former lover? Either way, could it be good for her to hear from him? Or could it only put up more walls between us? Remind her of what she has lost? Could he be the little dead girls' father? I feel prickly all over, I can't help but think that it will only further stall our progress, that I know that I'm trying to do what is best for her, and I can't know this man's intentions.

If she wanted to speak to him, she could ask me, could reach out on her own. And she hasn't. In the end, I trust that fact and also the discomfort twisting inside of me. It's my call, all communication -other than Jacob's with the superiors at home base- is on lockdown, for all of our protection.

I check my watch and realize that I'm behind schedule.

"No. And don't bring it up to her."

Chapter Three

I go down to the kitchen even though I don't plan to eat. Ceely opens the door to let me in, but I wave her out into the hall.

"Come on."

"What is it?"

"We're here. Come up on deck, I don't want you to miss it."

"I have a dish in the oven-."

"-It won't take long. Just come."

I can't help but to wrap my arm around her waist as we head up the hall. My hand rests at the soft spot on top of her hip. Her own comes up and touches mine, sending cold excitement coursing through me as she laces our fingers. I'm thinking crazy thoughts of marching us up on deck like this -claiming her and damn the consequences- when she removes my hand and arm. She puts space between us, giving me a conciliatory pat on the back.

I'm crestfallen as we reach the door and push through it out into the humid, overcast morning. I remind myself that she is just being smart, looking out for both of us. It shouldn't dampen this moment that I want to share with her.

Most of the crew is gathered on the deck already, at the starboard railing. A man named Ralph Edwards, salt and pepper bearded and wrinkly all over -a usually rambling and vacant man who has been on ships all of his life- is lit up and engaged. "Are we there, Captain?"

"I think so," I answer, and there are approving murmurs from the other men.

Ralph told me in his rambling introduction the first day that he wanted to die at sea. His voice like sandpaper around a worrying wet cough insisted, "Just feed me to the fish when I go, I'm not precious about it. Always knew I would die at sea, hopefully in my sleep, not drowned in some big storm or in the belly of the beast-."

Jacob comes up right after us and joins Roshin at one end. The darker man seems pleased to see him, has a smile on his face for maybe the first time since we departed weeks ago. I remember keeping an eye on him on our last assignment together, having been told to by my bosses. But when we reached our drilling site and I saw that same smile, I turned my focus elsewhere. It cut through all my worries about his background and the warning I had been given; he is no spy or saboteur. He's just a man haunted like the rest of us, without even a guilty verdict, and with an even more powerful fascination with technology. It's childlike.

I lead Ceely to the control room, park us in front of the navigation display. Everything shows me that we are where we're supposed to be. I give the men a nod though the window, and they jostle and clap in celebration. I check my watch at the same moment that Perry starts to ring the bell for six in the morning. Right on time with satellite-pinpointed accuracy. The men are twitching in place, rocking on their heels and leaning forward over the railing to get an inch closer to the horizon, hoping to see through the smog and clouds a moment sooner.

"Watch the eastern sky," I tell Ceely.

She stands with her arms crossed. She has no doubt figured out what we are waiting for, but her face holds its usual composure.

A few beams of light become visible first, falling on the dark waters roiling below. Then a massive disk shape appears behind them, with a long column stretching from the center almost skimming the waves as it approaches at a high velocity. The column is a set of tubes within one another, capable of stretching down, down, down to pierce the earth and bring up the oil. Set in the disk of the main level are four engines, efficient, powerful but nearly soundless. Only the slightest whir of the massive fan blades permeates the shocked gasp of the men and sends ripples out behind it as it moves so eerily and gracefully toward us.

It tilts slightly, leaning back as it slows, then powering down until it sinks the last few feet, splashes to float on the water, a stone's throw away. Ceely and the men are all watching it; I'm mostly watching her. Her face has changed, her eyes blinking and widening almost imperceptibly.

"Your engines," I prompt her, hoping that what she feels is pride.

"It is incredible to see…" But she is looking out across the horizon, then, in every direction, searching but trying to be nonchalant.

I sigh. "There's sonar and satellite imaging for miles. The creature is nowhere nearby." I flick my hand at the many displays around us, letting my irritation get the better of me for a moment. It's clear from my tone.

She glances at me, surprised.

"I'm sorry. I thought this would be a special moment for you."

"It was." She gives me a pat on the arm, then steps out of the control room and starts toward the stairs. "I need to get back to breakfast."

I do a quick scan. All of the crew are gathered on deck, so I let her go alone.

The flight rig is buoyant on the waves, still lit up along the outer edge of its main level, the perfectly round disk. A door opens and several figures emerge onto the catwalk that wraps all the way around. Two are big men, both black, one bald and one with a full afro. The last is a short woman, tan, with cropped black hair and a good set of lungs on her as she waves her arms and shouts across the distance.

"Caesar! Oh Captain, My Captain! Hello!"

She does a happy little jig that makes me smile. I can't help it. The men laugh and a few of them jeer.

"Oh Captain!"

"Captain, My Captain!"

"Mama's boy!"

I wave them off and move to the place where a Zodiac raft and hefty bundle containing a rope bridge are stored. I'll need help to secure it on the other side, and two on this end to double check the connections so we can be sure that we won't take a dip on the way back.

"Jacob, Ralph, let's cross over. Perry and Roshin, set up this end while we row over."

"Yes Sir," is Perry's dutiful reply, while Jacob and Roshin simply nod and move to their positions.

But Ralph is old fashioned, and so pleased to be asked. "Aye aye, Captain! At your service, Sir!"

I can't trust the old man with much, but I know he knows his knots. If every other rational thought spills out of his brain like sand through a sieve, knots and nautical terms will still be clutched tight like nuggets of gold. As we row over, he unravels the bundle of the rope bridge and feeds it out, singing a sea shanty all the while.

"What do you do with a drunken sailor, what do you do with a drunken sailor, what do you do with a drunken sailor…"

My mother is on me before I have even finished climbing the metal rungs welded onto the side of the flight rig.

"Amor, I missed you!"

"Jesus," I gave her a quick squeeze but then peeled her arms off of me. "Let me come aboard first, Ma."

"I'm sorry, I'm sorry. Do your thing, Mr. Man."

I crouch at the ladder. Ralph is balancing with capable sea legs on the bobbing inflatable watercraft, and offers the ends of the rope bridge to me. Metal hooks fasten securely to two latches on the catwalk, and failsafe ropes come along after.

Ralph scampers up like a man half his age and starts to tie one end while I work on the other. Pulling it taught, the whole structure rises out of the water, lightweight but sturdy, swaying as the wind blows, contracting and spreading as the ships drift minutely.

As soon as the bridge is secured, and I offer my hand and pull Jacob up onto the catwalk, my mother is on me again. I give her a more thorough hug, let her hold my face in her hands and kiss each of my cheeks and inspect me carefully.

"You look tired, Caesar. Have you been sleeping?"

"When I can. It's hard with a woman onboard."

Her neat eyebrow raises. "I thought there were no women on your crew."

"We found her out on the sea. She has quite the story."

"Tell me all about it while we sit down with some coffee. -Oh! And this is Shawn Jeffries, our pilot, and Aaron McIntosh, our security guard." She indicates first the very serious looking, bald black man. And then, indicating the broader one with the full afro, she places herself next to him and slides her small hand into his. "He takes good care of us."

The man has a small smile as he looks down at my mother. It looks sincere.

I reach out to shake each of the men's hands. "Nice to meet you both, thank you for the work that you do. Feel free to explore the ship, only avoid the yellow submarine in the hold. Let's have that coffee, Mom."

She starts to lead the way, but I stop and address Aaron once more. "I doubt I have to tell you this, but my ship -and yours, while we are tethered on this mission- is no place for a woman to be wandering alone."

"I'll keep both eyes on her."

"And both hands?" Regina teases, then cackles at her own joke as she walks away.

I follow, winding around the catwalk and then into the inside of the flight rig, a hallway leading first to a flight deck clearly labelled but also firmly locked. Its round track took us next past a security station, multiple displays at a single desk, no bigger than a closet on board the USS *Baton Rouge*. We go a bit further around the great circle and there is a break room, only a bit larger than the security station.

It has a microwave, refrigerator, single burner hotplate, coffee maker and sink. A table with three chairs.

"It'll be nice to have a full kitchen again, and just in time to make you your favorite spice cake." She is pouring two cups, collecting sugar and milk, and looks back at me over her shoulder, accusingly. "You thought I forgot, didn't you?"

I only shrug.

"Well I didn't, I told you, never again." She sets a mug down in front of me, rubs a hand up and down my bicep, giving it a squeeze. "Happy birthday, Amor."

"Thank you..."

"So, tell me about this woman."

I fill her in on the voyage so far, how Ceely turned up and an abridged version of her story. Regina shares the highlights of her own eight-day long quarantine and flight out, including some details of her speedy courtship with Aaron. Then we walk over the taught rope bridge for me to show her around the *Baton Rouge*. Traversing the deck from end to end, seeing the control room, she is amazed.

"I can't believe you're the boss of all of this. And you had enough pull to get me a job, too. I'm so proud of you."

It's the lowest of jobs, really. Clean a flight rig and prepare food for the pilot and security guard. She is a glorified stewardess, but even that she's grateful for. I feel the warmth of her praise, but it brings along a sharp edge of remembrance, too.

You were never proud of my hustling, my industriousness as a child, I think. *Even though it provided for you.*

As much as I have forgiven, the bad feelings will always walk hand in hand with the good ones. I just have to muscle through them, to be grateful -as she is- that we have some time together, now, while we are both healthy and still alive.

Her job is the safer one. The flight rig will pick up and fly away at the first sight of trouble. I have imagined more than once her standing on the deck, looking out the window and down at us as the creature from the San Andreas fault plows into our side, capsizing us and then smashing us to pieces that sink below the churning, white waters and down out of sight into the black depth. I feel it would be a fitting end to us. It's a sad thought, but a satisfying one, too, that my death would push her right back into the gutter where a part of me feels that she belongs. And another part of me knows she is so blissfully unaware in that state, that dooming her to it feels like a kindness. She would know as we were sucked from the waters into that creature's mouth that she had put us both on the path to wind up there. That it wasn't really that thing doing the eating. The mother consumes the child, consumes herself in the end. A mother is an ouroboros.

184

I have been adrift in thought all the way down through the floors below deck, through my 'impressive' and 'extravagant' quarters to the engine room and past Ceely's 'incredible' but 'depressing' submarine. I nod along and listen to my mother's rambling off of anything that comes to her mind, and finally guide her back up to the kitchen. Breakfast has already come and gone.

I knock and Ceely's face appears in the door way. She looks at me, then at my mother, and her eyes react, opening a bit wider. I should have warned her, probably, but did not know how to do that without implying some level of intimacy which would be inappropriate. It's all foreign to me; I've never slept with a subordinate before and I've never introduced a sexual partner to any of my mothers before.

She opens the door. "Hello." She's stiff.

Regina is much shorter than Ceely, blinks up at her. "Well, I'll be a monkey's uncle. Lucille, it's really you." She was smiling, shaking her head in wonder.

"It's been a long time, Regina... How are you?"

"Getting by. I wondered what kind of woman could build a whole submarine like that, and live on their own for so long-," I had left out the time travel when explaining. "-But now I understand. You were always that indominable sort, when I knew you."

Ceely does not seem to know what to say. She is as uncomfortable as she was during our confrontation in my office, concerning her daughters' bodies. I speak.

"You two knew each other."

"Oh, yes," Mom says. "Pretty well. But that was, what? Thirty years ago? Before the creature crawled up and ruined everything."

"Although it feels like no time at all," Ceely says, shooting me a glance.

"Ain't that the truth? I remember it like yesterday. I didn't know, then, and I don't know now how to tell you how sorry I am."

"I know. I am, too. I was angry, I was devastated-."

"-I know, of course. Of course you were." My mother puts her hands on Ceely's arms and gives them a rub. "I can't imagine. Let's just put it behind us." The two of them embrace, although Ceely looks quite uncomfortable in her face and body.

My mother wipes tears away as she finally lets go. "Well, isn't fate a funny thing? All those years on your own, and you wind up on my son's boat. You two have met already, but you didn't know he was mine, then. Of course, you met him once or twice when he was little, you remember? But now what do you think? He's so handsome, isn't he? And doing well for himself, too."

She's rambling, moves forward through the galley, toward the swinging kitchen doors, leaving us to follow.

"Very handsome," Ceely murmurs. "And very impressive..." A long pause. "She was my nanny. She was with my children when... when it happened. And when I found out, when she called, I was inconsolable...

186

I was furious. And she went off the rails, I guess, after that..." She looks at me with probing eyes, and the whole thing has given me a pit in my stomach, a queasiness that doesn't go away.

I see her wrinkles, her grey hair, her stretch marks, but I see through them all, too. They are just physical tolls of time. But imagining her and my mother -my birth mother- friends, close, apparently when I was still a child. And in another life, if the creature had never come up, or if her children had survived that cataclysm, they would be beautiful and strong women, like Ceely is. They would be just a few years younger than me. And if that creature had stayed dormant, and my mother had never been traumatized by it and all the loss it inflicted, perhaps they would have stayed friends. We all would have grown up together.

It's unnatural to think, but I could have been dating - or even married to- one of Ceely's daughters, right now. In that other life, maybe it would have seemed the most natural thing in the world. I could be someone else. Someone worthy of such things.

But, no. It hadn't gone that way. The creature came up. Ceely's daughters died. My mother -as I knew her- disappeared, and with her, my future.

I am here, now, having made what I could of myself despite it all. My mother has healed herself and Ceely has found her way here, too. It makes more sense this way. In any world, any version of our lives together, I know I would feel drawn to her, just as powerfully. It's chemical, biological.

I touch her on the small of the back to reassure us both. I'm sure she feels the same tremor. The twisting discomfort in my guts has worked itself loose. "It's ancient history. We're here, now."

"Yes…"

In the kitchen, my mother is investigating cupboards and tools, rounding up flour and eggs. She peers through the window of the large walk-in fridge and freezer.

"This is paradise, Amor! Lucille, you don't mind sharing today, do you? I need to make my little boy his favorite spice cake for his birthday."

"Of course. It's your birthday, Captain?"

I cross my arms. "Yes. I'm cooking dinner tonight, actually. I do every Friday. You're both welcome to help, or you can take the evening off, Ceely. I gave the crew the rest of the day, since we'll start drilling tomorrow…"

She shakes her head. "What are we making?"

"I was thinking chicken enchiladas with mole from scratch."

"Mm," Mom hums. "He always liked a challenge. We'd better get started."

I was already tying an apron on.

The three of us spend several hours in the kitchen. Mom helps me get the mole going, then splits off to bake a cake, while Ceely starts at first finishing a chicken noodle soup for lunch. She goes out to serve it with fresh bread. When she returns, I deviate from my sauce to help her clean dishes and wrap leftovers, then we begin the enchiladas.

With the meat simmering in a fragrant mixture, tortillas warming and ready to be worked with, Mom taps back in, and I go away to do my daily systems checks and reports. The two women had been getting along easily, making small talk and working well alongside each other; sharing space. They did not catch up or talk about the good old days, as I had thought that old friends would.

Once, Mom had started to reminisce, saying, "Ceely, you had that beautiful green cake dish, remember?"

But Ceely's face had tightened up, she had looked away. Regina had looked sheepish, collecting the unexceptional plastic cake dish which had started the conversation and creeping away.

Of course she would not want to be reminded of the life she had once lived. My mother is so thoughtless, sometimes. I hope Ceely will not be too uncomfortable, that Mom does not slip up again.

When my system checks all come back satisfactory, my report is sent in, I go back down. My stomach rumbles, I took only absolutely necessary taste tests while cooking the mole and chicken. I think every crew member is already in the mess hall, most already eating. Some look up as I enter.

"Delicious, Captain."

"Your best yet."

I nod to them, and sidle up to the line, behind Ralph. He scoops enchiladas onto his tray, then goes to leave, but Ceely intones from where she has appeared on my other side, "Eat your greens, or no dessert, Ralph."

He grins sheepishly. "Yes Ma'am."

It seems that she has thrown together a simple salad to go with the meal. She holds her usual tan colored coffee. I scan the room for my mother, realizing I haven't seen her. Her designated protector, Aaron, sits with the pilot.

I see JJ and Colson, the two documented rapists onboard. It takes the edge off of my worry but not significantly so. Any one of the others could hurt her on a whim.

"Do you know where my mother is?"

I'm spinning, looking around the room again, and Ceely's face reacts to my question, her brow raises and she starts to answer. Before she can, the door leading back to the kitchen opens, my mother emerges with a white-frosted cake held aloft in her tiny hands, a ring of candles around the top of it burning and half of them flickering out in the gust from the swinging door. She's singing in an uneven voice as she comes through the room, and the men look up in surprise at first. Then Aaron stands up and hurries over to her, adding his deep baritone to the song, waving for others to join in, too.

"Happy birthday to you…"

Most of the men are grinning, some make dramatic mockeries of singing along, others just grumble and eye the cake as Regina carries it over to me. My face is warm, I don't know what to do as they all look to me, then Ceely puts a hand on my back and her own low voice is joining the chorus, and my tension melts into a tight smile.

"Happy birthday, dear Caesar-."

"-Dear Captain," some of the voices stumble but then join back in.

"Happy birthday to you!"

Mom's dark eyes are shining with happy tears as she holds the cake up. I blow out the candles still flickering to scattered applause, then bend over the cake to kiss her on the forehead. "Thank you."

"Let's cut it." She sets it on the serving bar and takes up a knife.

"Did you make a wish?" Ceely asks in a murmur.

I look back at her and give her a small smirk that actually makes her smile in turn, and avert her eyes. But she knew what she was doing, asking me that in her small, sultry voice in front of so many people. Suddenly I didn't care about enchiladas or cake, but we each collected food and the three of us sat together with Aaron and the pilot.

My first bite of the enchiladas capture my attention again; hint of chocolate, rich layers of spices evolving as they pass over my tongue and down my throat. I hum and Ceely nods in agreement. I eat slowly, methodically, working my way through my food and savoring each bite, so that by the time I'm done everyone else has left but the four of us.

"Great cake, Mom, thanks. You two can head back to the rig."

"Oh don't be silly," she collects my tray and Ceely's, adding them to the pile on the bus cart. "It's still your birthday, you should get to relax. You shouldn't have to wait just to walk Ceely back to her room, so Aaron and I will clean up."

It gives me pause. Mom is clean and proud when she is sober, but I remember scrubbing vomit-soaked carpet on my hands and knees, food that I made left to attract flies by her bedside table.

Ceely answers for me. "Alright. Thank you, Regina. And you too, Aaron."

I give my mother a hug and kiss on the cheek, then we head for the door. In the hallway, just Ceely and I, I feel a weight drop off of my shoulders. It's strange; she is my mother, and she feels familiar, but she also makes me worry.

"Coming with me?" I ask, just to be sure.

Ceely nods, and we go. Closing and locking the door behind us, we stand silently in the office section of my quarters. I'm not sure if I should just kiss her right away. I want to, but I'm worried about impropriety again, power imbalance, her feeling obligated because of our positions and it being my birthday.

"I'd like a whiskey," she declares, breaking the silence.

"Of course." I go around the desk and pull the bottle out, pouring her a couple fingers worth. When I return to her and hold the glass out, she takes it in such a way that her fingers wrap around mine and linger for a few long seconds, her dark eyes look into mine, unnerving, arousing. Then she turns and heads into my bedroom. I follow.

She is wearing the outfit that she came to us in, not the crew coveralls she wore yesterday. It's a sophisticated blouse, teal blue, it might be silk, I'm not sure but she sits on my bed and while taking a sip, she undoes the top two buttons with one hand, almost absentmindedly.

Standing in my own room like an uninvited guest, I watch, waiting for an invitation.

"Dinner was delicious…" Her fingers reach under the blouse, rubbing along her collar bone, then the back of her shoulder. "A nice treat, wasn't it?" She undoes another button, the peek it gives me of more of her pale skin, down to the space in between her breasts, fills me with desire. I have to look away to keep myself from getting hard.

"Yes."

"The men liked it, too. Plenty of them had seconds. But not you. You never indulge in anything, do you? Not food, not drink…" She swirls the dark whiskey around in her glass to punctuate the statement. "I know, it's against policy to drink on the job. But you keep it nearby, why? In case the sirens go off and the end is near? Or because the temptation is delicious?"

She's leaning back on my bed, totally at ease, experienced, confident, in control. I find it all enticing, and she undoes another button showing her soft belly, a tiny glimpse of the top of her navel. Her shirt hangs open a bit wider, catching the inside curves of her mature breasts.

My throat is tight, I can hardly manage an answer. "It's fighting the temptation that makes us stronger…"

"Overrated," she replies.

Another button, her stomach on display, she goes ahead and releases the last one, too. Keeping half of her covered, she pushes one sleeve down her arm, exposing one breast and her stomach all the way down to the waistband of her slacks. Her nipple is soft at first, then starts to harden in the cool air. I wet my lips automatically.

Ceely raises the glass to her lips, takes a sip, then holds it precisely and tips it, letting a small rivulet of the dark whiskey spill from the tumbler and splash down onto her skin. The brown drops dye her white skin, then obscure on her pink areola, becoming a little waterfall off the tip of her nipple, down her stomach.

194

I surge forward, catching her grey head in my hand and stooping to kiss her. Her lips respond to mine, I can taste the whiskey on her tongue but it's not enough for me. Hunching over her, I lick up the opaque drops, suck her nipple clean.

Her fingertips scratch my scalp as she tugs my short hair. Her eyes shut and I know she wants me to do more. But she opens her eyes again, blinking sleepily, and offers me the glass tumbler. I accept, toss back a gulp of the burning hot liquor, then put the thing aside and go back to lavishing her with kisses.

Chapter Four

Waking up with a woman in my bed for the first time in a few years makes me acutely aware of my own heart beating. I wrap my arms around her, feel her soft skin, bury my face in her warm hair and inhale the scent of her. It's the same generic shampoo we all use onboard, but the added quality that is uniquely hers is delicious to me. I shut my eyes and kiss her neck and dwell in the euphoria for a few seconds, count to ten.

Then I have to let her go, climb out of the bed, head for the shower in the morning's low light. It's going to be a big day. We'll do morning system checks, then start drilling. A thousand things can go wrong. With machines, with people, the creature... I scrub myself clean to try to prepare myself for the day, but after a few minutes, Ceely opens the shower stall's door, steps into the steam and warm spray with me, and distracts my focus.

She's confident as she stands in front of me, but the moment I reach out for her, her eyes lower, a dark cloud of self-doubt passes in front of her face. I pull her in. The warm water runs in a rivulet down her neck and collar bone, and I run my tongue through it. She relaxes in my arms and we stay that way for a minute, then I turn her around. Her hand reaches back but I catch her wrist, stopping her from initiating anything, instead weaving my fingers into her hair.

She leans her head back onto my shoulder and shuts her eyes. I work shampoo into a lather, gently scrub her scalp. While she's docile, throat exposed, I trace my fingers down her trachea and the fragility is strangely erotic. It's an act, she's in control even with my hand around her neck. Whether she's in charge of my every move, making me wait, making me say please, or letting me feel like the strong one, the one in control, I want her just the same. Whatever role she wants me to play, I'll do it, if she's the one I get to play for, play with.

I leave her the use of the bathroom, a spare set of the uniform coveralls, happy that she'll be wearing my clothes even if nobody else will be able to tell. I get dressed in the bedroom, my own clothes, then I walk her to the kitchen, do my usual check for dangerous persons inside. I head up on deck.

The sun cuts through the smog up in the briny sea air.

I review my official plans, work flow charts, emergency contingency plans in the relative peace on deck. Men come up, some in groups, some alone, still munching on toast, drinking coffee. The bell rings out seven times, and the stragglers hurry up from below deck and form two lines in front of me. Seeing every crewman present, I nod.

"You know your assignments, I want maximum efficiency today. Any distractions, any chit chat or fooling around I see, you will be immediately dismissed. This job is only as dangerous as we allow it to be. Keep your eyes on your work and your ears open for instruction, or for an alarm. Do I make myself clear?"

A chorus of, "Yes Sir," and, "Yes, Captain."

"All hands to your stations, then. Let's make some money."

Affirmative grumbles and the men march off, going across the rope bridge. Jacob stands among the men, and I nod for him to come to me.

"Yes?"

"Stay close to me, today. If anything mechanical goes wrong, I want Ceely on deck in two minutes. That's your responsibility."

"Heard."

We are the last to go over. I meet Aaron on deck and we confirm our radios are on the same frequency. Mom is with him and hugs me, wishes me luck. I can tell that she's worried, I hope this isn't all too stressful for her. The pilot shakes my hand and then they both head into the rig's interior to their stations. The flight deck locks from within while in use, for security. If the sirens go off, my crew will race back to the *Baton Rouge*. Anyone who dallies or freezes will surely be flung from the railing of the rig as it zooms away, land in the water, fish food.

Men run around the catwalk, some carrying tools. Perry climbs up a ladder on the outside of the rig's main level, he'll perch on the highest point, a last line of defense if the higher technology all fails, to warn us of approaching danger. I'm not sure it's the right spot for him, in light of what he neglected to tell me, but I don't like last minute changes, and if his life is on the line, too…

Roshin and JJ unwind a massive hose stored in an outer compartment of the rig and haul it back to our ship. Using handheld electric tools they fasten their end in place with massive bolts to the spout which rises from the deck of the *Baton Rouge*. On our side, two men do the same, then switch positions and recheck the torque of the bolts fastened by the other without needing to be told to do so. Everything is checked and rechecked, with such high pressure and such high stakes. There can be no screw ups.

I squint and see Roshin and JJ on the deck change places and recheck their connection. Each stands and gives a thumbs up.

The engines of the flight rig have since powered on. They are nearly silent but their reverberations can be felt through the soles of my work boots, as well as the gain in elevation as we lift a few dozen feet out of the water. On my hand held, I switch between screens. On a camera, I see Ralph and Colson descend down onto a catwalk below the rig's main level, see the seals unlocked and the drill be released from its compartment like an unruly beast, like a tiger in captivity for too long. The bulk of the machinery stays above the water, but thicker metal encasements release thinner ones, on down, with a click each time. The slenderest drill bit of the string sinking below the water, and down, click, down, click, down, and we feel the impact eventually of it reaching the sea floor.

That small vibration may be enough. A dinner bell rung for the creature from the fault.

I switch to another program, which pulls up sonar, satellite imagery, seismic activity, thermal readings. All for miles around the ship. Each one hopefully capable of individually alerting me to the presence of the creature, of anything dangerous approaching my territory. And beyond the alerts, there are diversion tactics which will automatically deploy, which should tempt or scare the creature or the violent activists away.

Failing those, the ship is equipped with sizable weaponry, all at my disposal. A last resort which has worked maybe once in all of the company's missions since it acquired its government contract. So many layers of protection, and so often, they haven't been enough. I think of Ceely in the kitchen below deck. She knows to come up if the sirens sound, but a part of me worries that she will head down, further below the surface, to her submarine. It would take her time to get out of the bay, the threat would hopefully be diverted by the time she managed it. I have a moment where I wonder if the diversion tactics seem to be failing, if the sirens blare and the men all race for the life rafts, will I go to my position to help them have that little chance of survival? Or will I think of that creature slicing through the black water toward us and race down, to find her?

I can't entertain those thoughts, now. They are useless. They're distractions. Right now I can only switch between camera views and walk around the perimeter of the flight rig, ensuring multiple men at each station where they are supposed to be. Every place where processes occur to deliver the oil up from under the ocean floor and through over a mile of pipe, into a chamber onboard the flight rig for testing and filtering it, separating out the water which comes up with it, then sending it through the thick hose strung between the rig and the *Baton Rouge* and to its destination in the massive tanks below our own deck. Additional to the camera views of the crewman, I must alternate between readings of energy output levels from the engine's on the flight rig -Ceely's engines- pressure gauges at each section of pipe and tubing, heat gauges, and fill levels of the multiple tanks where the oil will be deposited, sectioned off and switched between for balance of the tanker and safety and loss prevention.

If one of the tanks is punctured, it will be dealt with, doused with extinguisher if aflame and potentially purged, even blown clear of us, taking a piece of the ship with it. Hypothetically, the *Baton Rouge* can stay afloat with multiple punctures or breaches, depending on their location. Hypothetically, we could limp back to port with one engine at half capacity, and riding low in the water with our sides ripped open, our tanks carrying hundreds of thousands of metric tons less than expected.

My pay and employment depend on not allowing that to happen. It's mentally taxing, like three games of chess at once.

Satisfied that everything is as it should be, I radio the flight deck. "Clear to begin drilling."

The sound and reverberations of the drilling beginning are much greater than those produced by the efficient engines.

Nobody -myself included- can keep our eyes focused solely on our objectives. Roshin, Jacob, JJ all look out at the empty horizon, their natures compelling them to look out for the waves that would break off of the creature, the white glint of it in the morning sun as it would twitch its mile-long, two fluked tail and come slicing through the water at us.

"Focus," I tell them, and they do look back down at their gauges, connections. I switch my radio briefly over to the intercom. "Focus, everybody." Then back to the private channel.

Jacob looks at his device which displays much of what mine does. It reminds me for a moment that he is technically the highest-ranking person aboard, apart from myself. If something were to happen to me, it would be his duty to take charge of the ship's crew and operations. I can't picture it. One of the more charismatic criminals would be more likely to take over, letting lawlessness run amuck, modern day pirates until the coast guard or the Navy blew them out of the water.

It's a lot of anticipation, a lot of room for anxiety as the drill splits open the earth's crust, plunges deeper for more than thirty long minutes. The entire rig feels a rattle, then, with every soul on it and the ship too leaving every body, the pilot's voice comes over the speakers.

"We've struck oil."

A few of the men hoot and cheer, a few clap. I feel just a bit less anxious, with the wind sweeping over the sweat dotting my forehead and cooling me. Maybe I can do it. Jacob has sighed, similarly relieved, and as we meet each other's gazes, he nods to me. I see hope in his eyes; faith in me, and it reminds me to bring myself back down to Earth. They're all depending on me. I've gotta keep my head in the game.

*

It happens suddenly.

Ceely has brought lunch of sandwiches and apples up on a cart, so that the men may eat while still minding their stations. She goes and a few more hours of focus and drilling ensue. I walk the perimeter of the flight rig, eyes always moving between my screen and my crew, with Jacob not far behind me. The whirring of the drilling and filtration systems, the almost soundless vibration of the flight rig's engine under my heels all become synonymous with calm to me. It's when the whirring turns to a grinding sound, then stops that I realize how loud it has been. The silence becomes deafening.

With dozens of eyes on me, the men all looking for answers, I swipe between different applications on my device. Pressure has dropped in the hose leading from the flight rig to the *Baton Rouge*. One gauge on a pipe in the filtration system of the rig is past acceptable ranges, in the yellow, climbing toward red. It's some kind of clog.

I grab my radio. "Halt all systems! Go, Jacob," I order, and he's moving before I've finished saying his name, feet clapping the metal of the catwalk, then he slows on the rope bridge, losing his perch and almost plummeting down between two boards. He makes it to the other side, then disappears in a flash below the deck.

It takes a few seconds for the pilot to radio back to me. "I'm halting all systems. Looks like we've got some sort of blockage."

"Heard," I answer, still favoring my first legit job as a line cook. "I have my engineer on her way up. I'll need Aaron and his keys."

Aaron patches in. "On my way."

They come, definitely not within the two minutes I had allotted them. Jacob moves quickly, nervously looking to me, then back to Ceely -who moves more calmly behind him- then back to me. She is careful on the rope bridge. I meet her at the end.

"Time to show me what you can do." I pull up schematics of the machinery where the troubled gauge is.

"Thought I already did," she breezes, and takes the device out of my hands.

"Some kind of blockage, we're climbing toward the red."

"I see that." She moves around the rig, taking the lead. "Can you give me access to these pipes?"

"Aaron is on the way."

"Should evacuate everyone from the rig."

I switch my radio to the intercom function. "Crew of the *Baton Rouge,* return to the ship. Wait on deck for further instructions." Passing by the place where the ladder leads down to the lower platform beside the drill, I offer Ralph a hand and help to pull him up.

"Sure there's nothing I can do to help, Captain?"

"Just get clear." I run to catch Ceely, then realize Jacob is still following us. "You too, evacuate."

"I should stay…"

"That's an order."

He goes. Aaron is coming around the rig from the other side. He searches a large key ring until he finds the one which opens the panel Ceely needs. She passes my device back to me, juggling a small toolbox and rolling up her coverall sleeves. I check the gauge again on the screen, then lean close to her to inspect the dial physically as well. "Pressure still rising, even with the drill shut down. And only a few hours into operations, on our first day. I'm thinking sabotage."

She shrugs, studying the system of pipes which run vertically within the rig. "Too soon to tell, but the timing is suspicious, isn't it? Either way, this amount of pressure can turn dangerous quickly." But you would never know it from looking at her. She was pulled on a pair of thick work gloves, a pair of goggles. "Nothing for it but to open the pipe and see what the problem might be."

I reach out and catch her wrist. "That sounds dangerous."

"Yes. So step back, Captain."

Her tone carries the cadence of an order, and Aaron puts a hand on my arm, pulling on me to get me clear. Probably thinking of my mother, who also would want me out of harm's way. Between respecting Ceely's expertise, being considerably smaller than Aaron, and also feeling the weight of my obligation to see the mission through to its end, I do lose some ground. But I plant myself when I am still close enough to read her expression, to rush back over should I need to.

My heart is hammering, and my mind is whirring as she reaches into the rig's guts and starts loosening a nut. Her arms are still toned and healthy with only a small wiggle of loose skin at the bottom of the biceps. Nothing about it feels right to me, even though this is her field, and she is an expert in it. If she had never come here, wouldn't I be investigating the problem myself? There are several with mechanical experience - Perry, Roshin, JJ- but I don't trust one of them so completely as to let them tinker with such important equipment at such a crucial time. Do I even trust Ceely that far? I thought so, this morning, but the trust of the mind and the trust of the body are two very different things. And my body is antsy, watching her loosen more encasing around the suspect pipe. Whether sabotage or just flawed design, the pressure is still rising, into the red, now, and it could burst at any moment.

Why did I call for her? Why did I let her take over? If she had never come, I could handle the task myself. If she had never come, would I have had the chance? Would there have been a need? Mechanical failures on these missions are rare. Rigorous checks are done before a ship or flight rig leaves its port. What are the odds that the mission she winds up on is the first in years to have a malfunction?

I've chalked the dead bodies in the freezer up to the unfathomable depth of love I'd like to believe can exist in a good mother. But what if they aren't even her children? Maybe she's only an unstable mind.

It takes her only a minute to get to the point where she is ready to alleviate the pressure on the pipe. I know because she glances at me before she does it. Her eyes meet mine and I feel foolish for suspecting her. She is just a bit afraid, just a bit excited. She doesn't know what is coming next. She isn't the one who caused this malfunction, of course not. Between when the rig landed yesterday morning and when we all came over this morning, Ceely had not been out of either mine or my mother's sight; cooking, eating, sharing my bed. If not her, who? My top suspects have to be those with mechanical experience. Perry, Roshin, JJ.

She tugs on the wrench she is holding, and a plume of steam shoots out, tousling her grey hair, then turning to a great woosh as the connection loosens further, then a spray of oil is bursting out, spraying Ceely's coveralls and splattering the metal of the catwalk at her feet. It's to be expected and hardly phases her, but my heart jumps into my throat, my body starts forward on its own, stopped by Aaron's firm grip.

A section of pipe comes off in Ceely's gloved hands, the gauge's needle drops to zero. She holds the pipe up to one eye, aiming in my direction, but the pipe is not hollow. "You can come over. I think we've found the problem."

Aaron is cautious. "That little thing?"

"Yes." She offers it to me, then thinks better of it. "Put gloves on."

I don a pair and accept the pipe. Holding it up to the light, squinting at it, it looks like a perfectly normal piece of metal from the outside. The inside holds a pale green substance, fungus-like, which has swollen up to completely block the pipe, and now has slowly begun to recede. Its wet shine is like plastic more than metal.

"Some foreign substance. Reacting to heat, it looks like?"

"That's what I was thinking."

"So it is intentional sabotage."

Aaron folds his arms. "Nobody did that since I've been on duty."

I nod. "It could have happened back at the hanger. Probably did. If we hadn't been watching closely, we could have ended up with a disabled drill."

Ceely asked, "What's the point?"

"There's not much of one, unless it had taken out multiple engines, which something this small is not likely to do, even if it had ruptured. But maybe that's what they were hoping for. Then we'd be looking at a mass casualty type event. Us all sitting ducks while some kind of signal draws in the creature. We have to stop drilling, treat every engine as though they've been compromised, analyze the chemical composition of this to know how to deal with it." I'm irritated, already making plans that will cost me a day, maybe two, since I can't trust anybody else to help me. But continuing to drill with this unknown element onboard is not an option.

"Maybe delay was the intention," Ceely says.

I consider, and nod. "It's possible. I need to contact headquarters, put them on alert, confirm my orders. Aaron will escort you back to the kitchen. Thank you both."

They go. I am left alone, still holding the pipe. Such a tiny thing, not even a foot long, fucking me over so thoroughly. I think that's the entire point. Some activists, given the chance to plant a bomb and blow the whole flight rig -multiple flight rigs, even the whole hanger if they had such access, and we have to assume that they did if they managed to pull this off- chose instead to plant this little bug, this glitch. They chose to fuck with me, in addition to the company. Maybe they see me as a traitor to humankind. If I had not been watching, the fault would fall on me, and on Jeffries, the pilot. It's either merely youthful, principled mischief or an unwillingness to take human life; maybe both.

Or maybe I was meant to thwart this first attempt at sabotage. Maybe it's meant to lower my guard. These people clearly don't know me. That's never going to happen.

Chapter Five

I order the crew to remain on deck. Jacob, alone, follows me as I head down to the medical bay.

"What's to be done, Captain?"

"First, test this substance that caused the disturbance. Write a report to send to the bosses and while we wait for orders, I'm going to search the ship from top to bottom, crew quarters and all, looking for trace amounts of the substance. That'll keep us busy late into the night, I think."

It gives him pause, but he quickly catches up again. "The crew won't like it."

"You'll be present for the searches of their rooms, as their representative."

"You know they don't consider me their ally."

I unlock the med bay door, step inside, close it once he has joined me. "You're right. I'll allow each individual to be present for the search of their room and belongings. It'll cost a lot of time to bring them down and back up, never letting them out of sight… but it's worth it to keep things from getting too adversarial. Go and tell Ceely that dinner will have to be served up on deck, while I run this test."

Obeying proper procedure to avoid any cross contamination, I take a scraping of the green substance, finding it spongey. I load it into a capsule and plug the thing into the computer. It whirs as the analysis is undertaken. I place the pipe inside a large plastic bag, seal it and lock it inside the drug cabinet, then return to my seat. By then, the screen flashes results.

The chemical composition of the thing is shown, no further information can be offered by all the vast knowledge accessible to the computer program; the substance hasn't been recorded anywhere else. Likely it was crafted in a lab by some scientist-turned-eco-terrorist, and that gives me pause as I stare at the screen. I'm used to being in opposition to authority, to cops and politicians and Karens. But finding myself on the side opposite science, I feel a bit ill.

Jacob is knocking at the door.

"Coming."

I sync the results with the handheld scanner I will use to detect any trace of the substance onboard my ship. Then I take a second, shut my eyes, and prepare for what is going to be a long night. Jacob must not have heard my reply, he knocks again. Pushing out a big breath, I stand.

I search the kitchen and Ceely's room first, as a matter of principle. I can't leave any room for any of the crew to accuse me of favoritism, or of prejudice. In her room are the makings of a little device she has been fashioning, with tools and wires spread out on the little desk. I look at her, and she looks back at me with her arms folded, and does not answer the question I have not asked. Her eyes dare me to. But I know I won't like the answer, and anyway I have bigger fish to fry. I scan the equipment and every surface, every corner, every inch of the room from top to bottom, with the yellow scanner making its baseline clicking and never indicating the presence of any trace amount of the green compound. Or any explosive or corrosive or in any way dangerous substance.

The kitchen takes hours. In and out of cupboards, the pantry, the fridge and freezer. Ceely asks permission to take food up to the crew on deck, and I must stop what I'm doing to scan her cart before I can allow her to go. As I do, she fixes two plates for Jacob and I. Leaves them behind. My eyes fix on the meal. Pork chop, cheesy scalloped potatoes and a salad. Jacob is staring when I glance at him. I can see hunger in his eyes.

"Go on. We're going to be at this all night."

We sit at one of the empty tables, across from each other, and eat for a few minutes in companionable silence. We drink water. Bone weary, we return to work.

Ceely returns after some time and starts to wash dishes. When the kitchen is clear, I deposit her in her room and insist that she stay put for the night; no midnight excursions for supplies or sleeping in the sub. We head up to collect the first man. On deck the air has gone rarely chilly, the sun has gone down and above us the sky is pitch black, with only a few stars able to break through the smog and cloud cover.

The men rush toward us before the door has swung closed behind me.

"It's freezing up here!"

"How much longer are you planning on keeping us?"

"This ain't right!"

"Yeah!" A chorus of voices.

Only a few -Perry, Roshin, Ralph- stand by silently and wait for instructions or news.

I wait until the ruckus has calmed down, until everyone is silent. Then I raise my voice. "For the safety of everyone onboard and the security of the mission, nobody will be allowed below deck until my search is complete."

They start groaning and complaining again. I turn my back on it, refuse to rise to it. I know they'll do nothing but what I've ordered. As a courtesy, I call back, "I'll bring some blankets up. Perry! You're first to bat."

"Yes, Captain."

The big old guy hurries after Jacob and me.

Perry's room shows no traces of harmful substances.

We bring stacks of spare blankets up on deck. I collect Roshin next, not only because he's probably smart enough to have created the green substance, or that he may have picked up some radical ideas while in Guantanamo or wherever he was, but also I want to get him out of the way, for Jacob's sake. The boy stands with his leather ledger squeezed tight to his chest, jaw clenched and eyes scanning the tidy little room ahead of my scanning. Roshin's body language is not nearly so worried. He looks tired. He always does.

I find nothing, not a trace, once again.

Up and down late into the night, nudging men fast asleep on the deck to wake them, then trudging them downstairs. Some gripe, but most just stand by sullenly while I turn over their things, root through their underwear drawers, their porno mags, scan the inside of the ventilation shafts, under the bed in dusty, cobwebby back corners where the white paint on the metal walls is often rusting away, and every other surface in their room.

4am comes and goes. Jacob is last, I need to be thorough. His bedroom and his office take a full hour. Nothing turns up. Standing in the doorway, he puffs out a big breath when I lower the scanner, leaning on the desk to take the pressure off my sore feet, and rub my tired eyes.

"I was scared," he admits, "I don't know why."

"Normal. Used to always clam up when CO's searched my cell. Worried someone might have planted something. You're clean though. Head on up, try to get some sleep. I don't need you for the rest."

"There's more?"

"Still hallways, supply closets, the engine room and all that."

"Jesus. Alright."

"When everyone wakes up, I'll be done with my inspection. They'll be free to move about the ship, just not onto the flight rig. They can rustle up their own breakfast, I'm getting some sleep and giving Ceely the morning off, too. Relay those orders to the crew, if you don't mind."

"Of course." He doesn't know what else to say, so he goes, looking sympathetic.

I could lay down and be asleep on the floor in five seconds flat, but there's still work to do. So much of it.

Headquarters are sending a few of their senior engineers to perform tests on the engines and treat them with some kind of chemical. Their ETA is around noon, so if I keep moving now, I can maybe get a few hours of sleep before their arrival. I'll have to supervise everything, keep the crew under supervision too, keep them on deck all day again. Exhausting. The longer I keep them sequestered from civilized behavior -and deny them creature comforts- the less reminder and incentive they have to behave. I'm risking mutiny.

I find a surprising amount of dust, checking nooks and crannies at the floor of the lowest level, opening the siding of the massive furnace unit and craning to get the upper half of my body inside, snaking an arm around its hot inner workings to scan the back corners, any possible hiding spot... I go wall to wall, every corner, then I go up and climb over the ductwork, having to drag myself along with my arms in places, gulping down more dust to check every surface and every inch.

I save the insides of the two submarines for last. The unmanned company vessel for underwater rig or ship repairs takes only a minute, it has barely any space inside for maintenance to the mechanical components. I move toward Ceely's submarine in the back, with a pit growing in my stomach all the while, and my tired muscles feeling heavier and heavier. I stand before it for only a minute. I wonder if I can make up an excuse good enough -at least inside myself- to not go inside.

I tell myself that I'm sure it will yield nothing. I tell myself it's a violation of her trust, of the respect I feel for her, of the privacy she asked for and deserves. I even admit to myself that I just plain don't wanna go in there. But it's not reason enough not to do my duty.

I haul the nearby table over and climb up. Scan the top of the submarine for any traces of the green substance, find nothing. Unscrew the top hatch, climb down. I have a flashlight on me, shine it toward the bow and the aft, feeling like there's someone down there in the dark with me, although I know there's not.

There's just them, the two bodies in the freezer. I move the clicking scanner over every other inch of the submarine's short tunnel body, under the control panel in the front, unscrew the panel separating the single engine in the back. The whole time, the rhythmic clicking stays steady, its arrow does not move to indicate a single particle of any harmful substance. I scan behind the chest freezer, along its sides.

Too soon -and not soon enough- it's time. I feel sick. But I won't let it get the better of me. I get a grip on the lid, the rubber stripping along it cold to the touch. I lift and the thing flings open like it's spring loaded. The bodies inside folded around each other are a strange mess of dried, pale, leathery flesh. I shine my light and can't help but to identify and study their sunken little faces. No eyes, lips withered away and teeth bared, the bigger one missing one of her front two. The way they are now, I can't see any resemblance to Ceely, but I try to imagine how they would look. Pointy chins, dark hair and eyes. Smart, discerning, full of life. It pierces me strangely, the image I conjure of the three of them doing normal things in some normal life together, one so different from this.

I almost feel like I miss them. Two little girls I never met. I feel my eyes starting to fill suddenly, static in the tip of my nose telling me I'm a goner, the tears are coming. I sniff, blink rapidly, wipe a few away before they can surge past the rim of my eyelid. Taking a few quick breaths, I swallow hard around the lump in my throat and direct the scanner toward the girls. It clicks indifferently all around the corners of the freezer, over the hills and divots in the flesh, the protruding joins, in the eye sockets.

I close the freezer gently, shutting the door on the parallel universe it awakened in me.

Man up, I tell myself. *You're just tired.*

I climb out of the sub, drop down to the floor of the ship and my legs crumble from the impact, sprawling me out. I press my face to the cool metal. I can confidently declare my ship free of any trace amounts of the green substance. There's nothing more to be done. I look out of the small porthole window and see the sky has begun to lighten. The sun hasn't quite crested over the horizon, but a halo of white shines through the smog out to the east. I don't care to watch the sunrise. I trudge up the stairs and my legs carry me to Ceely's room, feeling numb the whole way.

I tap before I can second guess it.

I listen closely, hear movement inside. She opens the door, one hand straightening her hair. Her eyes have dark circles under them as she takes in the sight of me.

"Alright?" Her voice is husky.

"Yeah. Search is done. Didn't find anything... Were you up late? Building things?"

She nods.

"I thought so. Take the morning off."

"Okay."

"Got a few hours before the company's experts get here to test and treat the engines..."

She nods again, then slides out of the way. "Come in."

I'm grateful, I'm not sure I would make it all the way to my office. Shutting and locking the door behind us, she puts hands on my shoulders and steers me over to her twin bed, which I collapse onto. I keep my eyes open long enough for her to crawl into bed behind me, snake an arm around me, and pull the covers over us.

Chapter Six

After dozing for what must have been a few hours, I'm woken by my full bladder, stomach gnawing at itself. Ceely's arm is still around me, I don't think she has moved a muscle. When I glance back, she is already wide awake, and blinks her brown eyes at me. I give her hand a squeeze as I move it off of me, then right myself and wait for waves of dizziness to pass. I lumber to the bathroom.

When I emerge, Ceely slides past me and goes in. I look out the window and wait for her. The sun is high in the sky, almost too high to see from the round porthole window. It's nearly noon. I'm needed on deck, but I have time to grab a bite first.

Ceely steps out, still drying her hands. She tosses the hand towel on the desk. "Good morning. Breakfast?"

"Brunch."

"Bottomless mimosas, quiche and French toast?"

"Eggs Benedict, I hope. That's my favorite." I head for the door, but she holds a hand up and stops me.

Moving ahead, she opens it. She leans out, looks up the hall, then down it, then nods and slides out. She is making sure nobody will see me leaving her room, understanding it is best and safest for both of us. I follow.

Opening the door to the galley, a smell of tomato, spices and cooking meat envelopes us. Past the empty tables and a bus tub still full of dirty coffee mugs from the morning, we head into the kitchen. There, Roshin is wearing an apron and brushing loaves of bread with a butter and herb mixture. A pot of red sauce is bubbling on the stove's back burner. Meatballs are baking, in neat rows, on a wide sheet pan. There are dirty mixing bowls, cutting boards and other small tools all around.

Jacob is sitting on the only clean spot on the counter, holding a cup of coffee and swinging his legs slightly. He is smiling and blushing when he hears us and looks back, smoothing his expression immediately.

"Good morning! Afternoon?"

Roshin murmurs, "It's not noon."

"Good morning, then. We weren't sure when you'd be up, so we thought we should get lunch going. We did what we could."

"It smells good," Ceely says.

His casual remark of not knowing when we'd be up gives me pause... Or does he just mean Ceely? Or just myself? But, no. Ceely would not need my directive to

222

get back to work. Maybe he thinks none of the other men would dare escort her to the kitchen without my approval, and so she would remain confined in her quarters until I woke. It could be nothing. I turn hard eyes on the clerk, and he blinks in shock at the inspection I give him, with red blood rushing up his neck and into his cheeks, he can't hold my gaze for long. He does know. He must have been snooping on the cameras again.

It doesn't sit well, but there's not much to be done about it. He may have shared the news with Roshin -a piece of delicious gossip- but neither of them is well liked or really desires to be liked by the rest of the crew. They are an insular pair. And if Jacob wished to use his knowledge against me, I would have an equal or greater card to play in turn.

I finally drop my gaze, letting Jacob breathe again. I move to the coffee maker, find two clean mugs and pour us both some, while Ceely puts bread into the toaster and finds peanut butter and plates. We sit in the galley, at the table closest to the windows, and enjoy our breakfast. I keep an eye on the horizon to the North, and when I see the glint of the high noon sun off of the black tinted glass of the approaching helicopter, I drain the dregs of my coffee and stand.

"They have things handled in the kitchen, why don't you come up with me and help the company experts with their tests?"

"Alright."

Up we go. The brightness blinds me for a moment, aggravates the blood behind my eyes and makes my whole head throb, but after a moment everything settles down and I survey the scene on deck. A few men are gathered in a circle playing cards. Perry stands in the control room, but steps out and meets me when I go to him.

"Good afternoon, Captain. I was just waiting to receive transmissions from the approaching chopper, if you didn't make it up in time."

"Well, I'm here, now." I move past him and radio the chopper, check their credentials against what corporate has given me and clear them for landing. I order that end of the deck vacated, and a few more crewmen come from below as the sound of the helicopter's blades chopping the air become audible. It coasts down and the gusts pelt and deafen the deck, stirring my shirt and making me shut my eyes until the whirling subsides.

Hopping out of the chopper -keeping their heads low- comes a string of grey-haired white men. It gives the effect of a geriatric clown car. The pilot is the only man under sixty, and he stays in the cockpit of the chopper, as is protocol. If the need should arise to beat a hasty retreat though, I can't imagine the shuffling old geezers making good time.

Four sidle up to me, shake my hand and make introductions before heading for the flight rig. One hangs back, hands in pockets, staring to one side of the deck. I notice him right away while I'm greeting the others; his posture is stiff, his salt and pepper hair is long and windswept, not corporate but more like an English professor who keeps his finger on the pulse of the culture, stylish despite probably being the oldest one onboard.

Looking around, I realize it is Ceely that he is staring at. She is staring right back, smiling softly, and it twists my guts like they're being squeezed by a cold hand. I remember Jacob bringing up an old acquaintance wanting to speak to her; an old flame, I was sure. And seeing them, now -how they start to cross the deck toward each other in the same moment, as if pulled like magnets- I know that I was right. He has come to take her away from me.

My body moves on its own, and I intercept him before he gets too close. "Hold it. Who are you?" What does it matter? It doesn't, but these are the things you ask.

"James Bender." He sticks out a liver spotted hand. "Nice to meet you, Captain...?"

"Alvarado. What are you doing on my ship and who authorized you to be here?" I want a name. Whoever allowed him to come is going to hear from me. I reject his hand, instead grabbing him by the shoulders and frisking him. He scoffs at the precaution.

"I'm a Carius shareholder, I called in a few favors, pulled a few strings. I think the final approval was from

Scott Stephens, or Stephen Scott. -This isn't necessary, Captain."

"Like Hell it's not." It isn't. He carries nothing, nothing in his pockets. Not even identification. "What are you doing here?"

Ceely has come up behind me, by then. "He's here to see me."

"Hey." He looks at her and clearly sees the same things I do, or close enough. It's unacceptable. He steps around me and holds his arms out, she accepts the embrace, sparing me a curtesy glance.

"We're old friends. It's been a long time…"

"More than thirty years. I can't believe it's really you, Ceely. I thought you were dead. I thought for sure I would come out here and find someone trying to scam the company."

"It's me. Let's go somewhere we can sit and talk." She looks at me, her eyes take in my folded arms and clenched jaw. "If that's alright with you, Captain."

It's not really a question, because I can't possibly say that no, it isn't alright with me. If I show any weakness now, she'll lose respect for me, and I'll lose it for myself. I can't act like a child, throw a fit. I grumble, "I'll escort you down to my office."

I force my shoulders down, they shake with the release of tension. I unclench my fists.

Bender, obviously picking up on my hostility, asks, "Is that really necessary?"

I stop. Look back. "This ain't Northwestern, Professor." It's a shot in the dark that they went to the same college. It lands. His face flashes embarrassment and he looks down.

"Of course. Lead on, Captain."

They don't say another word as I bring them down below deck, and the white metal of the hallways feels suffocating to me in a way that it never has before. I hold the door as they both step into my office. I'm not sure why I picked my office. I guess I didn't want to leave them in her room, and I had to afford her more privacy than the galley would provide. Part of me had also been territorial, I suppose. Let them sit a few feet from where we've touched and slept together. But as I close the door and cut off my view, I see my office for what it really is.

It's mine, and it has its few perks and fineries, but at the end of the day it is four cold walls, and everything in it is disposable. It's a temporary shelter, might as well be a cot and tent in the woods. It's a bone tossed to a middle manager of a floating death trap on the Pacific Ocean. I know it can't compare to Bender's house, and neither can my apartment at the company port in Alaska. He's a shareholder. He has put down roots and made something of himself in a way that I'm sure I never will be able to.

I remember that I never wanted her here in the first place, and why. Try as I might, I can't protect her, here. And I can't provide for her, even if we do complete the mission and make it home. Hell, she's still determined to come face to face with the creature, so far as I know. Of course, I have been hoping to change her mind. Thought maybe I was winning her over.

I should want her to get on that chopper and find a way to live happily for the rest of her days. With him. I should fire her and banish her from my ship, give her no choice. But of course I can't do that. Whatever happens, I can't take her choice away from her. I learned that lesson pretty young, watching mom refuse to accept help or move on for years and years, even if I flushed her stash.

I head back up on deck and cross to the rig. The old fellas are working on the engines, and I make rounds of the catwalk, surveying. They take a moment each to explain to me what they are doing, and I pretend to listen. But the whole time I'm wondering what is going on in my office. Are they holding hands? Driven to touch each other in familiar ways, the way that lovers are? Maybe they didn't bother with small talk or little touches. Maybe they're fucking on my desk, right now. Wrinkled skin flapping and grey pubes meeting...

Probably they're talking, and that's almost as bad. Catching up on the years. Him humbly bragging about everything he has and subtly implying how comfortable he could make her, reminiscing and teasing and tempting her. She will tell him the truth of her thirty-year disappearance. He will believe her, knowing what a capable mind she has, and he will ache for her even more once she regales him with the whole, sad story. I know I did. She will come to the present, and she won't detail her relationship with me. Maybe it will live and die in secret, sacred to the both of us... He will seize the chance to try to make me seem unreasonable, maybe even dangerous, asking, "What's up with that guy, anyway?"

I'm sweating and stewing, and feeling sorry for myself for a full hour, when I notice that the two of them have come back on deck. They cross to the helicopter, with her hand on his back the entire time, guiding him. His face is blank, he doesn't speak as she opens the door for him and says something. It's only once she hugs him again that he breaks out of his stupor. He takes hold of her arms, holds her. Makes a final, impassioned plea. She is unmoved, shakes her head and touches his arm once more as she encourages him to board the chopper. He does climb in, sitting on the bench seat, and looks content to sit there until takeoff, however long that may be. I can still see his face through the window. He looks so lost that it actually makes me feel sorry for him. If she leaves me, I'll know what that feels like.

A weight drops off of me, stops compressing my chest. I can breathe again. Ceely looks our way, finds me across the stretch of water. I can't really make out her expression, but I nod to her and I think she nods back. I see Perry run to catch up with her, and I know he will escort her safely back to the kitchen.

Lunch has long since passed. She will have a lot of cleaning and prep to do for a successful dinner service. I wish I could go and help her. Hear her humming along with the radio, know that she is alright. Is she? Have we both just made the biggest mistake of our lives?

No, I can't think like that. She came thirty years forward in time, to when I was ready to meet her, capable of giving her what she desires if not what she deserves. She found my ship in the middle of the ocean, not anybody else's. And given a few good chances to leave and claim almost everything a person could ever want in life, still she chooses to stay.

If the creature comes, and the ship goes down, I won't have time to bother with guilt, wonder if it's my fault she's here. I know I'll just be thinking of finding her so we can be together at the end.

Chapter Seven

I gave the order for the crew to rest up for a few hours, planning to drill through the night to make up for lost time. We could manage with half the crew, split into two shifts with pairs at the most crucial points. The old guys work fastidiously through the evening, stop when the dinner bell rings and one lingers behind to explain to me that with a reboot and a few more checks of newly applied sensors, their work will be done.

Before we make it to the stairs, Ceely comes up, with Jacob in tow. They each hold a tray of food. Dinner is homemade pizza and a salad. The slice she holds has the works on it. The one Jacob carries is plain cheese. She nods at me as she passes, I stop and turn to watch her.

Of course they are taking the food to the helicopter, to James Bender and the pilot, sitting unmoved after several hours. They come back to where I wait at the door, and we all go down together.

Some of the men sitting at tables are rubbing sleep from their eyes, having just woken up. They drink coffee and stare at the pizza, maybe wishing for eggs or toast, or just waiting for their appetites to surface.

I'm something of a pizza connoisseur, I like it classic, if it's good, and Ceely doesn't let me down. The sauce is sweet and multifaceted, the crust brushed with herbs and garlic, browned and crispy. I shut my eyes as I savor, nodding.

"Good?"

"Just like mom used to make," I say, glancing at Mom, who I haven't seen all day but is now making her way through the line with Aaron. They join Ceely, Jacob, Roshin and I, and we all crowd together at the table for our simple meal. I wish that I could stay to help Ceely with the dishes, but as the old engineers head back up, so must I. Aaron and Mom start to help her, anyway.

Engines put through their paces, varying degrees of throttle churning the ocean waters below the rig into a white foam. A portion of my crew watching from the railing of the ship turn their eyes to the horizon. The expert nearest me can't help but to glance out, too, but then forces his eyes back to his device, reading his gauges and chemical analysis.

He signals me to cut the power. Radioing the pilot on the flight deck, I hear the quiet whine of the engines fade. One by one, the experts sound off.

"All clear."

"All clear."

"Good over here."

The man I'm watching looks up at me through the metal mesh of the main level of the catwalk. "And mine, too. That means I can officially give you the all clear from Carius to restart drilling. And we'll be on our way."

Meeting him at the ladder, I give him a hand up. "Sure you don't want to stay the night?"

He chuckles. "Quite sure. Good luck."

"Thank you. Safe travels home." I hurry to the edge of the rope bridge to meet each of the other three, to shake their hands and thank them. They climb into the chopper, which powers up and then takes to the skies all while the first shift of the crew cross to the rig and take up their positions.

Aaron, Mom and Ceely all come up on deck. The older couple come across to take up their stations inside the rig, with Mom waving to me and calling, "Good luck, Amor!"

I watch Ceely lift her hand over her brow, squinting to make out the helicopter as it grows smaller and smaller. The sun is setting in the west, still predominantly above the horizon and reflecting gold and orange onto the mostly calm and slowly darkening water. Nonetheless, the pilot activates the rigs lights at my request, spotlights that are momentarily blinding. The whole rig is lit up in white, and multiple rings of the beams face outward, stretching at least half a mile in every direction. Those are only for our last line of defense, if radar and satellite fail, but better safe than sorry.

I switch my radio to the intercom function. "Alright, let's make some money!"

Affirmative responses from the crewmen at their stations around the rig and minding the tube's connection on the *Baton Rouge*. I instruct the pilot to switch on the machinery. The vibrations of the catwalk climb up through the soles of my shoes. Gauges rise, pressure and temperature, into acceptable, standard ranges. They stay there.

We're back in business.

Jacob has been hovering around, notes that everything is functional once again. He says, "I could monitor the second watch, if you wanted-."

I'm already shaking my head, and he cuts off, nodding his acceptance. He must have known -or should have- before even beginning that sentence what it would bring. "Walk Ceely back down below, please." Half of the crew is on deck, but half of them are below, probably in their own quarters, trying to sleep, but potentially roaming the halls, dangerous… I wonder if I shouldn't ask someone else to go with them, if Jacob isn't quite satisfactory as a bodyguard, but then he is gone, and the chance has passed. I watch for his return for two torturous minutes, and just when I have decided to run across the rope bridge and seek them out myself, to thwart whatever attempted rape I think must be occurring, his orange head emerges from below again.

His body language and gait are normal, and I am able to focus on my work once again.

*

A few grueling hours, it's not physically demanding but mentally, and the stress I carry in my shoulders and neck make me sore enough that when my timer goes off and I flinch -automatically scanning the horizon for the creature- pain ricochets around me. I rub my shoulders as I switch to the intercom function. "That's your shift, done. Good work. Get some sleep." The men start for the rope bridge, and I tell Perry, "Ring the bell when you go."

"Yes Sir."

The bell chimes but nobody comes up right away. The second shift will probably head to the kitchen and rustle up a 2am snack and some coffee. With the rig powered down, Mom probably sleeping, Aaron and the pilot maintaining their stations, I am the only one out in the night. With the warm breeze washing over me and the sound of the waves lapping at the hull of the *Baton Rouge*, it's strangely peaceful. It's also eerie. I feel a chill that comes from within, shakes its way through all my extremities.

I scan the black ocean as far as the horizon in all directions, but there is nothing.

235

Ralph is the first of the second shift to come up. I'm glad to see him, pat him on the back as he makes it to the rig after a torturously long trip across the rope bridge.

He salutes. "Reporting for duty, Captain."

"This isn't the Navy, Ralph."

"Just showing my respect. Should I man the manual shutoff?"

He means the lowest level, just above the water. I have a bad feeling about his old bones trying to climb back up that ladder in a few seconds' time, or even make it back across the bridge.

"Not tonight. Head back to the *Baton Rouge* and watch the connection site." There's not much to be done there. It would take all kinds of failures to require any sudden disconnection at that end.

Ralph looks disappointed, but he goes without another word. The others all come up together, in a big group. To my surprise, Ceely comes with them, holding a cup of coffee and what appears to be a homemade brown cake donut for me. I can't help but to smile as she comes across the rope bridge, swaying slightly and minding the coffee trying to surge over the rim of the mug. I meet her, with the men parting around me like a river past a rock and going to their stations.

"What are you doing? It's late."

"We need you at your best." She offers the coffee, then the donut.

I want to kiss her, but I can't. "Thank you. Go get some sleep…" I look behind me. The second shift includes both JJ and Colson, but I still don't want her walking back alone.

She reads my expression, or maybe my mind. "I'll have Ralph walk me down."

I consider, but it worries me too much. At least Jacob was young and able enough to run up for help in a few seconds. But he is gone, dismissed for the second shift. I shake my head, open my mouth to say that I'll escort her myself, but the engines power up on the rig and short circuit my brain.

The pilot's voice on the intercom. "Creature's on the radar, taking evasive action."

My hand comes up automatically, the screen of my device flashes red around the edges of the radar which shows a massive object fast approaching. No time for the intercom function, I whirl and shout at the top of my lungs, "Back to the *Baton Rouge*! Now, now, now!"

Men come hurtling, their footsteps ringing through the rest of the catwalk, luckily nobody had descended yet. Ceely has already turned and made it across the rope bridge by the time the first man reaches me, I wave them past, even with my blood rushing to my legs, pounding in my head, heart squeezed with fear, I have a duty to get them all off of the rig.

The engines have powered up. I feel the frequency that they put out increasing, the water churning as the blades spin and divert it. I steal a glance at my device again. The creature is closing the gap at an incredible speed, and why? The drill isn't even on. Was it just in the area, and the engines powering up rang the dinner bell?

The last man barrels past me, just as I feel the catwalk shift below my feet, the rig begins to elevate. I launch myself halfway across the rope bridge in three leaping steps. I slam into the back of Colson, who stumbles but makes it to the ship's deck with someone dragging him the rest of the way. One of the main support ropes snaps and I hear the cascade of droplets behind me as the rig lifts all the way out of the water. I swing and almost go over the edge into the ocean, but my grip is firm on the remaining rope. I haul myself back up as far as I can, one foot dangling and the other pinched between wood planks hungry to go racing down into the sea. I'm reaching for the ship's railing with no hope of reaching it, when the other support snaps and I'm in freefall for one second before a hand catches my arm. I am dangling.

My rescuer goes halfway over the side of the ship before a few of the other men snag him. Roshin's abdomen is slammed into the railing, his face contorting with pain as he does not let me go. But neither do the crew let him go, and as he is dragged back, I get within range of grabbing the railing, then one of the other hands offered to me, and I am hauled up.

I don't have time to catch my breath, although Roshin lays flat on the deck with all the color drained from his face and a hand on his ribs, probably cracked. Even in my scramble to get to my feet, I clap him on the shoulder and puff out, "Thank you," with what little breath I manage to catch.

The rig is rising up into the night sky, lights still shining in all directions, a flying saucer. I can't possibly make out any single person through the glass, but surely my mother is there, pressed against it, looking for me, and I wonder, *Is this it?*

My guts are heavy, but the rest of me feels light, buzzing with adrenaline, and my mind feels perfectly clear. The first line of defense activates without any clearance or order from me. The rig releases a flurry of small projectiles in the direction of the creature, which I can just see the wake of in the distance. We have half a minute, maybe. But the projectiles plunge into the water in an arch, deploy a moment later with booms that send plumes of water shooting up into the air. I look at the radar, and the creature stops careening toward us, it doesn't like the vibrations, the huge disturbance that the depth charges create.

The men have not raced for lifeboats or run below deck for shelter, in fact many of the first shift men have come racing up, roused from sleep. Perry lopes for the turret at the ship's bow, his station as the crew's official gunner, and I look for Ceely, but I don't see her in the crowd, and it brings my fear rushing back down on me with a vengeance.

"Ceely!" No answer.

"It's turning!" Someone shouts.

Jacob pushes his way past several gawking men and crouches by Roshin, who no longer lays back but bows forward, praying.

My eyes are dragged back to the horizon, where the creature's massive, oblong white face lifts out of the water and shines in the moonlight. It's long body seems to turn beneath the waves and then it's front arms appear, those horrible, mantis-like three jointed limbs with two claws each. Then, like a whale it slams back into the water and heads in the other direction. Its tail lifts above the water line briefly and sends it surging away, whipping up a massive wave that shakes us all once it pelts the ship.

The men are cheering, but the sound is cut off by the quick popping of gunfire deafening us all for a moment. Men cover their heads and hit the deck, although the bullets are aimed at the creature, they are still flying over our heads. I whirl and see Perry banging on the door of the gunner's station, bulletproof glass and metal, and Ceely is the one inside, a snarl on her lovely face and her hands wrapped on the complicated controls.

"Ceely, stop!" I shout. She can't hear me, or she doesn't want to.

I toss my device aside and run. In five seconds I am at the turret with Perry, and he has the latch pulled - there is no lock- but Ceely has it tied off to the welded mount of the chair inside. I wedge my fingers into the small gap afforded by her crude tie, and together we wrench and pull, with her firing all the while and the shots each like a blow to my ears with how close we are. I grit my teeth and strain every muscle until I'm sure something inside me is going to snap, sweating, aching, then there is a release that sends both Perry and I tumbling back.

I regain my feet and catch the door as it tries to swing shut, then I descend on Ceely, ripping her hands from the controls and getting an arm around her waist to drag her out of the gunner's chair. Her hands connect with my face. Ball into fists and smash into me repeatedly. She's not really seeing me, I don't think. She is kicking and thrashing too, and turns in my arms to catch the door's frame, screaming like a banshee, "No! No!" She howls and then dissolves into tears as I finally rip her free, still trying to make her realize that it's me -I want to hope that she doesn't know- and what is happening.

"Ceely, stop!"

She is sobbing, no longer fighting, limp in my arms as I drag her back across the deck. "No, no, no!"

I steal a glance out at where the creature had been, and I see nothing but gentle waves. The faces of all of the crew wide eyed and open mouthed as they watch us confirm that the thing did not turn back and race toward us once again, meaning to upend, capsize, mangle, eat. But it could have. Easily.

I stop dragging her, all at once losing all strength in my arms and legs going weak, too. We collapse onto the deck in a heap, and she curls in on herself, wailing with grief and with tears pouring out of her eyes. My own face hurts. She hit me harder than I realized. My knee twisted sharply as the rope bridge collapsed under me, my left palm is rope burned to the point that it seeps blood through the thin layer of skin remaining with each beat of my heart. But I pull her into my lap and wrap my arms around her, suddenly very cold and shocked and shivering, and her the only warmth in sight. I don't care that the men are staring, I don't care that this is all very bad, that I have to explain any expenditure of ammunitions to corporate. I breathe deep the salty air, bend down and murmur to her, "I'm here, Ceely... It's alright, Sweetheart."

Part Four
Mute

Chapter One

The boy is wet, but he no longer feels it. At first the smothering heaviness of his clothes on his back - warmed in the sun to the point that it burned, then chilled at night enough to make him shiver so hard his teeth rattled and he could not sleep- were irritating. But it has been so long, his mind is so fuzzy and far away that he no longer considers himself wet. He has been wet so long that his body has started to dissolve, and he is becoming part of the ocean, bit by bit. He welcomes the transformation. His body ached at first, but it doesn't any longer. His extremities feel numb. His legs had kicked automatically -sporadically- down in the water at first, but no longer. He lets go of the seat and brings one hand out from under the overturned lifeboat. His hand is dark brown on top, pink on the bottom, pruney and prickling as the blood flow returns; he grips the piece of metal that stretches the width of the little lifeboat too hard, he can't help it. Whenever he starts to drift off, rocked gently and warmed by the ocean around him, his fingers squeeze tighter, dig the edge of the metal into his skin, and keep him from falling asleep, letting go, and sinking down. It's not just sleep that wants him, it's a lack of consciousness he is drifting toward, and death, down there with the sharks and bodies of countless sailors since the dawn of man and the monsters, of course.

His body is numb, but his eyes and his throat feel raw and dry. It goes beyond pain. He's so thirsty that letting the water take him seems like it would be peaceful. He drank some of the seawater on the second day. It seemed like a good idea at the time, but then he expelled it from both ends for a few hours and learned his lesson. He shucked off his undies and let them float away, pulled his shorts back on when it seemed to be over. That was yesterday.

Then, last night, a chopper passed overhead. The night sky out in the middle of the Pacific was so vast and starry, it looked like the edge of the black sky and the top of the black ocean melted into each other. The water might as well be the vacuum of space. He was floating, dissolving into the ocean and the sky, dissolving piece by piece and thinking through the heavy fog in his brain that that wasn't such a bad thing, that it was so beautiful, that it would all be okay. He thought he remembered his mother, although he shouldn't, he was only two when she died. That was six years ago. But there was a voice in the back of his mind, and a warm presence accompanied it as it sang to him, like she had rocked him as she sang him to sleep. A song about a falling star, a rainy day. If it was his mother he was remembering, she had a lovely voice.

He closed his eyes and relaxed down into the water, with it kissing his cracked lips, making them burn. He knew the last part would be hard, would hurt for a minute, but then he wouldn't be scared or thirsty anymore. He just had to work up the courage to go under, or else wait out that stubborn last bit of strength and self-preservation that wouldn't let him let go.

He could almost pry his numb fingers loose of the overturned lifeboat. Maybe a few more minutes, he thought. But the sound of the propellor blades chopping the air created a dissonance in his struggle between peace and survival, made him flinch as they -along with a flashing light on the front of the thing- brought back the sirens that had blared when he was already adrift on his little boat, and the huge crash and boom that had hit him hard, made his ear bleed, and then that huge body moving through the water, making him feel so small and afraid. But it had twisted and its massive tail had propelled it away, sending a wave behind it that overturned the boat, upended the boy into the water among the pieces of wreckage from the ship.

He was too weak to wave an arm, his throat was too dry to let him call out. They wouldn't see his dark skin against the dark water, anyway, they wouldn't hear his hoarse voice over their own helicopter. It went zooming away, and he blinked in the once again dark and lonely night, unsettled inside, no longer able to hear his mother's voice or feel that acceptance of the end.

He hangs on a bit longer. The helicopter had to be coming from or going to something nearby. The dark stretches endlessly and uninterrupted in all directions, it seems hopeless, but occasionally he looks. After what seems like forever and also no time at all, the sky turns from black to navy to periwinkle, and the stars fade. Another day baking in the sun is upon him. As he has gone longer without food, the hunger has mostly faded. Now it is not an irritable gnawing, but a severe pain that racks him every so often, makes him wince and press his face to the lifeboat's hull. Little explosions echo around in his guts.

The water shines orange and gold as the sun rises, then clear and blue as it recedes behind the clouds and smog. He thinks that if he never sees the color blue again, that's okay. It must be near noon when the clouds and smog seem to part and the sun starts smoldering down again, baking him and his brain, drying him out, crisping him up. He thinks his skin must be a shade darker by now. The heat and the haze in his mind make him wish he had let go the night before. He could be down with the fishes right now, cool, at peace, one with the water.

The first day and night his mind was blank, with only thoughts of the crashing and fire and the huge monster drifting up to the surface. The second day and night he found himself clearer headed. He prayed to God that someone would find him. The third he just prayed for it to be over, whatever that meant. He doesn't bother to pray anymore.

A horn blares from somewhere behind him, one long, loud blast. It makes him flinch, he lets go of the lifeboat and whirls in the water, numb and sore muscles flooding once again with blood and adrenaline. Heart pounding like a final death rattle, the faint whisper of what should have been a scream living and dying in his ragged throat, the boy flails in the water and tries to crowd back against the boat, the only safety his body recognizes. But he has accidentally pushed it away, his arms are locking up anyway, he can hardly drag them through the water to keep him afloat another second. His feet won't move, they're dead weight dragging him down, and as his head sinks below the water, he sees the massive oil tanker that has cruised up right behind him. The monster is not slicing through the water toward him, at least not that he can see. Crewmen point and wave from the side railings, but they are small figures in the distance. Someone swan dives overboard with a round life preserver over one arm. Under the water, the boy's eyes are burning and his lungs being crushed from within. The figure of the swimming man is blurry, then fades to black.

*

The boy wakes and feels fuzzy. His brain, his eyes, his tongue, all fuzzy. The blanket that his fingers are touching, wrapping too tightly around him, he can barely wiggle in the white and grey room. Then he realizes why.

The cuffs around his wrists are designed to be soft and not to cut into the skin at all, to provide comfort to the prisoner. If his father woke up in cuffs, the man would be frantic, he would be furious. He would struggle and fight and demand to be let free, never acquiescing to any kind of confinement, never liking to be controlled, even told what to do. But he's not like his father, and besides, he is too tired to fight against the restraints. His legs are strapped, one single black strap across them, over the blanket.

The room is cool. It's small and the light coming in from the round porthole window is plenty for him to know that it is daytime. There is a needle in his arm, taped down, feeding from a tube and bag hung nearby, clear fluid. He doesn't really care about the restraint, but he can feel the needle move as he twitches his fingertips, remembering that they are all there, making sure he can move them, that he is still alive. He wants that needle out.

He can hear a beeping growing more urgent as he swoons, feels sick, and turns his face the other direction, shutting his eyes. Sweat breaks out on his face, feeling prickly and then chilly. There are sensors on him, reading his pulse, blood pressure. Those beeps are basically coming from him, reporting a malfunction. Like a robot in system failure.

Eventually the panic and nausea fade. He slumps back down on the bed, tries not to think about the needle. He thinks he's still dizzy from it, but then he realizes the rocking movement is just from the water. He's still at sea. On that oil tanker, probably. So the man did pluck him out of the water before he could die. And what for? So that he could see another ship demolished, and the creature swallow him whole this time, probably.

He shuts his eyes and tries to go back to sleep, to where he doesn't have to think about it anymore, but his body won't let him.

A tiny sound of tumblers turning in a lock, then the door pushes open. The boy had looked automatically, then slammed his eyes shut, pretending to be asleep, hoping he had not been seen. A man has come into the room, and now shuts the door behind him. He's distinct looking. Not tall but strong, covered in tattoos. They're a lot nicer than the ones the boy's dad had, and mostly got in jail. Bolder. Cohesive.

The stranger shuts the door behind him. Locks it.

Locked in the room with a strange man, the boy feels his heart start to pound, the machines respond with higher frequency beeping, betraying his consciousness.

"It's alright," the man says, keeping his distance. "My name is Caesar. I'm the captain of this ship. No one is going to hurt you, here."

250

The boy opens his eyes, but shuts them again. The captain has a confident voice, authoritative. He sounds like he believes what he is saying. As if. As if someone could protect him from that thing. Wouldn't that be something? If you could protect a person from everything that would ever want to hurt them...

He remembers breaking his arm when he was six. Just two years ago. Fell off a jungle gym, nothing for it, nobody's fault... His father -never perfect- had said with all sincerity while they lifted his mangled arm up for the x-ray and fresh tears poured out, "If I could take your pain on myself, I would."

If anyone could have protected him, it would have been his father. And his father is dead, now. He imagines his dad safe, somehow, alive inside the creature's stomach. But that's not reality. They'll be reunited when the creature comes, it will be a small comfort at the end.

The captain comes closer, moving slowly. He sidles up to the foot of the bed. Puts his hands on the white railing. "What's your name?"

The boy doesn't answer, doesn't see the point. He keeps his eyes closed.

"...Sorry about the restraints. You were out for a while, and you were having bad dreams. Scratching yourself."

That makes the boy open his eyes again, and look. His forearms are wrapped in bandages. That explains that.

"I can take the restraints off, if you show me you understand me, that you're calmed down and rational now."

He speaks slowly, keeps his voice soft, like people do when they don't have much practice talking to children, like they do when they think kids are stupid. The boy supposes he brought that on himself, washing up the way he did and leaving his will to speak in the ocean. He looks the captain square in the eyes for a torturous second; he feels shame as he does. He shouldn't be alive. He nods.

The captain's face changes, shows recognition. He starts to undo the strap around the boy's legs. He speaks, more casually, now. "Just don't feel like talking, huh? Well I have some questions I need answered, but you can just nod."

He releases the strap on the right wrist, then the left. The boy reaches across himself, going for the needle, but the captain catches his wrist in a flash. The boy struggles, a hint of a whimper rising as his anxiety spikes.

"Stop." The captain's voice is hard enough to make him obey. "You were out there for days, weren't you?" He doesn't wait for an answer. "You were dehydrated. You almost died. Your body needs those lost fluids replaced, so you're going to leave that IV in until this bag is gone. Then I'll remove it. Or you can rip it out, and I can restrain you and stick it back in." He lets go.

252

His muscles clenching around the needle has reminded him of how much he wants it out. But if he stays still, he can pretend it's not there. He relaxes back onto the bed.

"Okay. You came from a ship called the *Alessa*, is that right?" The captain is good at reading people. When he sees no recognition in the boy's eyes, he prompts. "A black yacht, owned by a Chester Osbourne, it was the only other ship in the area."

The boy looks away. Chester Osbourne, was that his name? The *Alessa*, that sounds right. A few days, his father had told him. He didn't know how many. The boy had to stay hidden. The rich people would hire him for indeterminate amounts of time, who knew how long their binges would last? His father couldn't get jobs at the nice restaurants that he used to, anymore. The best he could do was a penthouse, a party boat, living one job to the next on recommendations. He could still cook circles around anyone.

The captain reads the 'affirmative' in the boy's sudden thousand-yard stare. "Alright. Were there any other survivors?"

The boy shakes his head.

"Was it the creature?"

He grimaces.

"Billion-dollar yachts like that come with all sorts of equipment to deter and defend against the creature. They didn't work?"

The boy blinks, remembering. There was nothing like that. No guns, no drones. Just a siren and a minute later the creature appeared and rammed the boat until it was capsized and collapsing in on itself, bent metal and broken fiberglass, men screaming, being snatched and dragged down by the creature's long jaws. He saw it all from the lifeboat.

In the medical bay of the *Baton Rouge*, the boy shrugs.

The captain sits back, his sharp face troubled. "Sabotage, then." He looks at the boy. "You got to a lifeboat, and you were lowered to the water... you couldn't have done that yourself, could you? You can't be more than, what... Eight? Nine?"

The boy closes his eyes again, irritated, and his head aches dully. None of this matters. He chews at his crispy, sunburnt lips.

"So did you have someone looking out for you? A parent?"

The boy can tell by the captain's tone that he knows that isn't it. Those boats are designed so that they can be lowered from within, so that nobody need stay behind so that the others can escape. If his father had seen it coming, had been the one to put him in the boat, they'd still be together. He realizes that with sabotage being implied, and himself the only survivor, he is under suspicion. There's nothing he can do to prove his innocence.

The captain prods. "No? Someone else? Someone you'd met before?"

He shook his head. He had seen the man only once before, the day before. And the man had never seen him, not expected him to be on the yacht. He remembered the shock on his face, finding a little boy in a closet with a video game. The man was dressed in an all-white uniform like his father, either kitchen staff or a server. He was Asian and middle aged, probably.

He had closed the door all but a crack, instinctively, and looked around. Then he looked back at the boy. Then he closed the door without saying a word. The boy stayed in the closet with his game and his snacks for a few more hours, until his father came to get him, when it was dark outside. He rode under a serving cart back to their small room. That was the day before the monster came.

It was early in the morning when the Asian man came and opened the closet door once again. He held a finger up to his lips, his eyes were stern, ordering silence. He motioned for the boy to come. Feeling his guts twist with guilt, unsure of the penalty for sneaking on a ship -maybe his father would go back to jail- he climbed out of the closet.

There was nobody on deck, so early in the morning. They stayed up late and slept late. But the stranger did not march the boy to the kitchen, or to the master bedroom to turn him over to the owner. He brought him to the edge of the deck. Gestured to the lifeboat hung out over the edge, swaying slightly with the roll of the bigger ship below it. The boy felt a new swell of panic and shook his head, thought about running for the kitchen. But as soon as he glanced that way, to the stairs down to the next level, the man tapped his arm. Just the motion of him reaching out made the boy flinch.

Moving the white jacket they all wore aside, he showed a black shirt underneath, a black belt, and tucked into it, the handle of a black automatic handgun.

It made the boy's blood run cold. His mind went blank. It seemed like there was only himself and the man and the gun on the ship, in the world. Like God's own eyes were only on them, there could be nothing more important.

The man gestured once more.

The boy had not hesitated, he had swung a leg out across the gap, a few inches only but a long drop down to the water visible through it. He pulled himself out and settled down in the rounded bottom of the lifeboat, on hands and knees. He felt the ropes lowering at once, he began to sink. Soon he was rocking on the waves in the shadow of the massive yacht, feeling small.

He still feels small.

The captain rubs his face, he looks tired. "Do you know their name? …No? How about your own name? I need to know, so I can work on finding your family, and getting you out of here. You don't have to say it, you can write it down."

The boy stares at the offered pen and paper. He doesn't see the point. There's no family out there who can save him. He won't be leaving the ship. The monster is probably already on its way.

The captain sighs. Stands. "Alright. I'll leave you alone for a while longer. Are you hungry? You must be. We don't have a cook right now, but I'll try to scare something up."

The boy reaches for the needle still in his arm, but he doesn't pull it out himself, just points. The captain sees, nods, and takes a step back to the side of the bed. He gloves up, collects a cotton ball and segment of tape from the bedside table. Then he takes hold of the needle.

"Ready? One, two-." He doesn't say three, just slides it out. The cotton ball is taped over the bleeding vein before the boy is even finished wincing. "All done. Very brave. PB and J or ham and cheese sandwich? Stupid question, PB and J all the way, right? I'll be right back. This door is locked, it has to stay locked for now. You're safe in here."

He goes, shutting the door behind him, and the key turns the tumblers in the lock once again. The boy kicks his feet over the side of the bed right away. They are bare; he's in a hospital gown. The floor is cold tile, his legs are stiff. He makes it to the door but his knees are shaking, blood is throbbing in his temples. He grabs the handle and tries to twist it.

It's locked from this side, too. He's trapped. He's never leaving this place. He moves back to the bed and collapses down onto it. He hardly has the strength to pull the covers up.

Chapter Two

After eating the sandwich that the captain brought him and guzzling water, the boy goes to sleep again. He wakes partway through the night and his head feels full and buzzy. He knows his body won't let him sleep anymore. He stretches the sore muscles and joints of his legs out. Moves around the room, tries to wake the computer but it's password protected and won't let him do anything. The captain brought him a book -a boring western- so he reads for a couple hours until the sun comes up.

The captain returns with a few pieces of toast with jam, and links of browned sausage. He sits, mostly silent while the boy eats. He has a handheld device that he wakes up as the last crumbs are polished off. When he turns it around, the screen shows the boy's father.

"This is your dad?"

There's no point in lying, his father is dead, he can't get in any trouble now. He nods.

The captain's face is sympathetic. He nods. "He was a cook, huh? A pretty good one, if he was working on a yacht like that... Know my way around a kitchen, myself. Had to learn if I wanted to eat. What about you?"

Considering, he shrugs. He knows some stuff. Some things his father taught him, other things he just picked up because he pays attention. How to make a perfect omelet, how to sear a steak, berry compotes, his favorite on pancakes... But what does any of that matter, in a place like this?

"If Arthur Scott is your father, then your name is McKenzie Scott, isn't it?" He gets no response, the boy has turned to stare at the wall, but still manages to read a 'yes' somehow. "Can I call you that? McKenzie? Your mom isn't around, but you've got an aunt Genevieve in New Zealand. We already reached out to her, and told her what happened, and she's very excited to see you. She wants you to come live with her... Is that alright?"

He reads concern on McKenzie's face, surprise, as he looks back over. In the end, he just shrugs, again. He has only met his aunt once in his life. He knows she has a couple of kids, a couple of years older than him. But it hardly makes a difference. They are hardly going to materialize and take him away.

The captain takes it as a yes. Maybe he wasn't really asking. "We'll get you on a chopper out of here as soon as we can, but for now, I have to go to work. I brought you a pack of cards, I don't know if you know how to play solitaire… okay. I'll see you at lunch, then, and we can play some gin-rummy or something. Hang tight."

*

Lunch comes and goes. It's grilled cheese and a cup of tomato soup. The food sat heavy at first, but now energy seems to be flowing through McKenzie's body again, his muscles aching less and his head no longer staticky. He has had his first pee since being pulled from the ocean. Pungent and dark, but the second was a little better as his organs worked on soaking up the water he sips near constantly. Lucky he is young, probably.

Despite himself, he plays gin-rummy silently with the captain. It's not fun but it distracts him for a few minutes from the hopelessness sitting in his heart, and the horrible monotony of the white walls.

When the captain first popped back in, he took in the room with a quick glance. He noticed McKenzie has hung a pillowcase over the round window, not wanting to see the blue ocean, the empty horizon. He notices, also that the bookmark has not moved in the western since breakfast.

The captain is okay with silence but he does keep trying to spur McKenzie into a conversation. "Don't like that book? I liked it when I was young. Although maybe a little older than you. I like westerns. Characters in those books always live simple lives, with simple rules. I liked that, when things felt complicated. But maybe you'd prefer *Lord of the Rings?* Or some science fiction?"

He gets no answer, not even recognition.

The captain grumbles, "Should've made you play Uno."

McKenzie's lip twitches in a faint flash of amusement, but it's replaced with a grimace a moment later. He seems upset with himself for smiling.

The captain wins the game, then puffs out a big breath and stands, handing the collected deck of cards over. He looks very tired.

"Well, I'll bring you the first *Lord of the Rings* with dinner. They made those movies in New Zealand, where you're going to live with your aunt. It's beautiful, there. At least it looked that way in the movies... Is there anything else you like to do? Short on video games, unfortunately."

McKenzie looks at the door, back at the captain. If he is down here when the creature comes and smashes this ship up, he will die here, locked in, unable to fit through the little, round window. As much as he hates the idea of being surrounded by water, smelling that briny air and feeling exposed to attack from every side, he knows it is the safer thing. This white and grey room is false safety. Besides, he can't stand to look at it anymore.

The captain knows all too well what he wants. "I'm sorry. You can't leave this room. It's for your own protection."

He's either a liar -McKenzie thinks- or a fool. He can't honestly think that's the truth; that it's safer down here, locked in, that the creature is less of a threat than whatever else a kid might encounter on a ship. Machinery or strangers. And does he think McKenzie is some ordinary child? He'll never be an ordinary kid again. The captain doesn't seem like a fool.

He wants to keep me down here, McKenzie thinks. *Chooses to.*

As soon as the captain goes, McKenzie moves to the door. Presses his sunburnt ear to it, which prickles a little but then registers cold metal. He hears footsteps fading.

He tries the knob. Locked. He digs carefully in the trash for the needle that was in his arm. Finds it enclosed in the plastic case it came out of, still red with his own blood. It makes him swoon, but he is determined. He inserts it in the lock, fiddles around, tries to spring tumblers or turn the mechanism, but it doesn't work. He looks around the room. Takes stock.

The only other possible way to freedom would be through the air vent. It has a grate over its mouth that he could maybe get unscrewed, with the needle or a coin if he could get his hands on one. Small spaces don't bother him, he actually likes them. Closets, cupboards. If the monster came while he was in there, and the

263

water rushed in, and he was sinking fast with the weight of the metal dragging him down and he couldn't turn around, let alone get out… He might reach an end and not be able to get the grate off from the inside…

It will have to be a last resort. Maybe the captain can be persuaded to let him out, long enough for him to slip away. Or maybe he can get the keys out of the captain's pocket…

*

Dinner time comes. McKenzie is hungry by then. He waits by the door and listens, feels his heart start to pound when the footsteps approach. When it opens, he can see briefly into a white hall, the metal of the ship rusted in places or stained with age, and at the end, a cold looking staircase leading up on one side, down on the other. But the glimpse is short-lived. The door closes and the captain offers him a tray; he holds two.

It's goulash and lima beans. The food looks and smells lifeless. The goulash is oversalted to cover the burned meat, bland red sauce, the artificiality. The beans were surely just dumped from a can, and if they were warmed up at some point, it was long ago. The captain sees him make a face as he forces the goulash down, one chewy bite at a time.

"I know. We take turns in the kitchen. This is Ralph's best effort. We had a cook for a while -or, more like a week, I guess, it just felt like a lot longer- but she's in the brig, now. I didn't want to do it, but I had to. She broke out most important rule. She put everyone in danger. Tomorrow's Friday, so I'll be cooking. Maybe I'll bring you with me to the kitchen and we can whip up something tasty? If they haven't picked you up already. Alright. Eat up, though. You need the calories."

He dutifully takes another bite. Tomorrow. A big place like this must have a big kitchen, with plenty of exits and plenty of places to hunker down, so he doesn't get locked back in the room. And what then? He looks at the grey-red and grey-green food. He doesn't know what then. But at least he won't be locked in here.

Another game of gin-rummy, which the boy wins. The captain takes their trays, both still half full, and tells him goodnight. Alone in the room again, the boy tries the door, which is locked. He tries to go to sleep, but he can feel the rocking of the ship beneath him. the room is chilly -the AC is cranking- and his blanket is thin. And he is alone, which he is not used to. He is used to having a nightlight projecting constellations on the walls and ceiling, and his father being only a room away. In fact, on the yacht that the creature destroyed, they had been sharing a bed, and he had gotten used to his father's soft snores. Here it's too quiet.

He cries a little, trying not to let it turn into a full sob, and the effort strains many muscles in his throat, chest and sides. Eventually he has cried as much as he can. He turns the light back on and opens *The*

Fellowship of the Ring. It's much better than the western. Taking his pillow and blanket, he curls up underneath the bed, where the frigid air conditioning isn't blowing directly on him. He untucks the sheets from under the mattress and hangs them over the edges of the frame, sealing him in, a canopy, a secure cocoon. Eventually he drifts off to thoughts of the Shire, its safe and scenic landlocked gardens and fields, warm dirt and tall grass.

Chapter Three

Waking in his nest under the bed, McKenzie realizes that the door has opened. He peers out from under the swaying white curtain of sheets, blinking. His eyes are fuzzy, vision a blur, but it's not the captain who has come in. He stays still, under the bed, feeling anxious.

The red-haired man is tall and slender, and younger than the captain. He cranes his long neck and spots the boy in his hiding spot. "Oh! You scared me. I came in and didn't see you, and... I'm Jacob. You're McKenzie. It's a good name. The captain asked me to bring you breakfast today. I made you two poached eggs and some toast, and there's orange juice, too. It's from concentrate. Will you come up and eat with me?"

McKenzie is hungry. He climbs up onto the bed and sets the book down, taking up the tray.

Jacob's eyes light up when he sees the book. "*Lord of the Rings*, fantastic! Such good books..."

McKenzie doesn't give him much, just starts to eat.

Jacob tries to initiate conversation, telling McKenzie that he's the ship's clerk, that he spoke with the boy's aunt Genevieve yesterday and that she seems very nice. When that doesn't do the trick, he becomes a bit perturbed by McKenzie's empty stare, he changes the subject to the food, saying that he hopes the eggs are to the boy's liking; he made them with no runny yolks, the way that he likes them. He gets nothing, no recognition on the boy's blank face, peeling with sunburn on those high and distinct cheeks.

McKenzie doesn't know why he bothers. Surely the captain told the clerk that he hasn't said a word. Everyone thinks they're special, deep down, he supposes.

Jacob can't stop trying. "Our cook, Ceely -that's short for Lucille- she usually puts together a nice spread... But she needed some time to rest. She came out of the ocean and ended up with us, just like you. Of course, she was in a submarine..."

That makes McKenzie's brow raise. A woman, out on the ocean, alone like him? In a submarine, though. So she had shelter. How does that happen to a person? She didn't get forced off of some mega-yacht into her submarine at gunpoint so that some assassin could spare his conscience. She did it to herself, set out on her own. What kind of person would do that? A psycho, probably.

Jumping on that small flash of interest from the boy, Jacob rushes to explain. "It's incredible, she built it herself. She used to be an engineer."

But he has lost McKenzie's interest again. The boy sets his empty tray down, picks his book back up, and then crawls back underneath the bed again, bundling up and untucking the sheets to hang down around him.

"Alright, I'll leave you to your book. You'll see me again for lunch, the captain plans to work through it to make up some lost time. But apparently, he'll come and get you for dinner, so you have that to look forward to."

He goes, and McKenzie tilts his head, listening for the sound of the door closing, the lock clicking and the key scraping faintly as it slides out of the lock. He should have been prepared, he thinks, suddenly kicking himself. He was expecting the captain, and knew that the captain was observant, too aware to let any kind of escape attempt get past him, so he had thought he shouldn't bother.

When lunchtime rolls around, McKenzie has already been waiting in front of the door for a full hour, with the book in one hand, one finger slipped between the pages, hidden. Hearing the footsteps approaching, his heart starts to pound, his skin feels warm and prickly as the key turns in the lock, then Jacob appears, balancing two trays. He's easily startled, and not expecting McKenzie to be so close, and the hand holding the key and turning the knob shoots up to his heart.

"God! Hungry, huh? Here you go."

McKenzie takes the tray while swiftly tucking the book under one arm and pressing a piece of strong, white medical tape over the door's latch in the moment Jacob's back is turned. It closes almost silently, no click. Jacob doesn't notice, pulls up a chair at the foot of the bed.

Lunch is a hot dog, a side of green salad tossed in oily dressing, and an apple. McKenzie's father would never let him eat processed meats like hot dogs, spam, bologna, he had too much pride. Eating it hesitantly at first, he doesn't care for the texture, but the taste is good, salty and distinct. He eats the salad and saves the apple.

Jacob doesn't try to make conversation, just eats his meal, waits for McKenzie to finish, then takes their trays and goes. The door closes silently again, and the boy's ears perk up; it all depends on the next second. He can lock the door, but if he wiggles it even a little, it will give, and the jig will be up.

He hears the key turn.

The footsteps move up the hall.

McKenzie slides out of the bed and crosses the white and grey room. He presses his ear to the metal. There is a faint humming that is constantly present on the ship, magnified and echoing off his ear drum. Whether it's the engine or the air conditioning or even the machinery of the drill pumping oil into the hold, he isn't sure. There doesn't seem to be anyone around, out in the hallway.

Now or never.

He pulls on the door, and it gets stuck on the tape for a second but then springs free. Peering through the crack, he sees an empty hall. He props the door, reapplies a new piece of tape smoothly and securely, hoping it won't come loose or get stuck again. What if he needs to get back in, and he can't?

Up or down, that's the question. He was unconscious when they brought him on board, he doesn't know how many floors the ship even has. He doesn't know what he wants, exactly. He wants to be off of the ship and back on dry land, but it's not possible right now. There has to be a submarine onboard, if that woman came on one. If he can find it, maybe he can figure out how to launch it, point it north, toward land. If the woman was out there on her own, undisturbed, then it has to be safer than staying on the big, noisy ship, with the other monster bait. He brings his apple and heads out into the hall, taking the empty, metal stairs down.

The track lighting overhead flickers at the lower landing, where the stairs end and a heavy door is closed. He shoves the bar and goes in. The humming of the ship is louder, inside. The ceiling is high and the place is dim and dusty and spacious. There are two doors on the right wall, one labeled 'supplies' and the other unlabeled, with a light on inside.

McKenzie moves past them, by a massive furnace unit. In the back of the hold are some roll up doors, a small craft that looks modern and remotely controlled, and the much larger yellow submarine that was crudely made and rusted in some spots. There's a table nearby. He drags it over -with difficulty, it weighs as much as he does- and climbs up on top. The hatch is not locked, and he climbs down inside with no trouble.

Inside there's a white chest freezer right beside the ladder. At the front of the craft, there's a control panel that looks simple enough, but at the back he sees a big problem. A piece of siding has been removed, and a piece of the inner workings of the submarine, with it. A few tools and a few nuts and bolts lay nearby, whatever's left of what was ripped out. The sub won't run, not in pieces. That's plan A, ruined.

Too bad. It even has a freezer. Out of curiosity, he opens the thing. There are two bodies inside, little and Caucasian, around his age, or a little younger. Casualties kept for a later burial, or some kind of bait to lure the monster? He closes the lid, climbs out, closes the hatch and then jumps down to the cold floor. He thinks, next, of lifeboats up on deck.

The idea of being adrift, alone again, is a sad one. He thinks of what could make the voyage less terrifying. A flashlight or lamp of some kind, definitely. A blanket for warmth, maybe a tarp to keep rain off. A knife? A fishing pole? A flare gun. People have those in movies. If he had had a flare gun last time, the helicopter might have seen him. A stock of food, he could get some of that from the kitchen, when he's there with the captain, later. He will have to go back to the room. He will definitely be caught, if he tries to steal food; there must be people in and out often enough, with the cook locked up and everyone fending for themselves.

He peers into the supply closet, first. It's dark and narrow and long, with dozens of wooden cubbies containing small bits and bobs on one side and dusty metal shelves on the other holding larger pieces. There are pieces of pipe in every size, sheet metals and wood, tanks of gas, maybe flammable ones for welding, maybe oxygen for diving, there are several sizes of wetsuit and other diving gear around, too. And a lantern, which he finds does work, and spare batteries that will fit.

For a tarp he has to climb all the way up the metal racks, to take one off of the top shelf. They are heavy duty and bolted down, but the thing does wiggle perilously as he scrambles up. There's no flare gun anywhere, or a knife or fishing pole. With the lantern, the batteries and the tarp, he moves back to the door.

Scanning the basement, he checks that he is still alone and then steps out. The other room is lit from within, why? Surely there isn't anyone down here, in the middle of the day. He opens the door a crack.

The white wall extends into the room, he can't see much through the gap. He opens it a little wider, and the hinges creak. It sends a jolt of fear down the back of him. He remembers with perfect clarity the sound of the siren wailing and the monster's odd keening noise as it reared out of the water and smashed into the ship. His legs have gone numb, he should run but he can't move. He feels a hot flood of urine rush out of him and trickle down his pantlegs, uncontrollable.

A voice calls from within, "Hello?"

It brings him back to the moment. He's standing in the dusty bowels of the ship, outside of a room where a woman has heard him approach. His pants are wet and rapidly cooling, there's sweat on his face, and he is thirsty. He should turn and go, get back to the room.

"There's a mirror in the corner, I can see you in the reflection," the woman says.

He pushes in, why not? She's not lying about the mirror, he sees it ahead. The barred little cell stretches the length of the room along the back wall. The toilet and sink are in that corner, the bunk is in the other, he can see it around the corner of the wall as he steps further in.

She sits on the cot with a piece of machinery in front of her, and a dozen little tools. The faceplate is off of the thing, a device seems to spin inside, when it is operational. It's the piece pulled from the submarine, he's sure. She is trying to fix it. They're letting her work with tools, even in jail like this? It's odd, and so is the grey-haired old woman being locked up in the first place. It seems wrong, somehow.

Her dark eyes take him in, and her face softens visibly. "You're the survivor of the shipwreck, Caesar told me about you. McKenzie, right? Are you okay?" She has noticed his wet pants. It makes his cheeks burn with embarrassment. If she were not behind bars, he thinks she would take him to get cleaned up and changed, and he would let her, with a soft voice like that. It would be the most natural thing in the world.

But she is kept separated by the bars, which she now holds as she stands and surveys him. "Going somewhere? You don't want to do anything rash, I hear they're going to get you out of here as soon as possible... You really shouldn't be alone, in a place like this. Some of the crew are dangerous. You should stay here, until someone comes looking for you-." Hearing it, he immediately spins and walks out, leaving her shouting after him, "Don't! It's not safe! Hey!"

He goes, pushing through the heavy door that finds him again on the dim landing, and goes up the first set of stairs. At the next floor, he is back in the hall he came from, with the door to his room at the end. He starts to run, heart pounding, tarp crinkling under his arm.

But a door opens halfway, and a pair of arms ensnare him, sweeping him off his feet and wrenching a little yelp out of him. He squirms and kicks and he is lowered to the ground, the arms loosening but not letting him go far. Hands clamp down on his arms, a big, bald white man kneels down to his level.

"Hey now, what are you doing out on your own? Foraging for supplies, I see… Can't say I blame you. But let's get you back to the med bay, where you belong."

He walks up the hall looming behind McKenzie, steering the boy in front of him. The doorknob doesn't turn in his hand, and he smiles, gives the thing a shove and it does swing open. He swipes the tape off of the mechanism, which springs loose, and takes a long look at the provisions in McKenzie's arms.

"Gonna have to tell the captain you were out. No way around it. Can't have you wandering around on your own, no one wants to see you get hurt and there are some very unscrupulous characters around. I'm Perry, by the way." He holds out his hand, which McKenzie automatically shakes. The man has a slow, meandering way of speaking that comes off very forthcoming, he's saying what comes to mind as it occurs to him.

"And you're McKenzie… Boys have probably changed some, since I was one, but I bet it's still rough, having a name like that. I bet your mom picked that, because it sounded pretty, and she wanted you to be a sweet, sensitive boy. But like that old Johnny Cash song, you probably got tougher because of it, not sweeter… I bet you had your friends call you Ken. Is that right?"

Shocked, McKenzie nods. His mouth has actually fallen open, and he closes it when he realizes.

276

Perry nods to his pee-soaked pants. "Get yourself cleaned up, Ken. Hang in there."

He goes, shutting the door, testing the knob to make sure that it's securely locked. McKenzie is alone again. He stows the tarp up under the slats of the bed, wraps the lantern and batteries in a spare pillowcase and puts them in the back corner of the bathroom cabinet. He peels his pants off and soaks them in the sink, putting on a pair of sweats left for him that are much too big.

Then he climbs under the bed, pulls the blanket around himself, and reads. He's not sure what the captain will have to say about his excursion, whether he'll still be welcome to go to the kitchen and help make dinner. He hopes so.

Chapter Four

The captain shows up after a few hours. He stands in the doorway, and McKenzie is sitting on the edge of the bed by then, waiting. "Alright, escape artist, come on. Dinner service at six."

And that is all that is said, for the time being. McKenzie jumps off the bed and hurries out into the hall. The captain shuts the door, checks that the latch and lock are secure, then leads the way to the stairs and up. The next floor looks much the same as the one the med bay is on, white, peeling, rusting metal and track lighting and closed doors close together.

The galley is brighter, with tables and bench seats. A tub of dirty dishes waits, and the captain wheels it to the back, through swinging double doors. The kitchen itself is a lot of stainless-steel tables and counters, with plastic cutting boards, a large six-burner stove and four ovens, walk-in fridge and freezer. The place is made to feed several hundred, but if there were that many on the ship, McKenzie is sure he would have seen some around. He gets the feeling he has wound up on a ghost ship, crewed by the dead; they are either doomed to sail forever under the smog and the threat of the monster, or they get closer to Hell and its massive jaws every day… He wonders if the purgatory of it never ending isn't worse. Maybe they need to find their way out, earn their judgement through some act of attrition.

The captain opens an oven and the warm steam that wafts out carries the scent of delicious, spiced meat. He heaves a massive, foil-covered pan out and drops it on the counter. Inside is a trussed-up piece of pork, stewing in fragrant juices and herbs.

"We'll let that sit while we whip up some salsa… Wash your hands, I'll get you some veggies to cut." He collects tomatoes and onions, and a large knife, which to McKenzie's surprise, he is given. "Let me see your form?"

What he means is, does the kid know how to hold a knife? McKenzie does, it's one of the first things his father taught him in the kitchen.

Looking at his fingers on the knife's grip, the captain nods and pushes vegetables at him. "Good. Let me get a fine dice on these onions, then move on to the tomatoes, and then all into this big bowl, got it?"

McKenzie nods and gets to work.

The captain is charring up dozens of corn tortillas when a short woman with short, dark hair comes in. "Sorry I'm late, Amor. What do you need?"

"Help McKenzie with the salsa, please, Mom. Then maybe a salad."

She smiles a kind smile. "Nice to meet you, McKenzie. I'm Regina. Let's see, you've got tomatoes and onions. We should add some peppers, some cilantro and lime…"

The captain finishes charring tortillas and starts shredding the pork, right into the juices it cooked in. Regina gives McKenzie a couple of cucumbers to slice and collects greens and dressing. They toss it all together in a hotel pan and then dinner is ready to be served.

Out in the galley, men are already gathered, about a dozen. Several of them start to pound their fists on the tables, increasing the speed as the captain carries the heavy pan of shredded pork to the serving bar. Scattered applause breaks out and men rush to be first in line.

The captain nods his acceptance of the praise, and gestures to McKenzie and Regina. "My assistants. Dig in."

Men build heaps of tacos on their trays, jostling and joking as they do. McKenzie waits, he does not want to wade into the fray. The captain and Regina seem to feel the same way, although the former steps away for a minute. Before he goes -leading a rangy Arabic looking man back to the kitchen- McKenzie notices him scan the room, lock eyes with Perry, and nod to where his mother and the boy stand patiently.

Keep an eye on them, it denotes.

He wonders if there would be any point to sneaking away, even if he could. His stomach growls, and the pork smells so good that he knows there is not. Even if he found an unfindable hiding place, he would not have the strength to stay there for long.

Finally it is his and Regina's turn at the serving bar. He makes up two tacos, with plenty of the pork stock dripping off of them and big heaps of the salsa he helped to make, and a serving of the green salad, too. Unlike most kids his age, he will eat fresh greens any day, with gusto, providing that the dressing is halfway decent. He thinks of hobbit meals eaten in the Shire made from all sorts of fresh things, fresh breads and cakes and cheese, eggs and meats, berries and veggies with herbs and mushrooms. He takes a bite and decides the captain has them beat, the pork is falling apart, tender and with multiple layers of flavor, acid of citrus at the front, then one spice after another catching the tongue's attention, billowing out like a sail unfurling and catching a breeze.

He closes his eyes and all thought fades away. His father would be impressed. That was what his father loved about food; that it could keep you guessing. That anybody could make a meal that could knock your socks off, even in a place like this, for people like these.

Several of the crewman take up seats beside and across from Regina and McKenzie. Some stop as they pass and stoop to get a good look at him. They each ask him something, try to get him on the hook so that he'll talk. They think they're special; the chosen one to break the curse afflicting the poor boy.

"So, who made you walk the plank?"

"Hey, boy, do you want a dollar?" It's waved in front of him. "Just say, 'yes' and it's yours."

"I've got a candy bar. Only cost you one word."

One burly and mean looking fellow just stares him down for a few seconds, then orders, "Talk. I know you can."

Each time, McKenzie spares the man a glance, then focuses on his tacos again. The captain reappears and goes to the serving bar, where he starts to make up two trays of tacos and salad. The Arabic man has come out of the kitchen with a few tacos of his own, and as he sits at the next table over, McKenzie decides they contain chicken or fish. The captain holds two trays when he comes over. One has a mug of coffee on it. Apparently, he has decided that his recruiting his mother and Perry both to watch McKenzie is not enough.

He issues a stern order. "Stay here or in the kitchen until I get back. Help Regina clean up, please."

She says, "Go ahead, Caesar. We've got this."

McKenzie realizes that the other tray must be for the prisoner. The woman in the brig. What did they say that she did? Broke an important rule. Put everyone in danger. She must have nearly brought that thing down on the ship; what else could that mean? He will stay away from her, he decides. No matter how kind she seems. She is dangerous.

The captain goes, and as he is stepping out into the hall, Jacob steps in. He looks exasperated, and tries to speak to the captain, but the older man shakes his head and goes. Jacob looks after him, sighs, then comes into the galley. His eyes land on McKenzie, he gives the boy a smile but it's uneasy and doesn't last. He gets food and goes to sit with the Arabic man, seeming to immediately spill his worries, and then both of them glance over at McKenzie in the same moment.

Jacob and the boy's eyes meet, the man blushes and looks away.

A pit forms in McKenzie's stomach. Something is wrong, and it's about him. He must be in trouble for sneaking out. What can they do to punish him, other than putting him back in that room? Starve him? Torture? They are in international waters… Jacob looks sick from whatever he knows.

A tall black man wearing a gun in a holster on his hip and a button down blue shirt enters. He fills a tray, comes and sits next to Regina, scarfs down four tacos, gives her a kiss on the cheek and then goes.

Men of the crew go back for seconds, and some even for third helpings of the delicious tacos. Jacob and his friend do not, they finish their meals and then sit, and wait. McKenzie waits, too, and watches, until almost a full hour later it is only the five of them left in the room; the two young men, Perry, Regina, and himself.

The old man has drifted over to the window. He stands looking out. McKenzie watches him and sees a hint of a smile on the man's face, placid and open. The evening sun is dying out that way, and Perry looks ten years younger in the golden-orange light. He isn't scanning the horizon for signs of the monster, he's just finding his peace out there, somehow. He must be the bravest man to ever live. McKenzie wants to be like that.

"Let's clean up," Regina says, and takes McKenzie's hand. He lets her have it, although it feels strange. There are no leftovers at all. The two young men stand and automatically start to help them carry dishes to the kitchen.

The darker man introduces himself to McKenzie. His name is Roshin.

Perry, alone, stays out in the galley. The rest head to the kitchen, where there are two different two-compartment sinks, one on either side of the long room. They start washing dishes in pairs. Regina scrubs them in the soapy water, McKenzie take them from her, rinses them and stacks them nearby. He doesn't mind the work, although part of him is exhausted and actually longs for the seclusion of the room. That part of him has been tricked; it's safer out here where he can run if sirens blare.

He has forgotten his objective of stashing some food. There is very little out on the counter, but there are some bananas hanging from a hook. He tears one off quickly while Regina's back is turned, and sticks it in one of the sweatpants' cavernous pockets. She hangs mugs to dry on the further hooks underneath the taller cupboards. There's a box of protein bars in a cupboard under the sink, along with tins of tea and a huge tub of coffee. He sticks two of them in his other pocket.

He is still crouched in front of the open cupboard when the door opens and the captain comes in, holding two empty trays, two empty mugs. He takes in the sight of the boy -who has given the appearance of guilt, shooting to his feet and dropping his hands to his sides- but the captain says nothing about it, just walks over and starts washing the trays and mugs in the soapy water.

Jacob spins, not knowing what to say for a second. His eyes skip over McKenzie, then color rises in his face again. "Captain, I still need to speak to you."

"So speak."

"We should speak in the galley."

The captain looks at McKenzie, too, then nods, taking a hand towel off the counter and drying his hands as he goes. Jacob follows. As soon as the door has swung closed, McKenzie starts to go after then, but Regina catches his shoulder.

"Don't."

But they're talking about me, he thinks, and stands on his toes, craning his neck to catch a glimpse of the captain through the small window at the top of the door. His face is smooth, empty, and then it's cloudy, cold as steel. His heated reply can be heard through the door.

"I don't care what Scott says. Go over his head if you have to."

Jacob's voice was lower, impossible to make out. It sounded negatory, though.

"That's unacceptable! I'm gonna get those bastards on the phone right now."

"It won't help." Jacob speaks up, this time.

But the captain is going, and calls over his shoulder, "You and Roshin take the kid to his room, and my mother up to the flight rig. Go together. Make sure the damn door is locked, this time."

McKenzie's stomach drops. He goes back to the sink and finishes washing the last of the mugs the captain dropped in. There's nothing left, though. When Jacob comes in, Roshin is drying his own hands and Regina is going to shut the lights off inside the fridge and dry storage pantry, drain the sink.

Soon he is back in the white and grey hospital room, alone. He adds the supplies he smuggled to the bundle with the lantern and batteries in the bathroom cupboard. He knows he won't sleep easily. He curls up under the bed and can't focus on *The Fellowship of the Ring*.

What made the captain so angry? Something Jacob told him, pertaining to McKenzie. It has to be that they aren't coming to get him, of course. Leaving him to be monster bait on this boat, and the captain is angry for him, and for the hassle it is keeping him locked up and under surveillance at all times. He's never getting out of here. He's not surprised. He knew he would still be here when the creature came. He needs to be ready.

Chapter Five

In the morning the door opens and McKenzie jolts awake, only half-slept and banging his head on the metal slat of the bed above him. He hisses, rubs the sore spot. Peering out from under the hanging sheet, he sees the captain looking down at him, holding a tray out.

"Come out. Oatmeal and toast."

He marks his place in the book. He read until he couldn't keep his eyes open anymore, last night. He climbs up onto the bed, accepts the food. The oatmeal is instant, but not bad. It has apples and cinnamon in it. The captain watches him eat for a few minutes, looking troubled. He thinks he has to break it to the kid that he isn't getting rescued.

"Got word yesterday... From Jacob, first, but then I talked to some people myself who confirmed it... The company will not have you airlifted out. They consider it too high of a cost, and too much risk, since you were the only survivor of the wreck of the *Alessa*. I'm sorry, I really didn't anticipate this."

McKenzie shrugs, eats.

"Your aunt Genevieve is furious, she's appealing to the government and trying to stir up public interest. She's trying to crowdfund enough to hire a chopper herself, but the company doesn't have to let a private aircraft land with us to remove you, and they won't for security reasons…"

The only thing McKenzie finds surprising about any of this is that his aunt is trying so hard to get him out of here. This woman he has met only once in his life.

"I'm still going to get you out of here. It's just going to take a little bit longer. We'll fill her up with oil and dock back at the port in Alaska in a few weeks, and you're part of the crew until then. Alright?" He stands, holds out his hand, which McKenzie shakes. "Welcome aboard. Come on, and leave the tray. Got your work assignment."

He hops up. Hurrying into the hall to catch up to the captain, who moves with purpose, he is surprised when they take the stairs heading down, rather than up. Not going to the kitchen, then. The only things down there are the submarines, the store room and the prisoner.

The spacious, spooky coolness of the basement washes over McKenzie as he steps in, and he is suddenly aware of sweat prickling under his arms, chilling him. *There is no assignment,* he thinks. *He's locking me in with her so he doesn't have to deal with me anymore.*

The captain turns at that door, the way McKenzie knew he would, and holds it open, gesturing for the boy to go in. He waits.

McKenzie is frozen. If he runs, the captain will catch him, he knows it. There's nowhere to run, anyway. His father would tell him to be brave, make him proud, and it's the only thing that makes him move forward, step into the cold, little room.

The woman -Ceely- has her tools in hand and is tuning up the piece of equipment pulled from her yellow submarine. A mug of creamy coffee rests on the cot next to her. Her breakfast tray is empty next to the bars. She looks up, surprised, and scans the two of them. Swings her legs around and stands in a movement that is surprisingly fluid for someone her age, and her stance suggests she is ready for anything. She looks, momentarily, like a dangerous caged animal. A tiger. A lioness.

"What's this?" she asks.

The captain pulls out his ring of keys, steps up to the bars and unlocks the cell.

McKenzie automatically takes a step back toward the door.

"You're free. Relatively. I can't keep you down here indefinitely and I can't keep McKenzie in the med bay, so, two birds, one stone. You'll keep each other company. Look after each other."

Ceely's maternal mask sheds, she bares her teeth and snarls her reply. The change is instantaneous and shocking. "No. I'm not a goddamn babysitter!"

"You will watch him, though. You'll watch him like a hawk, because I've given instructions that no one else is to interfere if they see him wandering, or sneaking around, or anywhere he's not supposed to be. I'm making him your responsibility and yours alone. And you know as well as I do that some of these men would like to hurt him, just like they'd like to hurt you. If he gets away from you, he could end up hurt or dead, and you won't let that happen. You're too good of a person, of a mother, and you don't want it on your conscience."

She is more angry than anyone McKenzie has ever seen. She points a finger in the captain's face and seethes, "No! I won't do it! I refuse!" She spins on her heel and goes back into the cell, yanking the barred door closed with a clang and holding it so it doesn't just swing open again. "Lock me back up!"

"No."

"Lock it!"

He squares up to her and crosses his arms, as cold as she is hot. "No. You're due upstairs to start lunch prep. McKenzie knows his stuff, he'll be a good assistant for you. I expect you back to your old routine, providing three square meals for the crew, daily. Well-fed men are less likely to resort to rape, murder and mutiny, don't you think? Things have been dicey with the shit we've been serving."

Her voice drops to a furious whisper. "You're a son of a bitch. I know what you're doing and it's not going to work, you think you know me, but you don't."

"Then what are you so afraid of?"

She glances at the boy backed into the corner, observing the entire exchange with big eyes. Her face becomes a calm mask of aged, graceful womanliness again. "Fine. Let's go, McKenzie."

She marches out of the room, shoulders back and head high. But the sudden coolness is in direct conflict with the way that her fists are clenched at her sides. McKenzie knows the battle is over, but the war is not.

The captain gives the boy a push out of the room, after her. He murmurs, "Don't worry, she's not mad at you, she's mad at me. And she's actually really nice."

McKenzie feels ill. He's out of the room, but at what cost? He's going to be stuck in the kitchen all day, instead, stuck with her, locked in, from the way it sounds. And she is unstable, could snap at any moment.

Up the stairs they all trudge. The captain walks them through the galley, pushing the cart full of dirty dishes from breakfast as he goes. He checks inside the empty kitchen, even peering inside the walk-in fridge and freezer, the dry pantry. When he is satisfied, he nods to them, then leaves without a word.

Alone in the narrow kitchen with Ceely. She watches the captain go, her arms folded, and once he is gone, she sighs. Her hard, dark eyes turn to the boy.

When she finally speaks, she is no-nonsense. "I'm sorry you had to see all that. The captain and I are at an impasse, that has nothing to do with you, really, but you should understand he's trying to use you to keep me under control, and I'm not going to let that happen. If I have to keep an eye on you, I will, but that doesn't mean I'm going to be your friend. Think of me more as your boss. And your bodyguard, apparently." The words come out sounding bitter. She shakes her head. "Wash these dishes, please."

He starts filling the sink and gets to work, while she moves around the kitchen looking at what she has to work with. He can't relax, keeps an eye on her from the corner of his vision, and each time she passes by he feels himself stiffen. This is going to be his everyday, now, it seems. The only positive is that with plenty of time in the kitchen, he will be able to steal some more food, and maybe a knife and first-aid kit, too. And maybe she will let her guard down, eventually. Doze off or forget about him, as old people often do. Then he'll make a break for it, during a meal, hopefully when no one is on deck because they are all eating. Get to his supplies, get up on deck and lower a lifeboat or raft to the water and set out. The thought makes him feel nauseous but it's what he must do.

Ceely informs him that they'll make bacon, lettuce and tomato sandwiches for lunch, and potato salad, and some canned fruit cocktail. While she gets the bacon on sheet pans and into the oven, and potatoes and eggs boiling, he washes the dishes.

She gives him things to chop, and he chops them. Three feet away, up the length of the counter, she stands and mixes together an aioli for the sandwiches. Her shoulders are square, her jaw is clenched while she works, and she doesn't ever look over at McKenzie. Neither speaks. She only breaks the tense silence to give him instructions for assembling the potato salad, not that he needs them. She notices him add a few extra spices to the mix, sees him from the corner of her eye sniffing them first, making a face. They aren't as pungent as they should be; his father always stressed fresh ingredients, they're the building blocks, the foundation.

The sadness that pierces McKenzie makes his hands stop moving for a minute, where he is stirring the massive pot of potato salad with a wooden spoon. He doesn't like it, feels dizzy as he involuntarily is launched back to that lifeboat where he watched the monster crash into the ship, denting and tipping it and smashing it up. The screams in the distance, the halves of it sinking under the water, figures splashing and that long white snout full of prehistoric teeth rising out of the water and closing around them. He shuts his eyes and tries to catch his breath. The scent of mayonnaise, vinegar, sweet onion, black pepper and paprika bring him back to his reality. The lonely kitchen on the ghost ship, in between dead and alive, doomed and saved. His

294

nose prickles as tears rush up, his entire face reacts, his ears tingle.

"Taste test," Ceely declares, and pushes a spoon of the aioli into his mouth.

He blinks in shock, rolls the flavors around his mouth. It has kick. She has talent, or just dedication. This unhinged, potentially explosive woman knows her stuff and takes pride in what she does. Or maybe it's poisoned.

"Well?"

He nods.

"Alright, well, it's not going to spread itself on these sandwiches."

Sandwiches assembled, stacked on platters, potato salad and fruit cocktail in the serving pans. It all looks sort of cute, actually. Quaint. Surreal.

They wheel it out and the men troop in for lunch all at the same time. The captain comes, gets a mug of coffee. He walks around, seeming to just survey things, check in with the crew. His eyes keep drifting to Ceely, McKenzie notices where he has sat alone at a table. She doesn't look at the captain, not even for a second.

He makes his way over to the boy, who has a mouthful of fruit. "Everything alright?" Getting a nod, he sits. "What did you make? The potato salad? Looks good." He looks over at Ceely, again, who is sat with Jacob and Roshin, and the old man, Ralph. She is somehow more welcome among the crew than he is;

McKenzie actually feels sorry for the captain. He seems like he could use some friends.

Chapter Six

Dinner prep and service passed that first day of McKenzie's kitchen duties without any trouble. He and Ceely made chicken and dumplings and a cucumber and tomato salad for dinner, with him relegated mostly to the cleanup from lunch, cutting veggies for the salad, prepping ingredients to go into the broth which Ceely started early and simmered for a long time, letting the flavors grow while she made the dumplings.

There was no empty table at suppertime, so McKenzie sat with Jacob and Roshin, and Ceely joined them a minute later. The captain came in after the others, got a bowl of the chicken and dumplings and a scoop of the cucumber salad. He looked at their table, but must have decided he wouldn't be welcome.

He hung around afterward, though, and started washing dishes before the galley was even empty. Ceely did not go back to help him, instead wiping down tables and keeping herself moving. When the dishes were done, the captain shut off the lights in the kitchen, and they all moved silently out into the hall.

He took them to a room which turned out to be Ceely's quarters. She said only two words. "The boy?"

The captain opened the door, revealing a second cot on the wall opposite the primary bunk. She sighed, a hostile sound, and pushed McKenzie ahead of herself into the room, pulling the door closed sharply behind them. She had not slept there in some time, having been in the brig, and stood looking around the room. The captain had also moved her project onto the desk, the piece of equipment from her submarine, tools and all. A peace offering? She sits and goes to work with her back to the rest of the room.

McKenzie wonders what she would do if he spoke to her. Just ignore him, like a child sulking in the corner? He's almost curious enough to ask her something. Almost.

On the boy's new bed are *The Fellowship of the Ring*, a banana and two protein bars. So the captain found the bundle under the bathroom sink and decided not to let him keep the lantern and batteries, the tarp.

He reads for a while, then turns to face the wall and tries to sleep, although it's hard with her little tinkering noises and the light from her work lamp. At some point he dozes off.

He is still sleepy over a breakfast of banana pancakes, which McKenzie thinks are very delicious. For lunch, it's grilled cheeses and tomato soup. Ceely takes care with those, baking the bread and using a blend of cheeses, toasting them up nice. The soup comes from a can, it's concentrated but she tries to elevate it with herbs. It's much better than the ones they had a few days ago; he wonders if she has made an effort to show the captain up.

Breakfast and lunch are both simple meals, which she has done strategically, he thinks, in order to start the massive beef roast early. She takes care to cook it slowly, with butter and garlic and pepperoncini peppers, injecting the juices it stews in inside of it every couple of hours. The kitchen is sweltering the whole back half of the day.

Ceely ties her gray hair back with a red bandana, a little knot at the front over her left temple. In the blue coveralls much of the crew wears, she looks like Rosie the Riveter and makes McKenzie realize that she was once a beauty. She still has a strong jaw and taught cheeks for her age, a finely shaped brow over her dark eyes and a nose with just a bit of an upward turn at the tip. She looks like someone out of an old movie, from before faces all sort of started to look the same. She carries herself well, too, and cooks like she has something to prove.

McKenzie thinks that maybe she is aiming to out-cook the captain, as she injects the meat once again, crouching with a wince and taking hold of the enormous pan and lifting with her legs but still wincing again and setting it hard on the counter. There's a determination there that makes him think she might be able to do it. She adds potatoes and carrots and onions. She's trying to make the crew think of home, and of the good old days, trying to look like their mother or their first wife from long ago.

Why Ceely and the captain are so mad at each other, when they are so much alike, McKenzie can't imagine. He knows by now that it's not actually about him. He is just a pawn to them. His father taught him from a very young age that people would do so, and to look out. The captain had warned him, too. He had said, 'She's not mad at you, she's mad at me,' and, 'She's actually really nice.'

So he feels less tense around the old woman than he did the day before. She doesn't let him help much with the dinner prep. Cut these vegetables. Go and get me some more garlic. 'Please' is an afterthought. She makes dinner rolls from scratch, a floury, yeasty recipe that she has memorized, takes a lot of care with, brushing them with butter to crisp up the tops of them. She makes gravy with the drippings from the meat.

As she is whisking, he sits in one corner of the kitchen and reads. She had said only a sharp, 'No' when he tried to step out into the galley, even though it was empty.

She stops whisking suddenly, and turns her head, staring at him, wearing a troubled expression. He feels her gaze, and when he looks up, she sighs, looking upset. "You're peeling all over. Shedding. It's not very sanitary. Have you bathed since you came onboard?"

He shakes his head. It hasn't occurred to him.

"It must itch. You were just scratching your ears. Didn't he give you anything for the sunburn? Aloe?"

He shrugs. If anyone did, he can't remember. It does itch, especially on his ears and nose. His forehead, cheeks, chin and neck all burn somewhat constantly, and much worse if touched, so he avoids touching them. His arms are tender, too. His skin is cracked and peeling all over, he knows. He doesn't turn red like a white boy would, or a Latino boy, he supposes. Maybe that's why the captain didn't think of it. Or maybe he deliberately waited, knowing Ceely would recognize the need for it, and that worked to his advantage, somehow.

She certainly seems upset as she declares, "That's unacceptable. I'll make sure he gets you some, and you'll shower nightly, from now on, if you're going to work in the kitchen. And exfoliate. Rub your ears with a washcloth."

He nods, goes back to reading.

The topic of his dry, sunburnt skin is dropped until the crew arrives for dinner. Then storm clouds seem to roll over the woman's face. She marches out and McKenzie hurries after. He gets a front row seat of her accosting the captain with crew all around.

"You're supposed to be the ship's medical personnel and you couldn't see the skin peeling off the boy? Didn't you think of finding him some lotion? Or making sure he had a bath?"

He blinks, keeps his reply level. "I thought he'd been soaking long enough, I guess-."

"-In salt water. He's as dry as the Mojave Desert."

He sighs. His voice gets quicker. "I guess I was more concerned with him being in shock and so dehydrated that he almost died."

"Get him some aloe." Her voice is a furious whisper.

He turns and leaves the galley without another word.

Ceely brings the massive roast out, pushing the hotel pan on the cart. McKenzie doubts she could lift it and carry it all that way. Men clap at the sight. A couple rush to haul it onto the serving bar for her. She gives gracious thanks, tells them all to save room. In the hour before service, she had whipped up a chocolate cake with dark chocolate ganache on top, and McKenzie had hardly ever been so excited to eat something.

She had asked him before she got started, "Spice cake, or chocolate? I like spice cake, but the masses probably prefer chocolate."

He had given her a thumb's up.

"Chocolate it is."

And the captain had not made a dessert. Maybe he could cook but not bake. Baking is a much more rigid and disciplined pastime. Ceely made a big show of bringing it out, unveiling it to a humming of approval all around the room. The way that the men's eyes light up, McKenzie knows she has them in the palm of her hand. She cuts generous slices and passes them out personally. The captain is back, by then. He has made himself a tray, and sits with a few of the men, including Perry.

Ceely goes all around the outside of the room, serving cake to each man, going to the captain's table near the middle last. She passes pieces to every other person at his table, slowly, chit-chatting as she does, and with him watching her the whole time. Finally she puts a hand on her hip and takes a hard look at him.

"Dinner is delicious," he says, and offers her the white tube of lotion he has brought back with him.

She shakes her head. "Give it to him yourself. I'm not his mother." She scoops the last piece of cake out of the pan, plops it down hard on the empty square of the captain's tray, and wheels the cart around.

He finds McKenzie two tables over, meets his eyes, and throws him the lotion. The moist cake splattered on impact, and he licks some off of the back of his knuckle, dabs at the front of his shirt.

The two of them don't say anything as he helps with dishes at the night's end. The radio is switched on, and Ceely hums along at one point, then frowns. McKenzie is halfway through *The Fellowship of the Ring*. The captain asks if he is enjoying it as he walks them to their room, gets a nod. He says, "Goodnight," and Ceely does not reply, just shuts the door.

Then she points to the adjoined bathroom. "Shower. Give yourself a good scrub, then put that lotion on all over."

He does, even though his skin prickles and burns the whole time and for a while afterward. The new skin on his cheeks that is revealed by shedding the old is baby soft. He's like a snake, or a lizard. The aloe stings spectacularly on his ears and nose, feels cool and soothing after the stinging fades away. He puts on a pair of the crew coveralls, the smallest they could find and still hanging off of him, but they smell clean and block the worst of the chilling AC that constantly blows.

Ceely works at the desk again with her component of the sub. McKenzie covers himself with a blanket and sinks into a deep sleep with his moist, shaved head on the cool pillow.

Chapter Seven

In the morning, Jacob is the one who shows up to escort the two of them to the kitchen. "It looks like there's a big storm coming in, early tomorrow. We've been pretty lucky on that front, so far... The captain asks that you make something to bring up on deck to serve for breakfast and lunch. He has the crew working overtime to make up for what we'll lose. I'm to stick around and bring you up there."

"Alright. It'll be good to get outside."

She whips up a few dozen muffins, half blueberry, half cranberry-orange. She puts them on a cart with a couple pots of coffee, milk and sugar and butter. McKenzie doesn't get to help much, eats one of each type of muffin as soon as they come out of the oven and burns the roof of his mouth. He pours himself a cup of coffee, too, and Ceely raises an eyebrow at that, looks like she is going to object, but then doesn't. He tries it black at first -that's how his father took it- but it's bitter and awful, so he adds two sugars and a lot of milk, and then it's not so bad. Usually he wouldn't, knows it isn't good for him, his father never let him try it, but they are going up on deck. There may be a way for him to make his escape, and coffee gives you energy.

He doesn't have his supplies. Not the lantern, or the tarp, or a fishing pole. Not a flare gun. Not even the food he squirreled away. It will be another long, cruel stretch under the burning sun, through a harsh storm, from the sound of it. He can do it, is willing to try even though his body has been lulled into a false sense of security by these past few uneventful days.

This ship is still a great big sitting duck, full of monster bait. The only thing that really troubles him is the lack of a flare gun, of anything to signal to a chopper with to secure rescue. Life boats often come with them, or something like them and emergency rations, too. Life vests and rain slickers, too, for all he knows. He never got to check the one from the *Alessa*. It capsized immediately.

The idea of it happening again puts a pit in his stomach as the adults lug the cart up the stairs, and he follows. If being on the oil tanker is scary, it was almost as bad in the water. Not only not knowing what could be below at any moment, but toward the end when the visceral fear was no longer possible, when the arms of the ocean were gently hugging him, urging him to go under in his mother's voice... That is an eerie feeling that haunts him. He never will be the same again, after that. He's a person who has seen the end. He never wants to go back. He also thinks that if anyone can bring a ship through these waters and safely back to shore, the captain would be your best bet. It makes him take a hard look inward.

The air is a pleasant temperature, warm and not too muggy. Instead of that usual liquid dense in the air there is invisible crackling of electricity on McKenzie's skin. Coupled with the sugar and caffeine, it makes him feel wide awake and energized.

The morning is muted by the grey clouds rolling in, but what light there is feels good on his skin. He looks around and sees the mobile drilling platform, men walking around on top of its main level, a ring of steel and glass ten feet high, a flight deck full of controls visible within. It's a massive tower that reaches up out of the water, with a thick pipe coming out of it and descending below the gently lapping waves.

The captain's voice comes over the intercom. "Take ten for breakfast, use the bathroom if you have to, we're pushing through until lunch."

Crewmen troop over and start stuffing muffins in their faces, freshening up mugs of coffee. A few of them chat with Ceely, and McKenzie drifts away.

He has spotted Perry standing at the ship's bow, where its two sides meet in a point. To one side, an enclosed little room holds a chair and the controls to a massive gun mounted externally. Perry has his back to the crew. Stands with one leg hiked up on the railing.

His bald head catches the light. He hears the boy approach, turns and has the same contented smile on his face as usual.

"Hey, Ken. Storm coming. We're overdue. Haven't had a good blow the whole mission."

McKenzie likes storms back home, on land, but out here, he's not so sure. He must make a face, because Perry goes on.

"Storms are nothing to be afraid of. They're just the atmosphere sorting itself out. Air can have a lot of different densities, and temperatures, and when different currents meet, it becomes unstable, and we get a storm. And the rain, of course, comes from the sun drying up the sea, until the moisture is too thick. If you're worried about the thunder, you don't need to be. Loud noises only attract the creature when they're rhythmic, constant. Random booms drive the creature away, confuse it. It's our first and best line of defense. If I had to guess, I'd say it will dive down, deep to the ocean floor where it can rest in peace, tonight, until the storm is over. And right now, who knows what it's thinking, feeling? It probably has bigger fish to fry."

He has been peeling an orange all the while that he was talking, its citrus scent permeating the air. He offers a piece to McKenzie, who accepts, tips his head in thanks.

"You're welcome. Should head back over, report for duty." He gives no reason why.

McKenzie knows he has been dismissed. He pops the orange in his mouth, bites down, and juice floods over his tongue. He does not go back to Ceely right away, she and the captain are having a tense, not heated exchange. He goes to an empty spot at the railing on the ship's port side. There are no life boats hanging anywhere that he can see. Just panels clearly marked holding inflatable rafts.

He doesn't look too long at those, decides all at once he cannot go, just yet. Maybe after the storm. It will be good to know that they are there, the general layout, in case the sirens start to wail, and he has to make a fast escape.

He looks out at the horizon, the ripples throwing light more sharply further out, until they look like there is light coming from under the surface. He tries to see what the old man sees out there. The thing that gives him peace. Is it thinking of his family, back home? Or just how small it can make you feel, to not see land? Or maybe it's just emptying your mind to experience the beauty of it.

McKenzie doesn't last long, looking out at the horizon. It's boring. Ceely calls for him, anyway, and he goes over. The captain has taken an orange cranberry muffin and goes back to the drilling platform.

"Alright crew, back at it."

Men grumble and trudge back across the rope bridge.

"Crumbs everywhere," Ceely murmurs, wiping the cart off and discarding carelessly abandoned muffin liners into a small trashcan on the lowest level. Jacob waits, then goes to hold the door to the stairs. She pushes the cart, and McKenzie follows.

The loud grinding and whirring of machinery lurching to life pierces the quiet morning, makes McKenzie whip around to find the source; the drilling platform of course, and then he spins, scanning the horizon for the monster that he is sure is rushing toward them. His heart slams in his chest like a shrieking monkey bouncing off the bars of its cage, his legs move of their own volition, he stumbles back, away from the sound. It's no use, the whole place is connected to the drill, he can feel the reverberation in his feet.

The only thing in his mind is terror, he has to get away. Fuck the flare gun and food. His shoes squeak on the deck as he runs for the railing. Ceely has noticed his eyes go wide and moves to cut him off, but she's a little too slow. He wrenches one of the panels off the siding of the ship, gets his hands on the plastic bundle, then feels the hands on him and screams as he is swept off his feet. The ripcord on the life raft was already in one hand and he yanks it. It hisses and expands on the deck, while Ceely wrestles with the thrashing, screaming boy out of his mind with fear.

"Stop! You're okay!"

The captain has come scrambling over the rope bridge and runs across the deck. He says into his radio,

"Cut the drill!" His hands manage to stop McKenzie's kicking feet, and he gets his arms around his wriggling torso. "Give him to me!"

He's still screaming his throat raw as the captain carries him down the stairs, struggling the whole way to hang on to the wriggly boy. McKenzie is aware enough that he knows it when he is dragged into the med bay once again, and his screams turn to sobs. The captain sets him down hard on the bed. He is stunned for a moment, then goes right back to fighting Ceely as she takes over pinning him down.

"Hold him!" The captain opens the medicine cabinet, loads a syringe with a sedative, and moves back over to them. His hand is like an iron shackle pinning McKenzie's arm down, sticking the needle into the muscle.

The crying stops first, then the fight goes out of him slowly. He slips into unconsciousness and the two adults sigh as they relax, crowded close on the single bed, sweating and catching their breath.

"He doesn't like the drilling," Ceely states.

"Yeah…"

"He's pretty messed up."

"Seems that way."

He's looking at her heaving chest, watches as she pushes her hair back behind her ear. His eyes land on her mouth, and her eyes meet his and realize it, and then she pushes herself back and swings around to sit on the far edge of the bed.

"So what now?"

"We leave him here for a few hours and I escort you back to the kitchen."

"We'd better hurry, so you can get back on deck." She stands, but he catches her hand as it slides away on the sheets.

"I'm sorry, you know?" His voice comes out sounding rough. He clears his throat, looks down. "I wish things had gone differently in your life, even if it meant that you'd never met me. But you did, you're here now, and you can't honestly expect me to watch you destroy yourself and do nothing to try to stop you."

She removes her hand from his. "That is what I expect. You have no right to ask me to let go of my children. I'll never do that. If I did that, I wouldn't be a person worthy of your concern. Do you understand that?"

He tips his head in acknowledgement, but his lips are pressed into a tight line. "Kid's messed up."

"Yeah. And so am I. You can take us or leave us, for as long as we're around, but you have to take us as we are. Don't try to make us into something that we're not."

"Understood."

Chapter Eight

When McKenzie wakes, his eyes and mind are bleary. Someone is gently shaking him. The captain.

"There you are. How are you feeling?"

He sits up on the bed in the infirmary. *Nuts*, he thinks. *Back here again.* At least there is no needle in his arm this time, although he sluggishly starts to remember them jabbing him with something. Ceely and the captain. A sedative, that was what it was. That's why his arms and legs are heavy, he still feels tired even though he has just been asleep, it's still daylight outside but not for much longer. The sea is roiling with heavy grey clouds overhead, the sun is a single brilliant spot of gold dipping under the horizon.

The captain tries again. "McKenzie?"

McKenzie blinks, shrugs.

"Alright. You're a little foggy right now, but that'll pass. Let's go get some dinner. You missed lunch, you must be hungry."

Next thing McKenzie knows, he is seated in the galley with a beautiful fillet of white fish in front of him, on a bed of tomatoes, onions and olives. It's coated with a buttery herb blend and decorated with charred lemon slices. Mediterranean fish. It's beautiful and delicious, but McKenzie feels like he isn't really appreciating it as he eats. He's just going through the motions, and quickly. There are eyes on him, the galley is quieter than usual. He wants to get out of there, even if it's just to the back to wash dishes.

Outside, thunder booms in the distance.

He thinks the crew is not just uncomfortable around him, or thinking that he is weird after his outburst, but they are also nervous about what is coming. And if these hard men are nervous -when many of them are seasoned seamen- McKenzie realizes that he should be, too. He can't really muster it, though. He goes to the back and starts to fill a sink.

Ceely and the captain bring dishes. She pulls out a massive turkey from the freezer to start defrosting. He helps rinse and stack the dinner trays to dry. They're done in no time. Shutting off lights, they all step out into the hallway.

There, the captain stalls. "Think I should keep an eye on McKenzie tonight. There could be side effects of the sedative, or the storm could set him off again."

He hates when people talk about him like he's not there. He shuts his eyes, sways a little in place. He wants to lay down.

314

Ceely murmurs, "So you're taking him, then?"

"Only, it wouldn't be appropriate for me to have him in my quarters overnight, unsupervised."

"Mm-hm. I guess I'll have to supervise, then."

They all troop to the captain's office, and upon stepping inside, McKenzie sees a cot is already laid out against the back wall. Past the desk, under the window. He goes to it and collapses. His heavy eyes close.

A few seconds later, he feels hands on him, and it startles him. His heart jackhammers in his chest, but it's only Ceely draping a blanket over him. Her old hand is soft and cool as it rests on his forehead. "You're a little warm..." She strokes his head, where hair has just started to sprout. It's a surprisingly tender gesture that makes him think of his mother. He closes his eyes and feels calm again. "The bathroom's right there, if you need it."

They both disappear into the other room.

In the dark little office, the sound of rain pelting the window and the metal side of the ship is a constant pinging, like static. Thunder booms and when lightning flashes, the shapes of the chair, the coatrack in the corner start to look like squat monsters, looming figures. McKenzie squints in the low light, his heart starting to pump harder.

In the other room, the adults have a quiet conversation.

"What is that thing you're working on? For the sub?"

She doesn't answer for a long moment. "Like a big taser. Two barbs fire from the harpoon guns, embed in the creature, cables connect them to the ship, creating a closed circuit. Rig up an extra battery. Fry that son of a bitch."

"Why, though?"

"When it sent me forward, it used electricity. I think if I give it a shock, I can spur it to replicate the event… send me through time again. Send me back, maybe."

"Or send you another thirty years forward, to when you're a hundred years old, if you even survive another round. The world will have taken some shocking, awful new turns by then, I'm sure. Manmade horrors beyond your comprehension. You'll be bald and toothless and incontinent…"

She seems to speak out loud what he hasn't: "And I won't have you."

"…You'll have me. If I'm alive, you'll have me. Even toothless and incontinent."

She brushes past the declaration. "I hate hypotheticals. If it's not the life you lead, then, in the end it doesn't matter."

"Your entire premise is based around a hypothetical, though. And you're taking an awfully big risk."

"Trial and error. It's a necessary part of the scientific method. There was a doctor in the 1700's who infected himself with syphilis to try and prove his own hypothesis. If people didn't take those swings for the greater good, we wouldn't have the knowledge that we do today. There would be unnecessary loss of life."

"You're grasping at straws to try to rationalize this. A doctor who gave himself syphilis? You're a seventy-year-old woman who has experienced something horrifying, you're traumatized and acting irrationally so that you don't have to grieve."

"You've got it all figured out, huh?"

The silence is heavy in the time between the lightning strike and the clap of thunder in the distance. The churning waves make the ship roll underneath McKenzie, who is somewhere between awake and asleep. His head spins, he might as well be rolling down a grassy hill in the Shire.

The captain says, "Time heals all wounds."

Ceely says, "Cliché."

"It's not," he insists. "It's the wisdom of the ages. A week ago, you were furious with me for throwing you in the brig."

"Maybe I still am. Maybe this is all a ploy so I can slit your throat in your sleep and commandeer your ship." There's a smile in her voice.

"You're rushing this so that you don't have time to heal. Or to realize how tired you are. Or how happy I could make you, if you'd let me."

"You have no idea what it's like to lose your children. That's a kind of pain time can't heal. I know by now that I could learn to live with that pain, make room for it, but it will never go away. And there is a

317

chance that I can save them and get my life back. It's a small chance, I know... One in a million, maybe. Practically hopeless. But I can never stop trying. I'm their mother."

McKenzie feels ill, the ship is heaving beneath him, and images of the ship breaking in two and sinking to the ocean floor fill his mind. What's worse? To be dragged down with it, with the air escaping and the water rushing in, and a few torturously long minutes knowing that the end is here? Or getting to the raft, the only survivor, a small toy bouncing on waves of dark water as tall as sky scrapers, and then in a flash of lightning it appears, its shiny head lifting up out of the water, its white snout arching downward and closing around you... He shudders and shakes, he's not sure if he's having a reaction to the sedative or if he's just getting himself all worked up. He misses his father. He lets the tears fall.

A long silence. The captain sighs, defeated. When he speaks, it's with the cadence of an order, he's reasserting himself as the captain, the one in control. "Come here. Lay down with me, while we still can."

"Yes, Sir... You were right about one thing: I am tired."

"Me too. And scared."

"Time will take care of that for you. You have a lot of years left."

"Too many."

"Hush."

*

The sun rises red in the eastern sky, the waves
having died out completely and the air tepid, still. It
gives the impression that there could not have been a
storm last night, with waves that pummeled the ship,
winds howling and carrying spray across the empty
deck, whistling through split seams around the windows
and keeping everyone awake, making Ceely and the
captain hold each other tighter, and each getting up to
check on McKenzie twice during the night.

Just after dawn, the crew is already on deck,
looking like a horde of zombies. They chug coffee, and
Ceely is prepared for this, has every pot and carafe on
the *Baton Rouge* full. They munch through bacon, egg
and cheese on toasted English muffins -no bacon for
Roshin- with sluggish determination. The captain tries
to rally everyone.

"Extra systems checks today, we have to make sure
there was no damage from the storm."

McKenzie eats a sandwich, skips the coffee this
time. He carries *The Fellowship of the Ring*, as he
always does lately. wanders over to where Perry stands
on the bow with a ripe pear, mopping juice from his
lined mouth as he turns to greet the boy. He is smiling,
at ease, even with the natural bags under his eyes darker
than usual.

"A red sky in the morning is a sailor's warning, you know. Old superstition. If I didn't know better, I'd say we were heading for another storm. Of course, in *Lord of the Rings*, the elves consider a red sunrise to be a sign that blood has been shed, the previous night. A sign of danger past..." The old man's face turns scrutinizing as he looks at the boy. He looks around, making sure that no one will hear what he says, next. Although he keeps his tone light, there is a warning carried on them.

"I always liked reading, especially when I was a boy. Reading helped me figure out who I was, what my place was in this world. I related to Tolkien's Elves. They were the first children of Ilúvatar, they invented poetry and music, were called *Eldar*, or People of the Stars. They had special bonds with nature, living simple lives in the woods, giving back what they took, harming no one. Until outside interference corrupted some, and called others to war to save the Earth that they loved.

"Melkor, and Sauron. The Dark Lords. And man. The greed of men almost brought the Earth to ruin, in Tolkien's world as well as in our own." Perry turns the husk of his pear around in his hands, and kneels, so he can lower his voice. "This place is like Mordor. Like Saruman's tower in Isengard. The dark forces are using this place to rape Mother Earth for their profit. Just like the people who owned the yacht that your father worked on. The creature from the deep isn't being summoned, this time. If this ship is shattered like that

320

one, it will spill its filth into the sea, and that's the last thing we want. It has happened before... too many times.

"Death is coming, though. Quickly, and silently and thoroughly, it's coming to every man and woman who operates this ship. So I'm going to ask you something, Ken, and I want you to answer carefully, because it's the most important question of your entire life."

McKenzie is covered in cold sweat. He is frightened, but also intrigued, excited. Adults never talk to him this way, about serious things. He thinks he knows what is coming.

"Are you an Elf? An innocent, and a child of nature, for whom danger has already passed? Or are you one of them, a man, a sailor, and an instrument of Earth's destruction? Doomed."

He wants an answer. McKenzie lifts the book, starts to tap the cover, but Perry's voice calls out a sharp, "Speak!" And makes him jump halfway out of his skin.

"Elf," he says, and his voice surprises himself. It's a rusty croak from his unused throat.

"Good. Head back to the kitchen witch, now. I'll come find you when it's time."

He goes, feeling wobbly and full of guilt. He agreed with the things Perry said, wants to be like him, so calm and unaffected, but he feels like he just made a deal with the Devil.

Chapter Nine

With the massive turkey still more or less frozen, burgers are what is for dinner. Well-seasoned, charred up nicely, served with the usual toppings plus a spicy aioli and grilled onions if a person should so choose. The sides are a salad and a vat of golden brown, crumbly and gooey homemade macaroni and cheese.

McKenzie wants it all at first, and builds the perfect cheeseburger and a full tray along with it, but then he loses his appetite when he sits down with Ceely and the captain, his mother and her boyfriend, Jacob and Roshin all crowded together. They talk about when they will fill the tanker; tomorrow or the next day. They talk about going home, and what that will mean for each of them.

Regina and Aaron are giddy like teenagers, they say that they'll move in together once they're back in Alaska. They know it's soon -they only met a few weeks before the start of the mission, entering into their mandatory quarantine, but she had to let her own room go to take the job, and they want to give it a shot.

Jacob is unsure as he gives his answer. He looks at Roshin, looks down, looks at everyone else, and blushes as he speaks. "I'm due back at headquarters after a few days of rest and recouperation. I'll be glad to see my cat, Nicodemus, and, if I'm being honest, I might be looking at a promotion pretty shortly. This mission should make me the standout. It's boring work, but it seems like what I was made to do."

Roshin watches him intently as he speaks, then his pinkish lips with earthy undertones purse in deep thought. He doesn't speak to what the future might hold for him, and gazes sheepishly redirect around the table, for someone, anyone to speak.

Jacob prompts, "What about you, Captain? You've almost beat the odds, it seems, three missions under your belt. Will you be seeking a more comfortable assignment, or is it more danger and daring?"

The captain smiles a little at that. "I'm not sure. I've never been good at planning ahead. My commission is probably going to my mothers, mostly, keeping them comfortable. I might be eligible for some safer jobs, that would make them happy-."

"-And me too," Regina chimes in.

He looks at Ceely from the corner of his eye. "-Or maybe I could find something closer to them, more permanent, in a different field, even. Settle down." It all sounds up in the air, like he's not sure of anything. It's surprising, coming from him, who is always so confident. McKenzie supposes that the future can frighten anyone.

When prompted, Ceely sips coffee. "My repairs to my sub are almost finished. I don't think I'll be travelling back to Alaska with you all, though I'm sure it's lovely... My business lies in warmer waters."

"Somewhere tropical?" Regina speculates. "I suppose you could buy your own island, and drink mojitos on the beach for years, with the kind of money you're owed. Private villa, maid service, cabana boys." She nudges the grey-haired woman, who manages the ghost of a smile, and shrugs, and lets her go on believing it might be so.

Ceely is the one who remembers to include McKenzie. "McKenzie is heading to the airport after the ship docks in Alaska, isn't he?"

"Yes," the captain agrees. "I'll probably take him there, myself. Put him on a plane to New Zealand, his aunt will be waiting and hopefully him and his cousins will get to see the sets from *Lord of the Rings*, pretty soon."

His burger is mostly uneaten on his plate. None of them know that none of these plans, these hopes are going to materialize. None of them know that Death is coming. It makes him feel sick. He looks at Perry, sitting a few tables away and smiling, listening to someone tell a funny story, and eating his own burger. How can he do it?

If that inner calm leads to this, McKenzie thinks, maybe he doesn't want it after all.

Ceely and the captain wash dishes, but McKenzie can't read, just sits and watches and chews peeling skin off of his lips until they bleed. Ceely asks if he's alright on the way back to the captain's quarters -where apparently they will sleep again with no pretense- and he only shrugs. He knows he should speak, warn them, but the words won't come out.

Perry had to scare it out of him, and now has scared him into silence again, without even being around. He lays down when urged to, in the captain's office, on the cot under the window, and pulls the covers around him. He watches Ceely and the captain retire to his bedroom, closing the door behind them. He thinks he will never see them again.

What will Death look like, when it comes? Will it at least be quick, peaceful? Or will it be white water whipping up, and screams, as it was for McKenzie's father, and the rest of the people onboard the *Alessa*?

His father wasn't bad, he knows. He was a man who made a few mistakes, cracked under the pressure society placed on him, and had to take a job that few would want. Just like a lot of these people. Not all, maybe. But most. His father did not deserve his fate, McKenzie knows, and neither do they.

But what can he do, against something like Death? Perry is going to summon it, the way that the Asian man summoned the creature. And McKenzie is only a boy.

He sits awake in the dark. Several hours pass that way, but it feels like only minutes. By then he has started shivering, gone numb and still, and started shivering again three times over. Just when he starts to think he can't keep his heavy eyelids open anymore, the tiny scrape of tumblers from a key turning in the door make his heart leap into his throat. He sits bolt upright in bed.

The door swings open in perfect silence, and though McKenzie is sure by then that it will be Death itself coming from the hallway, the big figure is Perry's. In the dark, he raises a finger to his lips. *Sh.*

Then he motions for McKenzie to come.

The boy puts his feet on the floor, which is cold even through his socks, with the AC blasting like usual. He leaves his shoes. He brings only the book. Tiptoeing out into the silent hall, Perry shuts the door behind them.

They head up the stairs and onto the deck, where the night air is warm and a little foul. The clouds have mostly dispersed and over the ship, stars shine brightly and beautifully. Some people can navigate by the stars. McKenzie knows only one thing about it: the North Star is at the tale of the little dipper, but it's all he really needs to know. The nearest land is north.

There is a raft already inflated, Perry shows him. He feels timid as the man guides him over to the railing, but he sees a rope ladder leading down to the little boat riding the gentle waves. There are supplies inside, rations and water bottles and an orange case that McKenzie is sure contains a flare gun. Everything he needs to make it.

Perry nudges him when he hesitates at the railing. As he swings his feet over, *The Fellowship of the Ring* under his arm, his hands are clammy on the rungs. It feels wrong. It's what he has wanted, but he's not sure it's the right thing anymore. Leaving them all behind.

"Good luck, Ken."

He reaches the raft, it's soft under his feet and then sinks and shifts uncomfortably below him. He feels nauseous. The ship looks immense, much larger than it ever felt while he was trapped on it. It looks sturdy, all that metal, it looks safe compared to the endlessly stretching water, tame though it currently is.

It's an illusion, and he knows it. Safety is an illusion either way, whatever he does. Perry has gone from the railing. McKenzie is alone again. He disconnects the tether keeping the raft near the ship. He does not pick up the small oars and begin to row, but the water slowly starts to carry him out, away from the *Baton Rouge.*

He thinks of the Fellowship. Crossing Middle Earth together, climbing mountains together and, in the chapter he is currently reading, descending into mines of Khazad-dûm. They are bonded, sworn to each other, would never abandon each other. And if he hasn't sworn any oath to the people on the ship, he is in their debt. They pulled him out of the water, when he was almost dead. Actually, it was Perry who dove in and saved him. But the captain saw to his recovery, and Ceely stopped his itching and tucked him in, and the pair of them cooked delicious meals with him and kept him busy, tried to keep him safe in their own way.

The waves gently lap at the plastic of the raft. He is drifting outward. North, that's lucky.

Soon it will be too late to go back. He feels paralyzed, unable to think clearly, or move. What would Aragorn do? That's too much. He would come in, sword swinging, and save the day... What would Frodo do?

Chapter Ten

In the night, Ceely wakes with cold feet; Caesar has stolen the covers once again. She puts her cold feet on his, searching them out under the blanket, and he grumbles an objection, half asleep, even as he pulls her closer and nuzzles his nose into her hair. She almost lets the strong arm around her lull her back to sleep, but then something nags at her; maternal instinct. For a moment she is transported back in time, to when Josie was a colicky baby. But as she sits up, the present crashes in around her; she is on the ship, her daughters are dead. McKenzie is in the other room, and although she doesn't want to care for the boy, there is something about seeing a child sleeping and safe that her body needs at the moment.

Only, when she leans out of the captain's sleeping quarters, the cot under the window on the far wall of his office is empty. The rest of the room is dark and still. She checks the bathroom, the door is open and there's no one inside. Her heart starts to pound faster in her chest, she hurries into the bedroom and shoves the sleeping man, then starts pulling on her shoes.

"Caesar, wake up! McKenzie is gone."

He sits up, rubbing sleep from his eyes. His words come out slurred. "That's impossible."

She hurries to the door and tries it, but it seems to still be locked from the inside. She calls, "Hurry!"

Caesar comes, keys in hand, he tries them in the door and the handle turns, but the door itself does not move. He puts his shoulder to it and shoves. He speaks aloud what they both suddenly realize. "Something is wrong."

"Yeah. Could he have disabled the lock somehow?"

"It's not the lock, it's the door. It's like it's blocked or jammed." He puts his weight into hitting it once again. It goes nowhere.

"Is there another way out?"

"Smash the window and get a rope around the railing? Maybe you could fit through and climb up to the deck."

She huffs. "Have you seen my hips?"

"Once or twice… Gonna have to be the ventilation system, then."

"Let's move the desk."

They push the solid and massive desk to the far wall with a few shoves and determined grunts. He knocks everything off of it with a sweep of his arm, jumps up and gives her his hand. Up she goes and they stand close together on top of the desk, inspecting the metal, mesh mouth of the ventilation duct. A screw in each corner, rusted.

"Grab and pull."

They lace their fingers inside the grate and pull. The metal bends outward, groans as they strain. One screw rattles, but Ceely and Caesar let go in the same instant, catching their breath.

"Again."

Without having to discuss it, they focus on the weak corner. The thin metal stretches, Ceely winces as it digs into her fingers, but she pulls, and Caesar is so tense that veins stand out on his tattooed arms, they shake at the elbows. Sweat dots his face. It snaps off all at once, and she stumbles, would go over the edge of the desk and hit the ground if Caesar didn't snag her wrist. The grate hangs by one corner, swings down.

"Up you go," he says. He kneels and cups his hands.

She takes the boost, even as she's shaking her head and muttering, "Here we go."

It's hard work pulling herself into the ventilation shaft. The metal is cold, slick on her coveralls, she has to shimmy to get her bottom-heavy back-half into the tight, square space. She can't get on her hands and knees, has to just lay on her stomach and use her forearms to pull, her toes to push herself forward a few inches at a time, like a worm.

"Coming up," Caesar calls, when she has moved out of the mouth.

The metal of each section dips under their weights and snaps back into place as they shimmy forward. It's taxing work and getting warm in the cramped space. Sweat prickles on Ceely's crown and starts to drip down her face; the AC is not on, for once.

She passes over the grate of the next room; that's only Caesar's bedroom. Jesus. She shimmies on, panting and sweating. She feels seventy years old -give or take- feels truly old for the first time. Has to stop and catch her breath when she reaches the intersection of the ducts and can turn left to find her way toward the hall. It's tight around the corner.

It's a long drag to the midpoint of the wide, white hallway. It's empty below as she peers through the grate. In the distance, she can see a bar welded across the door to Caesar's office.

"I'm at a grate."

"Keep moving, I'm coming."

"Someone wants to keep us in."

"What?"

Ceely has wiggled further up, keeping her toes at the edge of the grate. Looking over her shoulder at Caesar, who is army crawling toward her in the dark air shaft, she says, "A metal rod welded to the door."

"You don't think McKenzie could have done that, do you?"

"No. Welding is too tricky for an eight-year-old."

"Alright, get your foot on there." He takes a few deep breaths, while Ceely twists in the dark and gets the sole of her boot on the corner of the grate. Caesar pushes himself up, palms on the metal mesh and broad shoulders bending the metal top of the ventilation shaft upward. He doesn't count, just orders, "Push."

They push. He pushes as hard as he can, sweat dripping off the tip of his nose and falling through the grate, to the hallway floor. Ceely pushes at first, then bangs her heel down on the corner, trying to make something snap. It's no use.

Caesar stops pushing and collapses into a heap, head spinning. "Shit. I pulled something." He rubs his shoulder.

"Are you dizzy?"

"Yes, and my head is pounding. It's hot, too."

"This one isn't budging, should we try another?"

"Unless we wanna die in here."

"Try one of the rooms, or to the next grate in the hallway?"

He thinks for a moment. "The vent in our room slopes down, that's probably for easy access, and condensation might drip onto the grate and corrode the screws over time. The one at the opposite end of the ship is probably the same. The library. We'll try there."

He shimmies backward, Ceely follows. The shafts don't run length wise up the hallway. At the corner he backs down the shaft the way they came, then starts crawling up the entire length of the ship. Ceely lags behind, breathing heavily, worried that she may have a heart attack. She is dizzy, and resting doesn't make the feeling go away. She feels like she can't breathe; it's the air. It has turned poisonous, smells of combustion, faintly burning fuel.

She starts to think she won't make it. That it will all end in that fucking metal coffin, and none of it will have mattered. Her building the submarine, shooting the creature, getting transported here, through time. Meeting Caesar. Fighting him every step of the way. Her struggle to get back to her girls, their bodies in a chest freezer... It's all pointless, it's all random, there was no greater meaning to any of it, if she dies in a ventilation shaft, poisoned like a rat. She's not sure she ever thought any of it had meaning, hasn't thought about it. These are the kind of things that just don't matter, anymore, once you've lost your children, but she still feels indignant, somehow.

"I can see light," Caesar calls. "Keep moving."

"I can't." Her arms have lost all strength, they're limp noodles.

"You have to. Come on, we're almost out."

Black dots swarm over her vision. She presses her face to the cool metal underneath her.

"Hey. Ceely." Caesar shimmies backward, he tries to turn in the small space but can't. He cranes and folds himself as much as he can, reaches, and his fingers can only just touch hers. She is nearly unconscious, grumbles when she hears her name, but her fingers stretch out and her hand fits into his. He pulls, dragging her although it's not easy, and she groans again as she slides up the metal ventilation shaft. He drags her into his lap. Pressed together, they hardly have an inch to move, but he manages to push them both toward the grate with his feet, then gets a hand through the grate and drags them the last stretch.

Both of their faces crowded at the end of the vent, he touches her cheek and gives her a little shake. "Hey, we made it. We're almost out, but I need your help. Ceely!"

She doesn't stir. She is still breathing, faintly.

He braces himself, gets both hands on the vent, which doesn't slope downward the way that he thought it would. It just ends; he can see shelves of books and boardgames, tables and cozy armchairs all in faint glow of twilight coming from the window. He can see the door that would lead to salvation. He takes a few seconds to breathe. It does him no good, the air is tainted. He pushes, face contorting, muscles crying out, the thing bends but doesn't give, nothing snaps. He realizes all at once that no human being could push their way out, he yanks and wrenches and finally bangs his fists into the metal at each corner, hoping just one screw will bust, breaking skin and maybe his knuckles, drawing blood that drips down onto the dusty metal.

A last-ditch effort, he shouts out of the vent. "Help! Anybody!"

He winces; his head throbs. The desperation sinks in, it's all over. He pulls Ceely closer, squeezes her tight against him. He can't save her, but he was never going to; at least they are together at the end. He gives her a kiss on the head and hopes she feels it somehow.

Eyes shut, he relaxes into his fate.

A scratching at his ear and his brain draws him up, out of the oblivion. His vision is blurry, but he blinks in the dark and looks out of the grate once again. And is startled to find a small, dark face looking back at him.

"McKenzie! What the hell is happening?"

He doesn't answer, just keeps unscrewing the grate, it takes a very long minute, then the thing falls and clatters to the ground. Caesar scrambles out, then drags Ceely out after him, it's tricky lowering her while standing on a chair and with a hurt shoulder is tricky, clumsy work but then they are on the ground, and he is shaking her again to rouse her.

The air is not so foul in the med bay, with the door open out to the hallway.

"Ceely, come on. Wake up."

McKenzie appears with a tank of oxygen; not the kind stocked in the med bay, but the kind for scuba diving.

"Good job!" He straps the plastic mask to her face, and sees her breath fog it up a moment later. It eases his fear enough for him to look around, at the open door, and his mind starts to turn again. McKenzie didn't do all of this. He came to save them, he knows what is happening. "Hey! Who did this?" When the boy stays silent, blinking and wide eyed, he prompts him, "Come on."

"Perry."

"Do you know where he is?"

McKenzie shakes his head.

"Okay. You stay with her."

He sets her head down gently, then climbs to his feet and runs up the hall. Pounding on the door to Jacob's room, he finds his key and flings it open. "Jacob!"

Inside the room, two figures jolt upright in the bed. Roshin is a dark blur, jumping to his feet and flinging himself against the wall in a defensive stance. Caesar takes in the sight, meets Jacob's gaze as he is still trying to wake up, sitting on the bed. Throws him the keys.

"Get everyone awake and out of their rooms. Bring them up on deck. Ceely's in the med bay with McKenzie, bring them too, and hurry!"

He runs up the hall, to the stairs, and takes them, going down. The AC hasn't been on the whole while that they were crawling through the ducts, but the ship's engines are on, and they shouldn't be. He thinks he knows what Perry did, hooked up the ship's exhaust to the ductwork. Carbon Monoxide could have killed all of them while they slept, if Ceely hadn't woken up.

At the door to the lowest level, he slows down. Keeping his eyes peeled, his stance wide and his hands ready, he eases in. The cavernous room is dark. He doesn't switch on the lights, taking a few seconds for his eyes to adjust.

The door to the engine room has been axed and kicked in, it hangs off of one hinge. Perry must have managed to get his hands on a replica of the captain's master key, which could control almost all other locks on the ship, but not the engine room. The engines are too important; too expensive. It was Caesar's worst fear that the engines might be tampered with, and that they would all be dead in the water. It would have been disastrous, emasculating. He changed that lock out with his own two hands, their first day at sea. Good thing; if Perry hadn't lost precious minutes taking an axe to the thick metal of the door, they might all be dead, poisoned, right on schedule.

The engines are massive and unharmed. No figure moves in the dark, there is no whisper of breath, Caesar can feel no eyes on him. Perry has come and gone. The only change to the engine room is that the exhaust has been rerouted up into the ductwork, as Caesar had expected. It's a sloppy job, the exhaust hose is ripped from the outlet on the wall, not carefully disconnected, the bolts are still in place, but mangled. It is duct taped to mouth of the ventilation system, while the outlet is left uncovered, a gaping hole looking out at the dark waters and grey sky of the twilight, lightening out to the east.

Caesar rips down the hose, drags it to the outlet, and wedged the edges back inside of the remaining pieces.

338

It's not a good seal, but it's much better than it was. He can ask Ceely to repair it, later, if she is recovered.

He heads out of the engine room, up the first set of stairs. Men are standing in the doorways of their sleeping quarters, some pulling on clothes as they step out into the hall. Jacob and Roshin have woken them all, and probably gone to collect Ceely.

Caesar looks down the hall, but he can't linger; he thinks he knows where to find Perry. The murderous rat. Taking the stairs up in a few long steps, he rushes past crewmen who are still confused as to what is happening, and up the stairs, heading for the deck.

Dark fury is taking hold of him. His fists are clenched, hungry.

Chapter Eleven

The air on deck is salty, a relief after the fetid air below. A couple of men are already on deck, and start to ask him what's going on. He waves them away, marching up the length of the ship, to where Perry stands at the bow. The older man hears the footsteps approach, and turns, folds his arms. He doesn't hold his usual piece of fruit, apparently having lost his appetite as he set himself to the task of killing more than a dozen people in their sleep.

"Captain," he says, while Caesar is still approaching, "Very well done." He holds his hands out, as though he is ready to be cuffed.

But Caesar winds back and throws a punch in the same motion that he steps up to the bow, sending the bigger man reeling away. The only thing that keeps him going over and into the ocean is the captain, catching his arm. He turns and heaves the man onto the deck, and he goes down, sputtering.

"Most unkind." He spits blood, his eyes are incredulous and amazingly judgmental for an attempted mass-murderer as he looks up at the captain. "I surrender."

Caesar kneels and seizes hold of the older man's shirt, yanking him upward and cocking back his fist again, just to see him flinch. He stops himself, shuddering as he exhales. If his knuckle wasn't broken before, it definitely is now. From the bald man's self-righteousness, he deduces his motives. "You're an environmentalist."

"A protector of the Earth, by any means."

"Yeah? You can tell it to a jury. Move."

More men have gathered, and still look on in confusion. McKenzie comes up on deck and freezes in the doorway as Perry marches, with the captain's hand tight on his collar. The old man smiles a bitter smile, seeming unbothered by his impending imprisonment.

"A sneaky little human, after all."

Caesar gives him a shove. On the stairs heading down, they meet Roshin coming up. His face, usually showing nothing, flashes a deep concern. At the sight of it, Caesar freezes, his heart drops.

"Ceely?" She is old, he thinks. She was more afflicted by the carbon monoxide than the others. Did she die on the floor of the med bay, without him?

"She came to," Roshin says, "Then raced down to the basement. Jacob was trying to stop her and asked me to find you."

Caesar takes the rest of the stairs in one leap, dragging Perry with him, now. "Move it!" The older man stumbles, but climbs to his feet quickly and keeps pace with the captain, heading down another flight of stairs and once again into the basement, which is cool, but bright and loud. The overhead lights are on, and an arch of white light along with a fine mist of salty water seeps in as a wave strikes the main bay doors, closing on a grinding gear. Jacob hurries over.

"She launched, I'm sorry, I couldn't stop her."

"Dammit. Move!" He shoves Perry toward the brig, and barks orders at Jacob, who follows. "Get everyone to their posts, now!" The clerk goes, while Caesar painstakingly locks the prisoner up in the little cell, where he once locked Ceely. He can't believe or accept that she is gone, though she told him that she would be, dozens of times, in so few words. She saw her opportunity, and she took it.

He races back up on deck, where men await orders. "Disconnect from the rig! Disconnect everything!"

A few of the men are standing at the railing, staring in the distance, where Ceely's yellow submarine slinks through the water, faster than it was when first they spotted it, out that same way. She heads away from them, now, and the vessel sinks lower, disappearing under the waves.

An alarm blares. Caesar is confused for a second; he has forgotten all about his responsibilities. He has left his handheld device in his quarters, but the same sensors are linked to the mounted panels in the control room, along with the ship's wheel. He races into the little room, feeling eyes on him as the crew awaits more specific orders.

Jacob follows. "Captain?"

He speaks his thoughts aloud. "There's a frequency transmitting nearby. Moving northwest. Ultrasonic and pulsing rhythmically. Ceely's submarine, it has to be."

"Ultrasonic? And rhythmic? That will draw the creature."

"That's the point." He bows his head a moment, it's still pounding. It's so far out of the purview of his responsibilities to go chasing after her that his next move may lose him his job and commission, even if he returns with a full tanker of oil, but he can't do anything else. "We're going after her."

"To what end?" Jacob is frightened. "You can't apprehend her with the technology at your disposal. Not unless you put a hole in her sub, first. You might disrupt whatever she built that's creating that frequency if you rammed the sub, but she would never let you get close enough for that. She can dive and we can't."

"Our defensive systems will drive the creature away. They've done it before."

"Maybe! You can't be sure!"

"She'll stop when she sees that I won't give up. She won't put us all in danger, she cares too much. She'll come back." He cranks the wheel hard to starboard to bring the ship about. Feeling Jacob's incredulous gaze on him still, he snaps, "Take a raft back to the rig, if you don't like it. Take McKenzie with you, if you do." He says it and then wonders if he should make them go; he thinks Ceely will do the right thing, but he has seen her be irrational around the creature before, and these people are all his responsibility... She is his responsibility, too. She signed on, is a part of the crew.

The *Baton Rouge* builds speed and regains the ground that Ceely had earned with her head start. They are the faster vessel, even fully loaded, ripe with oil. They would have hit their quota, most likely by the day's end. They still can, Caesar tells himself. After they get Ceely back.

Someone patches in on the shared frequency with the flight rig. "Caesar! What's going on?" It's Regina, her voice thick with worry. The connection is already staticky, and getting weaker.

"It's Ceely," he says into the radio. "She needs me."

He switches off the radio, focusing on the screen that pinpoints the source of that ultrasonic frequency projected from her vessel, beeping as it updates every second, his only link to her as she's rushing away from him under the waves. It doesn't make sense to him. How can they have shared all the moments they have, and yet she doesn't feel what he feels? If she does feel what he feels, how can she leave him? It's the kids, he tells himself. Some people love their children more than anything else, as they should, and he loves that about her. He knows that it's the natural order of things that he should be second, in her heart. It's still hard to wrap his head around, though. Especially when her daughters are gone.

The sun rises behind the ship, the rig gets smaller and becomes a dot on the horizon. Most of the men go below deck to scrounge up some coffee and breakfast. Some come back up still munching on toast, which is what makes Caesar aware of his own hunger. How they can all eat with such danger barreling toward them, he doesn't know. Maybe they don't quite understand what is happening. Maybe most of them trust him to save them.

An hour passes and each minute he grows more and more uneasy about what he is doing. The fever of desperation has passed. He tries to picture turning back, never seeing Ceely again, but he just can't.

When the sirens start to blare it clears his mind in an instant; too late for second thoughts, changes of heart. It's coming, and fast. A murmuring of panic runs through the men. He speaks over the intercom. "Here we go." He has already told them to have a raft ready, and the remotely piloted little repair ship, too, in case he needs to hook up a tow line and pull Ceely's submarine in. With Perry in the brig, he has stationed their only other former soldier, a black man called JT in the gunner's turret. He looks unsure but has taken to the task of familiarizing himself with the weaponry, and sits ready to be their last line of defense.

Jacob stands with McKenzie, with hands on the boy's shoulders, on top of an orange life vest. They watch the horizon and Caesar hears a gasp. He is watching the radar, which shows the approaching figure, the smaller shape of their own ship the central dot on the computerized chart, and the tiny dot of Ceely's submarine in no man's land, in between, all alone. It's closing on her, fast.

He looks out at the real scene as the volley of explosives leave the ship. The creature's white body is visible just below the surface, and massive waves break off of the flukes of its tail; Ceely is down there, somewhere. He hopes the small blasts will not harm her, but it's mostly chance, now. The missiles impact the water and plummet, then depth charges activate and spray fountains of mist in a wide arch.

The figure of the creature only rushes past the little echoes of the explosions on the beeping screen and in the distance, it disappears as it dives deeper under the water. Men of the crew are panicking, now. Several are inflating life rafts, pulling on vests as the next line of defense activates. A torpedo fires from the ship's bow, under the water, and Caesar can see it on a separate screen, hardly anything visible under the water, just little specs zooming past the camera, then the flash of a white, oblong and toothy skull that rears and dodges the torpedo, which then buries itself in the creatures white abdomen.

The largest dot on the screen pauses, he wonders if they may have actually hurt, or killed the creature. But Ceely goes toward it, still, recklessly. Overhead the sky changes from a mostly clear morning with some white clouds in the distance to a roiling grey spiral of rainclouds, them forming too fast, impossibly fast, promising a killer cyclone. The sun disappears, and Caesar sees that Ceely must be within range of the creature, which moves, starts to retreat.

He runs from the control room to the bow, pushing past the crew. "No…"

She must hit her target because the thing rears in the water, its massive head breaks the surface and its body follows. As it breaches, Caesar can see a length of curly wire, razor thin but with a sudden crack of lightning glinting off of it, dangling and disappearing under the whipping and foaming white and black water. He grips the railing. His legs want to go limp under him, he feels as helpless watching as if he were in the creature's jaws, or under its shadow as the top half of it hurdles back down.

She must give it a shock -as she said she would- because it shrieks, a piercing, awful sound. It smashes into the water, displacing huge waves as it does, the sound almost deafening. Dozens of pillars of lightning light everything up blindingly white in the same moment that electricity courses through the railing, up Caesar's arms, and into his brain.

Everything goes dark.

Part Five
The Doldrums

I come to slowly, taking note first of the warm sunshine on my skin, second the cool earth underneath me, molding to my body as though I have been laying in this field for several hard rains, or all of a dry planting and sowing season; or maybe someone planted me when they planted the corn, and I grew here. The corn has an earthy, sweet smell. It groans as the tall stalks bend in the wind.

My grandfather used to say that corn grew so fast that you could hear it growing, and now I do. I open my eyes and I can see it grow, too. It's all around me and the silks that escapes some of the husks whisper in the pleasant breeze. The stalks extend in little spurts, grow inch by inch until they've all but blocked my view of the clear, blue sky.

I should get up, I think. There is no reason to, and my arms and legs feel like warm Jell-O, amazingly relaxed… but I think I was trying to get back to someone. I don't remember who, but they are not here.

I push myself up. My head spins, it takes a moment to orient myself, but then I stand on bare feet. I wiggle my toes, and the cool dirt sifts between them. I'm wearing a floral sundress, white with little red flowers.

I remember wishing that I looked better in soft dresses like this one. They tended not to suit my square shoulders, and strong arms. Just nothing dainty about me. But it doesn't really matter, on a day so beautiful. The hair that bounces into my line of sight is brown and wavy, and that does give me pause, but I can't remember why, just like I can't remember who I was looking for, or how I ended up in this corn field. I'm not worried about any of it, my body knows it will all work out.

I pick a direction and start walking, knowing it will be the right one. The rows of the corn field are wide enough to walk through if I turn sideways and step carefully. I hear flurries of bird song up ahead, carried on the wind. Then the chirping and tweeting turns to giggles, little girls' laughter, and my heart reacts, a smile grows on my lips. I would know those little laughs anywhere.

I push through the last rows of corn and find them sitting there, on a green grassy hill, in the shade of a big tree, I think it's a willow. There's a swing made of a single plank of wood and fraying rope hung from one of its lower branches. The land slopes down to a sparkling pond a stone's throw away. It's beautiful, and so are the three figures enjoying a picnic on an old plaid blanket. Caesar, Astrid and Josie. The girls are in matching dresses, white with red flowers, the same as mine.

"Mommy!" Josie's face lights up.

"There you are," Astrid taps her Hello Kitty watch after climbing to her feet. "Where were you?"

"I'm not sure." I open my arms and pull them to me, squeeze their little bodies tight and swing us gently back and forth. "I must have wandered off." I'm emotional, suddenly, absolutely pierced by the joy that swells up in me, and my tight throat makes my voice come out sounding high and girlish.

"That's alright," Caesar says. "We waited for you." He's wearing a finely made blue button down rolled up at the elbows, and jeans, and leaning back on the blanket with a content smile of his own. He looks delicious.

So do the assortment of foods spread on the picnic blanket. "Here," he says, seeming to read my mind. He builds me a plate. "Try some of everything."

There are quartered cucumber and chicken salad sandwiches, fresh grapes and pineapple, fresh veggies with a homemade dip, and a sponge cake with strawberries and cream. I try the dip first, on a green pepper, and it has a pleasant kick.

"Mm."

"Tea, Mommy?" Astrid pours for me without waiting for an answer. She pours a little too much;

when a sugar cube is added a few brown drops spill over the rim of the teacup. "Oops."

"That's okay." I pick it up and lift it carefully to my lips, taking a long drink. It's lukewarm, but sweet. "Very good, thank you."

"Try the cake, Mommy. I helped Caesar make it." Josie is already eating a big piece of cake, herself.

Caesar smiles, cuts a piece and brings a bite to my mouth. "Yes, she did. She helped measure all the ingredients, cracked the eggs, arranged the strawberries…"

"There might be some shell," she admits. "Eggs are hard."

"I think we got it all."

"Delicious. Very well done, all of you."

"Can we go swim?"

"Stay in the shallows, and where I can see you."

They shuck off their dresses and race down to the water in their swimsuits. Caesar repositions himself so that he is leaning back against the willow tree, and facing the pond. He pats the space next to him, and I slide over, fitting myself against his side, laying my head on his shoulder and lifting it only when he feeds me a bite of something from the full plate. When it is my turn to feed him, he reaches up and takes hold of my wrist, guides my hand closer, and holds it there, sucking pineapple juice from my fingers and kissing the tips. He kisses my wrist, where he can surely feel my pulse on his lips, a long, slow kiss, then up my arm. He

353

kisses my shoulder through the fabric of the dress, then my bare neck. Shivers course down my spine and race out through my legs. I shut my eyes for a moment, enjoying the feeling.

I pry them open a moment later, when my heart jumps into my throat and I jerk upright. I forgot to watch the girls, and am suddenly sure I will open my eyes to see them both facedown, floating, their dark hair fanning out around their tiny corpses, and their skin sallow and sunken, changed by the water -and miraculously so- in that one unsupervised second.

But they are splashing and laughing in the shallows, just as they were. Josie sputters, getting a little more water in her face than maybe she bargained for, and starting to whine. Astrid shushes her, stealing a glance up toward us under the tree on the hill, and then they troop off though the reeds to catch frogs that I can hear croaking.

"It's alright," Caesar gently pulls me back against him, wraps both arms around me. "They're safe here. We all are."

It scratches a part of my brain that reminds me that this is all strange. Parts of it are not right. My body knows it, keeps waking to the fact in little ways and feeling either unease or panic. It's like a dream, but it's not. I can feel, taste, smell, all vividly. But it's not reality, either.

I can feel Caesar's arms around me, they make me feel safe and loved, just like the real Caesar's. His

354

presence -that intangible thing I was drawn to and intrigued by from the start- is as clear and sharp as in reality. I almost think it should be impossible to fabricate. But I'm not sure. Maybe if you love someone, you can make a perfect replica.

Maybe this Caesar is even better than the one I know, or, at least is better suited, if he is untroubled by life, status... If he is content to sit and relax and watch my girls play, have I robbed him of some complexities, and done him a disservice? Or are we the same, just in a world where none of that matters? Heaven? I decide to just ask him, even if I'm scared of the answer, because this all suddenly feels fragile, existing because I believe it does, choose it to...

He notices my furrowed brow, or maybe he knows everything I'm thinking because he exists in my mind. "What is it?"

"Are you really here with me?"

"Of course."

"Not just as I remember you, as a figment of my mind, or, whatever this is?"

"Yes, Ceely. I'm here. Don't pick it apart. We're all together and safe and happy."

"Right." I try to take his advice and enjoy the moment as Astrid and Josie come running over to show us a frog. Josie holds it, fearless, and Astrid won't touch it, declares that it will give her warts. They launch into a debate fit for the presidential stage, mostly shrill cries of, 'No it won't!' and, 'Yes, it will!'

Their dark hair shines in the sun, their little face scrunch in anger, their voices are sharp and healthy. I think that if they are mirages, they are damn good ones. I created them once, there's no reason I shouldn't be able to do it again, if only in my mind.

I don't know if it matters if they are real, or not. The hole in my heart that that they left was real, I remember it even though I don't remember much else. Without them I'm something gaping and wounded, dead on my feet, unnatural like a beast of prey mauled viciously and somehow still alive. While I am here, that hole is gone, filled by their presence. That's real enough.

*

The house is a two-story farmhouse, which hasn't been updated in decades. Antique appliances in the kitchen, floral wallpaper, upholstered furniture with fine wooden accents. Chair rails and crown molding, fine china in a large cabinet, a decent collection of books in the study. The only modern touch is a flat screen mounted over the fireplace. I know where everything is, and everyone else seems to, as well.

The girls go upstairs to their rooms, to change and then seem to occupy themselves. They do not come back down. Caesar picks a book and kicks off his shoes, stretching out on the sofa. I move around from room to room, not sure what to do. I go halfway up the stairs with every intention of finding something to do with the girls, but I hear them talking, hear Josie's giggle, and realize I'm being silly. They need their playtime, it's good for their imagination, expands their minds. And all parents need to enjoy a little alone time, when they can.

But there are no dishes in the sink, I am not needed for work anytime soon, there's not even a project on my shoulders, with a deadline near or far. It wrinkles my brain. I make another lap around the first floor. Caesar looks up from his book.

"You really can't enjoy the peace and quiet for long, can you?"

"I need to feel like I've done *something* today."

"Alright… you could clean out the fireplace. And I'll chop some wood."

"You can relax, it's fine."

"Not while you're working, I can't. I'd feel lazy. It's alright. I could use the exercise, and then we'll have a fire going and we'll relax together."

"Okay."

He goes, stripping his shirt off as he does. I watch his broad shoulders, the muscles of his back and the dimples at his hips as he goes out the glass double doors at the patio. There's a large stump and an ax out there, along with a small stack of wood already chopped. I think he's doing this mostly for my benefit. It's plenty warm out, but not so warm that a fire is unthinkable. A fire does sound cozy, and it will get colder once night falls. I watch him take a few swings, his tattooed muscles rippling and powerful.

Only a minute, I allow myself to watch. Then I get to the dirty job of cleaning the ash out of the fireplace. In no time, I have it spotless, ready for Caesar, who carries in an armful of wood. His skin is glistening. I think that I could lick the sweat off his chest with no qualms. I listen upstairs for the girls. All quiet, there. Maybe they have fallen asleep…

Caesar stacks the logs in the fireplace, leaving it unlit for now. When he stands, I am right beside him, and run my fingertips down his spine. I wrap my arms around him, propping my chin on his shoulder, and he smiles, and leans his head back against mine. His hands reach for me, finding bare skin on each thigh at the hem of my dress, then sliding up and squeezing my hips, pulling our bodies tight together. He has a fantastic ass. He's almost flawless. I feel hunger, like I could take a bite out of him, want him between my teeth.

I do get my teeth around his earlobe and give him a little nip. Then a slow, firm bite on the skin where his shoulder meets his neck, making sure to leave an imprint of my teeth. I have a good view of where his hairline ends, and of the little mole there. I give it a kiss.

It's the kiss, not the bites that gives him pause. Maybe he isn't in my mind; maybe he was taught to see moles as ugly, imperfections. "What are you doing?" He tries to turn, but I hold him tight.

"I've wanted to kiss that mole a hundred times. But I couldn't." I don't remember exactly why, but I have an inkling. We were in a place less forgiving; I was fighting myself, as I was fighting the world. Here, I can be as soft as my heart always meant me to be. I kiss the mole again, long and slow. When I look at him next, Caesar has closed his eyes, seeming to enjoy the feeling.

"Do we have time?"

"All the time in the world," I assure him. I am beginning to understand this place.

"Alright then." He stoops, grabs my thighs firmly, and I don't understand what he's doing until I'm hefted into the air, landing astride his back and instinctively throwing my arms around his shoulders to hang on. I hear myself laugh, a real laugh, completely free and coming up from my chest riding on a surge of joy, and I think it has probably been a long time since I laughed like that.

He carries me to the bedroom, as easily as if I weigh ten pounds, and drops me on a soft bed of clean sheets.

We undress and explore each other with patient reverence. I have never exactly been shy, or inhibited, but I do remember being close to those things, the first time that we were together. I didn't really care for him yet, so I didn't really care what he thought about me, but I was uncomfortable in my old skin, grey hair, thicker body. Now I am thrilled for him to experience

359

this body, in its prime, and he is as mesmerized with me as I am with him.

Every touch lights us up, turns cells to live wires, we're charged and buzzing and vibrating at the same frequency. Even his slow, tender movements send me to an overwhelming place, over the edge and crashing back down for more, pleasure is limitless and yet somehow still builds higher, until we both are satiated and slouch into restfulness with our bodies feeling pleasantly stretched like cats in sunbeams, used, spent, and with the slight ache that often accompanies long and passionate sessions of love making the only twinge of physical discomfort I have felt since waking in the field. It doesn't last long.

I spare a thought to pregnancy with more than a bit of longing. I don't know if this place would let us change so much. Sex in this place has, however, helped us channel our words. Finally. And we say it again as we hold each other after the frenzy has passed, just to make sure they still stick.

"I love you," I murmur. It's a whispered promise that I hope will stay with him forever, or reach him, if he is, in fact, not really with me in here.

He strokes my hair. "I love you. I adore you."

If I have been loved before, I know with certainty that I have never been adored. I have been wanted, chosen, and appreciated, but never with Caesar's specific brand of knowing and treasuring the unique depths of me. And with such ease as to make me feel proud and beautiful and damn near perfect. It starts me crying happy, warm tears.

It rains outside. Drops ping down onto the skylight over our bed. The day is dimmer, with the rainclouds, but time does not rush by. We lay like that awhile, hours should have passed, but the girls don't come looking.

Eventually, I hear their voices in the living room. We dress and go out. Astrid has gotten an apple for each of them, slice and smeared with peanut butter. Offered slices, we accept.

"What's for dinner?"

"Let's go have a look."

We all troop to the kitchen, where we find we are working with a fridge and pantry fully stocked with fresh and dry and canned ingredients.

"Soup," Caesar declares. "We have guests coming, best way to feed them all."

"What kind?"

"I see corn, and black beans, and chicken. Let's make a southwest style chicken tortilla soup."

The girls approve, and eagerly follow him to the counter with all the ingredients. They follow Caesar's instructions, Astrid is older so she gets to chop things, Josie helps by measuring seasonings to add to the broth base he puts together. He tells Astrid to chop an onion and they both gasp.

"No onions!

"Ew!"

"What?" he is aghast. "No onion? Onion is delicious."

They start to chant and pound their small fists on the counter. "No onion! No onion! No onion!"

"Alight, fine, you win."

They cheer.

I have been working on a dough for fresh bread to accompany the soup. "That's just about the only thing they don't like."

"Maybe someday they'll appreciate the beauty of an onion…" He has started to trail off at the end, realizing as he says it out loud that it's the wrong thing to say. The girls don't notice the way that he stops stirring the peppers and garlic cooking in a pan, or when he looks over at me to see if I've noticed, or if that simple sentence has shaken me the way that it has him. I knead dough and glance over, then down, continuing to work.

"Chicken," he says, refocusing.

It's interesting. I find a dry spot on my lip and pinch it in my teeth and pull. Blood wells up, metallic. When I go to poke the sore spot again with my tongue -so the pain can keep me in the present- it is gone. This place is endless and pleasant, unchanging and still in time. It is also trying to make me forget the outside world, and forget my reservations, but I can't let that happen. I am enjoying this all for now, it feels as natural as breathing, but I need to keep my faculties and make sure I don't fall into this uncanny valley.

Caesar misspoke, he didn't do that for my benefit, he is not manifesting my doubts. He regretted it immediately, reminding me that the girls will never grow and never change in here. I am sure now that this *is* the Caesar I know. His consciousness is here with me. It is not just my mind, or his, it's some neutral secondary location. Knowing that he is really here with me is comforting, but also disconcerting. The real Caesar can put up a fight. He has almost convinced me to do things I didn't want to do, before. On the ship. He almost convinced me to stay.

We are going to have to have a hard discussion, soon.

But not while the girls are still around, not before the guests arrive and the soup is served. I knew they were coming, too. I can feel it.

*

They all arrive at the same time, right after the girls finish setting the table with the fine china. Caesar frowned when I suggested using it, probably knowing where my head was at based on the suggestion, or maybe just finding the idea of serving such a simple meal in them preposterous. But the girls are excited by it, and he lets it slide. Regina and Aaron bring a bottle of wine, she gives kisses to everyone as though my girls are her real grandchildren, and the resemblance is there, if I really look for it. The girls are tanner than I am,

363

with shiny, black hair. I think they are perfect replicas of what they were, so maybe it is a coincidence, or maybe this place is infecting my memories, too... spreading deeper into my brain. Maybe they will call him 'Daddy' if we stay here much longer, and we will all forget the truth.

Tommy and Jessica are our other guests for the night. She is a round, blonde woman with a pretty and brightly shining face, glowing, actually. Her belly is big with child. She offers us a red velvet cake, and we find a place for it on the table.

Tommy offers his hand in the same moment I go for a hug, blushes fiercely and accepts, grumbling, "Oh, sure. How you doin', Ceely?"

"Wonderful. It's good to see you. And congratulations."

I'm remembering, now. This was his house, but I guess not here... He let me stay, it was a business arrangement on my end, but he was lonely, glad for the company, and cared for me right away as if it were his duty. Really, it was just his nature. I remember him helping me off the dusty ground, carrying my jacket, strapping me into the seat of his bush plane. Bringing me sandwiches and tacos and beers, refusing my money. I suppose I consider him the best of us. I'm glad to see him, proud to introduce him to my girls, even if it's only in this place. "This is Astrid, and this is Josie."

He shakes each of their little hands in his big, meaty ones. "Pleased to meet you, ladies. Did you help make this dinner? It sure smells good."

"Yes, we did!" they exclaim in unison, and it sends a little pang through me.

They might as well have been twins, for how similar they were. Astrid small for her age and Josie big for hers. Always thinking alike, wanting to be like each other, reinforcing each other. I was glad for it, their closeness, but knew they would grow out of it, eventually. I couldn't wait to see them change, find divergent paths, become their own people. They would have been exceptional women, someday.

Everyone gathers around the table. Caesar gets me to serve, ladling out two big scoops of the fragrant, creamy, orange-brown soup into a bowl and then passing it off. The bowls make their way around to our guests, while the basket of fresh, warm bread goes the other way along with the butter dish. Caesar pops the cork off the wine bottle, starts to pour for the adults.

He sits at one end, I sit at the other, with a daughter on each side and a couple further down.

"Toast, anyone?" Aaron holds up his wine glass, looking around.

Tommy offers, "Good food, good meat, good God, let's eat?"

"Boo," Jessica jeers her husband, making him go red again but then kissing him on his flaming cheek.

Caesar stands and holds his glass out, looking at me. "We're together, and we're safe, and we're happy. That's all that matters. To a beautiful life. *Salud*."

"*Salud*," people toast around the table.

They sip, first, then try the soup and sing its praises.

When asked what he is up to, Tommy tells of a fine crop for the season, and building a crib for the expected little one. Nothing fancy, he says. Jessica puts a hand on his and assures that he is being too modest, that he has built their little boy a beautiful and safe crib, from a tree from their own backyard, and that they have painted the nursery, gotten him lots of toys for stimulation, and that their son will know right away that his parents are proud, and that he's loved. It sets Tommy to crying, almost. He hides his face in his napkin and sniffles.

I feel an ache again for my friend, for all that he deserved and lost come back around to him in this place. It's the righteousness of it that is most tempting, I think. A place where people get what they deserve, based on the kindness of their hearts, and nothing can hurt them or take what's theirs away. No sickness, no bad luck, no Fates twisting and spinning and snipping threads for their own amusement.

I think I know what this place is, now. I think Tommy, and Regina, and Aaron, and everybody will end up here, someday. I also think that the way my mind can still reach outward, back, mans that I am not truly here, yet. Not for good. I am still in between.

366

Everyone laughs at something, their joy is loud and infectious and makes me smile even though I was not listening to what was said. Caesar beams with white teeth the entire length of the table away, but his smile turns troubled when he looks to me a moment later.

The guests don't overstay their welcome. Eat and drink and laugh and then leave.

I tell the girls it is bed time, they whine to stay up longer, but I have always been firm and stick to my guns. Structure is important, even in this place. We troop upstairs, while Caesar puts the food away. He joins us a couple minutes later, after the girls have put on their nightgowns, and I have called them over to sit on Josie's bed with me. I pull them close and hold them tight, smooth their hair and inhale the scents of them, remember the way they feel, every detail, hope I can recall the feeling when I need it. How holding them makes me feel whole. They start to fidget, want to be free. Tears rain down my face. I have to let them go. It doesn't come naturally to me, not at all.

"A story?" Caesar suggests, earning their cheers and distracting them so that I can mop up my face as I pull away. "Go ahead and pick."

Astrid picks, gives him the book as he wheels a chair in between their beds. But he stoops and covers Josie up first, makes sure she is tucked in tight while I do the same for Astrid. He sits, then, and pats his lap for me to join him. I shake my head. I stand watching, in the doorway.

He reads them a story about an angry, purple platypus. His voice is normal at first, low and urgent as if he's riveted by what he is reading, as though it's some urgent dispatch. But when he gets to the place in the story where the platypus itself speaks, he pitches his voice up bizarrely, his face scrunches and makes the girls giggle. I smile, watching, loving him more every second and also falling deeper into sorrow than I have ever felt before. I am looking at my family, but I've never felt so alone.

Josie has dosed off moments after the story is over. Astrid tells us goodnight and turns over, heading for sleep herself. Caesar turns off the light and shuts the door, and we stand close together on the landing. I fold my arms, take a deep breath. Before I can work up the courage to suggest that we talk, Caesar speaks.

"We should get to those dishes."

I blink. "Sure."

He puts his hand on my lower back as we descend, then splits off to the living room, where he starts a fire crackling in the hearth, and switches on the radio to a classics station, just loud enough that I can hear it over the rushing water from the faucet as I fill the sink.

Where, usually, one of us would wash and the other would rinse, here Caesar comes up behind me and wraps his arms around me, laces his fingers through mine. We grip the sponge, the dishes, and wipe and scrub in the same movements as though we have one set of hands, as though we are the same person. We can sort of read each other's minds, whether by virtue of being in this place or just knowing each other and being so in love, being in no hurry.

Caesar kisses my cheek, my neck, my temple every so often. As if there were any risk of me forgetting he is there, or that he adores me. It makes my heart ache. My loins, too, but I can't let him distract me for much longer. It's like a Band-Aid. Easier to get it over with.

"We need to talk," I remind him, pulling the stopper to drain the sink as the last dishes are stacked on the rack and drying.

"Shh," he whispers. "Not yet." He takes my hand and pulls me into the living room, over to stand in front of the fire. He pulls my body tight against his, arms wrapping around me, a hand on my ass and one between my shoulder blades. I lean against him and let him lead me in gentle swaying. On the radio, Bob Marley is crooning, "Stir it Up."

I let him have that one song, hold him as tightly as he is holding me. I wish I could give him the world. I wish I could give him the life and the family that he deserves. Another resounding ache in my chest, all for him this time. It's enough to make me start crying again, burying a little sob in his chest that tears its way out of me.

It's his cue to stop, as the last seconds of the song die out. He sniffs, I hear emotion in his voice and pick up on him trying to stay strong. "I know. Chin up, kid. Let's have that talk."

369

He switches the radio off. I wipe my face and leave the warmth and coziness of the living room for the empty formality of the dining room. I sit at the narrow end of the table, and he takes the nearest chair, reaching for my hand across the top. He squeezes mine in both of his for a long minute. Then he lets me go, leans back and crosses his arms, ready to do battle it seems.

"You're going to have to start," he says. "I don't know how to."

"Alright… I think I know what this place is. I thought it was the afterlife, for a while. But it's not. It's not a final state, you can feel that too, probably?"

He nods. "What then, Purgatory?"

"No. I think it's what happens when anyone dies. It's where the tunnel of light and peaceful presence and our lives flashing before our eyes all happen. Synapses firing in the last moments, memories resurfacing, and that last bit of energy -the one that makes us what we are- carries it all onward so that the last moment feels like it lasts forever, if only in our minds. It's comforting to think that Astrid and Josie experienced the same thing, that they're living their perfect days, forever-."

"-Astrid and Josie are upstairs." His voice is a low murmur.

"No. They're dead and stuffed in an ice chest, right next to where I'm lying unconscious or dead. Even if the power didn't short out when we were struck by the creature's defense mechanism, it still won't last forever. If I stay here, they'll start to rot. So will I. So will you."

"I've never been a philosophical person," he says. "But what does it matter, Ceely? Those are just bodies, they're not what makes us who we are. I fell in love with *you*, not your body. Everything that we are is here, along with everything that matters, it's- it's everything a person could ever want. At least a sane, normal person. We could be happy here, forever." He stabs his finger down on the table to punctuate the word.

"We could. Part of me wishes that I could." I hope he can hear it in my voice. *Here's a man who can actually keep up,* I think. *Thirty years too late.*

"Then just do it!" He captures my hand again. I realize that he is angrier than I have ever seen him, hardly able to hold in his rage and desperation. "Stay here, with me, with us. It might be hard at first, it might make you sad, sometimes, but I'll be right there with you to help you through it. And I know that if we stay, you'll forget eventually. It will be like this is the only life we've ever had."

"I can't forget. I know it would be easy, and good, but being a mother is not about taking the easy way out. I brought my children into the world so that they could have life, it was hard and painful, but I did it with my eyes open. This is going to be even harder, even more painful, but I have to do it for them, for that slim chance that I can bring them back and give them the possibility of changing, and growing, and everything that is supposed to come with life. Good and bad."

His mouth is a tight line. "There's nothing I can do to change your mind?"

"No. I'm sorry."

He nods, I can see that he is processing it all through his dark, expressive eyes. "If you weren't such a good mother," he says, after a long minute, "I wouldn't love you so much. I saw this coming, I just hoped I was wrong."

"If you wanted to stay, I'm sure it would seem to you that I never left. You would forget. You would be happy. I would understand-."

"-No. If you're going back, I'm going back. I told you, you'd always have me... If there's no version of this where we get to be happy together, then I'll just have to chase after you while you chase after that thing."

"I don't want that for you. I want you to salvage the rest of your life. I'll be fine."

"Beggars can't be choosers."

I huff. I reach across the table and he takes my hand again. I know that asking him to give up on me is almost as hopeless as asking me to give up on them. "If things were different," I say, slowly, "...nothing could keep me away from you."

"I know."

"Do we just leave?"

We both look at the wooden door.

"I would think so. Are you really ready, though?" His thumb traces softly across the lines of my palm.

"No. I never will be. We have to do it, before I lose my nerve." I look back at the stairs. They're sleeping up there, and they will stay that way while I live the rest of my life, trying -and probably failing- to get them back. Someday I'll come back through the door, go up there, and it will be morning. We'll have banana pancakes and we'll all be together.

I push myself to my feet. I slide the chair back into its proper place against the table; always leave a place better than you found it. Caesar stands, too. He brushes himself off, takes a deep breath. I watch him for a moment while he's lost in thought.

"What's on your mind?" I can't help but to ask.

He sighs. "I'm thinking of how lonely it's going to be. Good thing I grew up lonely; I'm pretty much used to it."

"That makes two of us." I hold my hand out again and he takes it. He would never have said something like that out loud, in the real world. I hope I remember it all when I wake up. If I wake up. "Do me a favor?"

"Anything."

"Remember me like this."

He looks at me for a long time, memorizing little details, I hope. "You'll always be a knockout."

He kisses me. I breathe in deep the scent of him, savor the taste, the softness of the kiss, the warmth of his tongue. Lightheaded, I tear myself away. Without another word, we make for the door, which he holds open for me. I see nothing but darkness outside. I keep hold of his hand and we walk out into it together, squeezing tighter as the feeling of each other fades.

Part Six
Sowing

Chapter One... and Only

Caesar comes to with black spots swarming in his vision, but knows immediately where he is. He is on the *Baton Rouge,* after being shocked by the creature. He squints at his hands, blinking to clear his eyes. They look normal, not wrinkled and sun-spotted. If the sobbing of his mother as she leans over him and holds onto him was not enough to clue him in, those are. He has not been thrown thirty-some or more years into the future by the shock, the creature's defense system. Nor has the ship, nor has anyone else. He can feel the waves rocking the deck infinitesimally below him. He thinks as he sits up and pries his mother off of him that if he had anything in his stomach, he would vomit.

"Captain, are you alright?" Jacob is crouched at the front of the crowd of spectators; were none of them affected at all?

"I was so worried," his mother manages, mopping up tears. "Your heart stopped for two minutes! Then you wouldn't wake up. I thought we had lost you."

It makes him drag himself to his feet. If his heart stopped, did Ceely's, too? "Is everyone else alright?" He hears the words come from his own mouth, a sluggish afterthought. He staggers to the railing and feels a rush of relief; the little, yellow submarine has surfaced, the hatch is open, and since Ceely is the only one onboard, that means that she is alright. Or alive, at least.

Come back, he thinks, without a prayer.

"Everyone is fine, although Regina says that the pilot of the rig already reported the ship's deviation from the mission."

The pilot, the flight rig floating in the distance. That's right. He looks back at his mother, and sees an inflatable Zodiac raft with a motor tied to the ship, bobbing on the waves. She commandeered it and came over, she broke protocol, too. She sticks to him like glue, reaches up to feel his forehead. He pushes her hand away.

"You have to go back." Thoughts are forming slowly. He remembers everything from the shock-induced dream state, in vivid detail, clearer than any memory. He can still feel the last, soft kiss on his lips, the squeeze of Ceely's hand as they left that place together. He remembers how much he wanted to stay, but now he's here, and it leaves a bitter taste.

A part of him thinks that he just gave up his one chance for salvation; the only peace he'll ever know. But he's not entitled to it, nobody is. Certainly not him, with the life he has led. He pushes the feeling down.

"What's going on, Caesar?"

"I'm not completing the mission. I'm commandeering the ship." He watches a white hand emerge from the open hatch of the submarine, bring it closed. That's it, then. She's not coming back, even though she knows he's willing to do this with her. She thinks he will grow out of it, grow up, move on. She has another thing coming.

"You can't mean that," Jacob sputters.

"I do," he insists without hesitation. "You all need to evacuate the ship, if you stay, you'll be considered accomplices. You could be looking at federal charges. Treason, even."

The crew lingering around the captain are shocked at this sudden development; it's just about the last thing that they ever expected to hear from the straight-laced hard-ass they have come to know over the past few months. They have also come to trust and admire him, and Ceely, too. They talk, when they gather for meals or during down time, playing cards, doing their cleaning tasks and other busywork. They have all heard about the bodies in the submarine by now, and the woman's almost rabid need to kill that creature. They saw her fire on it, break down in the captain's arms afterward. They know that she designed the engine's on the flight rig, she's a certified genius, as well as a certified mad woman. Not everyone understands her rage. But most respect it.

The silence carries for a minute. The crew exchange looks with their friends. Ralph is the first to speak. "Treason, huh? That sounds like fun-."

"-No," the captain tries to shut down the idea, but the others are chiming in.

"There's no one I'd rather follow into delinquency."

"Sure. If the captain's doing it, it must be the right thing to do."

"I'm onboard, too."

They're chattering among themselves, now. "Always wanted to be a pirate."

"Every boy's dream."

"No, no! Listen to me," the captain says. "She's not going to stop chasing that thing, and I'm not going to stop chasing her. We'll be safe from the government sinking us, with our holds full of oil, but the company could launch an assault and try to reclaim the ship. And we will come into contact with the creature again, and we will run out of defense mechanisms. It's a fool's errand, and I can't ask any of you to be a part of that. I can't allow you to be. You'd be throwing away your lives."

"I don't have that long left, anyway," Ralph retorts, crossing his arms stubbornly. "I want to die at sea, you know that. And with the way my lungs are rotting in my chest, they would have to be out of their minds to let me out on the water again. Doesn't matter what wavers I sign, how strapped for men they are... If you want me off this skip, you'll have to throw me overboard."

"Me too," Regina pipes up, and when Caesar tries to interject, she steamrolls over him, with her face set, determined. "I wasn't the mother you needed, when you were growing up. I can't ever change that. But I can be here for you, now. -And even more than you, I owe that woman a debt. If we can help her, in any way, I want to try."

"No," he insists, getting a hand around her arm and fully intending to drag her to the life raft and put her back in the water. She yanks herself away.

"Keep your hands off me, Caesar. You don't have it in you to hurt me, and it won't do you any good, anyway. If you throw me over, I'll come doggy paddling after you. I swear I will."

He exhales, starting to shake in all his extremities. He can't let it happen, but he believes what she is saying. She has always been a bit irrational. "You were going to move to Alaska, with Aaron. You were starting over."

"I still am."

A few of the men chime in, again. "We can't get fresh starts, not really. Step out of line one time, and you're blacklisted for life."

"The only jobs we can get are shitty ones. I mean 'shitty' literally. We'd just end up working another oil tanker on this same beat, waiting to get smashed to pieces and eaten. I like my chances a lot better, with you at the helm."

A few agree with weak affirmations.

JJ is in surprisingly high spirits at the morning's turn of events. "Who isn't down for a little pillage and plunder, huh?" He gets a few chuckles.

"Do you know the reward for killing that thing? Split ten ways, it's still a fortune."

"Enough to make any charges against us disappear. We could own land. Never have to work again, or if we did, we could buy a fishing boat or some trucks, landscaping equipment. Work for ourselves."

"You're all out of your minds," one single man dissents. He heads for the inflated raft, tossing over his shoulder as a courtesy, "Good luck to you, though."

Another man wordlessly goes with him.

Jacob and Roshin have been having a conversation with just their eyes. The clerk speaks, finally. "I'm sorry, Captain…"

"Don't apologize. You both were fine additions to the crew."

He shakes each of their hands, escorting them to the raft. He can't argue with the logic the rest of the crew has presented, either. If they go back, there's no good work for convicts, no fresh start. He knows it well enough. If Ceely kills that thing in her attempts to aggravate it, or if they do, all will be well. Nothing has been able to, yet, and almost everything -short of a nuclear bomb- has been tried... It's almost hopeless, but no more hopeless than returning to their old lives.

"Do one more thing for me, and make sure that McKenzie gets home safely?"

"Of course."

"And Perry will have to be taken, to be brought to justice."

Roshin nods. "I'll go and retrieve him."

"Beacham and Jinn, go with him. McKenzie?"

The boy hurries over. He shakes the captain's hand, when prompted, looking confused and suspicious.

"Looks like you'll be back on land by sundown. Thanks for saving our asses, kid."

He gets a solemn nod in return, and then McKenzie climbs over the railing and descends to the raft. It's a shame, Caesar thinks, watching him go. He knows that once a childhood is lost, there's no getting it back. The boy had to grow up early, and he'll probably make a lot of bad choices, if he's anything like Caesar was. He can only hope that McKenzie will find someone or something to set him on the right path. Or maybe saving more than a dozen lives will have done that, already.

Perry comes from below, with his hands cuffed in front of him, and lifts his face to the morning sun, smiling. He doesn't seem interested at all in what is happening, why he is being set afloat on a raft with a handful of the others. He doesn't care that a few of the crew spit at his feet as he passes. He just slowly descends the ladder as he is told and settles down onto the raft.

Jacob hesitates, exchanging another meaningful look with Roshin. "If you're really going to do this, there's something you should know…"

When he can't get the words out, Roshin says it for him, in his usual tone, low and perfunctory. "Just before lunch, on Ceely's second day on the ship, JJ and Colson attacked Ceely and Jacob in the galley. If Perry and I hadn't gone early to keep an eye on things, as you asked us to, things could have taken a dark turn."

"I followed Ceely and Perry's lead about the whole thing." Jacob's face turns red, he can't look up. "I should have told you, but I'm the one that she let in, I left the door unlocked, because it was so close to lunch time- I didn't think it mattered… I was ashamed. I'm sorry."

Caesar has to forcibly unclench his jaw to speak. "It's not your fault. I'll handle it, thank you both." He watches them both climb over the railing, joining McKenzie and Perry and the other two deserters, then cuts the line tethering them to the ship. He has felt fury rolling inside him, like storm clouds in the distance, the entire, agonizing minute. Then, looking out at Ceely's submarine, he sees it descend beneath the waves, and the knife in his hand feels as light as air. He flips it over, shifting his grip.

As he walks back to the crew, the men see the look on his face. The smart ones part like the red sea, so that he can get to JJ and Colson. Colson is a big man, all brawn and no brain. He follows JJ around, does his bidding. Caesar kills him quickly, gets an arm around him and slices his throat, making him collapse into a big heap on the deck, choking for air as blood sprays from his wind pipe, pools around him. A sudden intake of breath that is not a gasp runs through the men, it's not quite surprise, just dismay, and if he loses their support now, he thinks, all the better.

"Caesar, what are you doing!?" Regina has certainly never seen him violent before. When JJ leaps back and pulls a knife of his own, she exclaims again. "Oh my God! What's happening?" A couple of the men hold her back.

The two men face each other with knives in hand. JJ is fast, slick and small. He's the one who likes to push people and take anything he can. He keeps his feet moving, a dancer's feet, or maybe a soccer player. He faints in and skips back, jumps from side to side, but Caesar is not putting on a show, or playing games. He has a cold pit in his stomach and his blood is boiling, pounding in his head. He advances, takes one swipe across, makes JJ jerk back to avoid getting his own throat or face slashed, putting him off balance, and Caesar pushes in another step. The man frantically jabs out, but Caesar's hand closes around his wrist, an iron bracelet.

There is a moment in time for the shock and fear to flash across JJ's face, and during it, Caesar reconsiders killing him quickly. He flips his own knife around in his grip, then drives it down, into the meat of JJ's thigh. In the next second, he gets an arm around the villain's neck, and wrenches the arm he is still holding until bones crack and the captive man's knife clatters to the deck.

JJ has finally managed to draw a breath, and he screams with every bit of it, a wounded animal kind of wailing and thrashing, it makes a few of the men watching wince, cross themselves.

Live like an animal, Caesar thinks, *and you can die like one.* He drags JJ kicking and screaming across the length of the deck, it's not easy. He starts to sweat and becomes aware of the pleasant sea breeze washing over them. It would have been a lovely day. The crew scuttles after, watching. At the back of the ship, there are various chains and ropes for anchoring, or towing, or rescue.

Caesar picks a thick rope, unwinds a length of it, and throws JJ to the ground. Then, looping the rough, braided rope in his hands, he wraps it around the man's neck, tightening it until it crushes the air from his windpipe, cuts off his last desperate pleas.

"Help-!"

But the crew have not moved to help him, they aren't going to. The captain ties an expert knot to keep the rope securely in place. He drags JJ a few more feet, then heaves him over the railing and sends him flipping head over feet down to the water. A splash a second later. Caesar hopes it doesn't knock him unconscious, that he will flounder in the water and suffer, feeling every second of his dying, starved for air. He hasn't ever taken joy in hurting someone before, but he is different, now. Ceely is not just his woman, she's his family. He wishes he could have kept that waste of life alive and fed him whole to the beast.

But a bleeding body on a line will have to do. Like a worm on a hook. They are the faster vessel, he can overtake Ceely's submarine in no time, stay ahead of it, track her movements, as long as she is projecting that high frequency to try to attract the creature. But he won't be able to force her to meet with him, not until she is out of food or water, desperate. It might be days or weeks. They might meet the creature several times in that stretch.

It fled after the shock, is nowhere on the displays as he flips through them on his handheld. Probably miles away, by now, but it will come, drawn by the frequency and then, hopefully, distracted by the presence of death and drawn to dinner...

Catching his breath, he cleans blood off of his knife with a wash rag from nearby, then throws it overboard. "If anyone wants to leave, this may be your last chance. I want to believe that that thing can be killed, or that this will all work out, somehow... but I can't promise anything. I can't guarantee your safety, if you stay."

Nobody moves. A few consider leaving, he can see it in their faces.

Ralph says, "JJ was a dirty cheat at cards, you know."

"Owed him my whole paycheck," Beacham agrees.

"All our paychecks are goners, now."

Chatting amongst themselves, they move to their positions without having to be ordered to do so. It was already a skeleton crew, now halved. But with a halfway decent captain, they'll do fine.

They have nowhere better to go, are the definition of the desperate times in which they live leading to desperate measures. They have a vague hope of valor and riches, enough to set themselves up for the rest of their lives. Probably they also dream of becoming a legend, a bedtime story; modern day pirates hunting a sea monster, like Captain Ahab's crew on the Pequod.

Nodding, Caesar heads to the control room. Ceely is a blip on a monitor. She might as well be a missed shot on a game of Battleship he played as a child, or a sea monkey. An ancient museum exhibit behind glass, untouchable and getting further away by the second. With an ache in his heart, he sighs, hangs his head, and pushes the lever to accelerate forward. There's nothing else he can do.

The End.

If you enjoyed this book,
Please consider leaving a review on Goodreads and
Bookbub, or wherever you buy books.
It's harder than ever before to make a career out of
writing books, and every review helps.

Turn the page for a look inside Monster Midwife…

Chapter One

I live in a land of monsters and I am just a woman.

I have been alive in this realm for twenty-seven years, and that fact still manages to shock me. It shocks me that I have made it this far. It shocks me that I still have the ability to become complacent, to forget my station. The reminder comes sometimes in small ways, sometimes in large ones. Today or tonight -I'm not sure which it is, inside of the pitch-black labyrinth- it is a big enough and terrible enough thing to make me sob with my hot face pressed against the cool stone.

Swirling rage and terror threaten to climb up my throat. I'm going to either scream or puke. I grab the hilt of my dagger, squeeze until my fingertips are numb, force everything down inside of me, and then exhale. I have to move.

It's echoey in here so it's hard to tell, but the hoofbeats sound like they are getting closer.

About a day ago, I was in my room and the prince came in. My room is not much, just four walls, enough room for my bunk which is thin and definitely only suitable for one. I have a small chest for my few changes of clothes, and a small desk which barely fits, its corner touching the bed's simple frame. It holds my books and journals where I can study and record my findings by the light of the window. I am luckier than most slaves in the King's castle, who sometimes bunk two, four, six to a room, and still I was embarrassed when I opened the door and saw the prince standing there. Embarrassed and flustered.

He would always direct me on my missions from his own chambers, which were richly decorated and comfortable in every way. Visiting a slave would probably reflect badly on him. Although I also wondered if, like the prince himself, the other members of the Court weren't starting to see me as more than a slave, and as more of an equal.

But of course, he had come without any of the servants who surrounded him most of his days. He had looked each way before stepping over the threshold. He had shut the door behind him. So probably it was wishful thinking to imagine that any of the fairies could see me as a person. I was just their biggest cash cow, to trot out when it suited them.

And I know now why Prince Killian was so reticent in sending me to this God-forsaken place. Maybe he is a bit fond of me, but mostly he is just worried for the investment that his father made. The knife is strange in my hand, heavy. I hurry on.

I have run too much and now I can only manage a brisk walk. It has been hours, down in the dark. My thighs are heavy, my knees shake with every step. I had to run; I know that. I don't know what sort of people have been sent down here with me, but at least two of them were in cahoots, I saw matching tattoos on the back of their necks, when their dark hair was swept aside by the whipping wind on the sea.

Humans, like me. A man can be dangerous alone; I tend to keep an eye on them. A pack of men is almost always a bad thing. I avoid them at all costs.

I unravel a thread as I go so that I can find my way back if I survive. It looked like a spindle of spun gold when Killian presented it to me, along with the dagger which he pulled from his own belt. Now in the pitch-black darkness, where I can't see my own hand in front of my face, it seems to give off its own, tiny amount of light.

"My mother spun this when she was young, in the trials to be my father's wife. It's unbreakable," he said. "Nobody but she -or someone from our bloodline- can cut it. It will help you find your way home." His dark eyes had turned fierce as he said it, then he had seemed embarrassed, and turned to go. But something he had left unsaid had frozen him with his hand on the doorknob. "When you return, there is something very important you and I need to discuss. I'll see you soon, Alanna… Good luck."

I unravel thread. Come to a corner and follow along its outer wall. I keep my eyes turned toward the ground, looking for the hint of gold on the stone ground that will let me know I have come to a path I have crossed before. I reach a place where the wall falls away under my fingers. The tunnel branches out that way. I shuffle across the width to the opposite side, and find it is the same. Straight forward, I fumble in the darkness. A wall. I have come to a T-shaped intersection.

Squinting although it doesn't help, I drop to my knees. On the right, I can see a small glimmer. The golden thread, telling me it is not a new path.

No sooner have I straightened than a man's scream comes echoing from the right tunnel. A grisly wailing that turns into a gurgle and a cough, with an animal's bleat and then silence. It freezes me in place. The hoofbeats come from that direction unmistakably, growing louder each second so that I barely have time to scuttle back along the ground. My backside hits the wall of the tunnel I have just emerged from and then I curl myself against it, burying my face.